Metamorphosis

Greg Lundberg

This is a work of fiction. All of the characters, organizations, and events portrayed in this novel are either products of the author's imagination or are used fictitiously.

METAMORPHOSIS
Copyright © 1997, 2010 by Gregory M Lundberg.
Edited by Sarah Herbst.
Cover text design by Cheryl Lundberg.
This is an original publication of Quicksilver Books.

All rights reserved.

No part of this book may be reproduced, scanned, or distributed in any printed or electronic form without permission.

ISBN-13: 978-0-615-56804-1
ISBN-10: 0615568041

Visit the author's website at
www.authorgreglundberg.com

DEDICATION

This book is dedicated to my father, whose voracious appetite for Sci-Fi inspired me; and to my mother who taught me how to write.

CONTENTS

ACKNOWLEDGMENTS

Cheryl, my love, who patiently kept after me to pursue my dream and encouraged me not to give up.

i

PROLOGUE

ONE THOUSAND YEARS BEFORE PRESENT DAY

THE dark ship emerged from the black cloud of the nebula, leaking copious streams of plasma. Wide gashes coursed the length of the battered hulk. Glimpses of tiny space-suited figures could be seen through great rips in the hull. In the distance, an asteroid field glistened, its tumbling rocks reflecting light from a distant star.

100 kilometers to the starboard, a white disk of light expanded into view. From its center, a silver starship emerged. Like a bullet, the newcomer accelerated toward the dark ship. Only half the mass of its quarry, the silver vessel bristled with weapons.

Alarms began to sound on the dark ship as it began to flee toward the distant asteroid belt.

A bolt of energy reached out from the silver vessel and touched the rear of the retreating ship, exploding into a gigantic display of lightning. The dark ship's rear shield collapsed just as asteroids began pelting the forward screen.

"The Others have found us, oh Great First One," spoke a short, squat creature hovering over a tactical display, "but we are too damaged to fight."

The horribly mutated leader of the dark ship stood at the console, his face, or what was left of it, trembled with rage. Thin tentacles of tissue connected his body to the computer console. He felt rather than viewed the scan readouts of the attacker, and anger boiled up from within. "I am the Alpha!" he shouted, "I will not yield! We are the superior ones, the Others are weak and puny," lectured the leader. "Commence evasive maneuvers, but not too evasive! We want them to follow us in." He added, "I have a plan." Maneuvering among the asteroids, the dark ship's navigator was careful to keep larger rocks between the attacker and himself. The hunted craft pressed deep into the belt, taunting its pursuer.

On the silver vessel, bridge officers refocused their efforts to pursue and destroy their prey. The captain cajoled his crew, "Don't let them get away!" He thundered, "That ship is all that stands between us and the end of the war." The captain was well over two meters tall, dressed from head to toe in dark blue. He was a gray-skinned biped, vaguely resembling the mutated leader of the dark ship. Unlike the dark ship's commander, however, the silver vessel's captain wasn't disfigured and in fact, was considered handsome by members of his own race. "If we don't finish this here and now, this blasted war might well continue until there is no one left alive who gives a damn."

The silver vessel hurled two more bolts at the dark ship. One detonated prematurely against a small asteroid. This time, fireworks played over the screens of the hunter disabling shields and taking out main gun turrets.

The dark ship's sensors reported the catastrophe to its leader. The one who called himself, "Alpha," twisted his alien face into what can best be described as a smile. "Open fire. Target sensors only," he commanded. "It's only a matter of time before they make a fatal mistake," the leader prophesied.

Acrid smoke filled the silver vessel's bridge. "Sir, they are targeting our sensors," choked the first officer, "we must withdrawal or we risk serious damage!"

"Can't be helped, we must stay with them at all costs. No reduction in velocity," replied the captain. "And clear this smoke!" he ordered. As he was speaking, from out of the darkness an asteroid bore down on the spaceship. As luck would have it, the first sensor array destroyed was the only one that could have detected the rock in time. The big rock struck and immediately half the starship went dark. Gravametric dampers failed, knocking most of the silver vessel's crew off their feet and causing chaos below deck.

"All stop!" shouted the captain. The silver vessel slowed, order returned quickly to the disciplined crew.

On the bridge of the dark ship, a number of ugly, misshapen heads swiveled to gaze upon the 'First One.'

"So predictable," the alien leader shook his bulging head in disbelief. He would have broken off the attack and waited for superior reinforcements. The dark ship wasn't going anywhere fast. The Alpha looked up from his console and ordered his ship to close on her foe. "Attack them now! Forget all the repairs and send everyone to crush them. I want the Other's starship intact. Success is ours once again!" There was a rush of activity on the bridge as all the creatures attended to their orders.

Grapples were flung across to tie the two starships together. Gantries extended. A mish-mash group of space-suited figures clambered across to the surface of the silver vessel.

A cargo hatch on the silver vessel blew outward in a cloud of gas. Metal spheres 1.5 meters in diameter were flung into orbit and, after orienting themselves automatically, they established overlapping orbits around the two ships. Instantly, all 240 of the spheres opened fire with anti-personnel disrupters, cutting the first wave of attackers to ribbons. A second wave appeared, some clothed in space armor, others in deep space repair suits, and others in relatively lightweight emergency suits. The suit material was dirty and disheveled sporting neither insignias nor consistent styles. The suits had come from many different sources. Those in armored suits attacked first and managed to pick off several of the spheres. The machines responded with concentrated fire and quickly overcame the armored attack. The spheres then wiped out the remaining space suited creatures. No more figures came forth from the dark ship.

The captain wiped blood from a wound on his brow and turned to the first officer, "Thinks he's so damn smart does he? He wasted over half his crew trying to board us. What he should've done was blown us to bits. He has the weaponry, but now we are tethered; we're too close for him to bring them to bear."

The first officer replied, "May I remind the Captain that our main weapons are offline? We cannot destroy them, either. It's a standoff. What do we do?"

The captain sighed, "We have no choice; we can't flee, we can't destroy them outright, our only chance is to take the battle to them, before they have a chance to organize. Our troops don't have much time. We know how fast these creatures can regenerate." The first officer nodded and gave the order.

Crew from the silver vessel assembled outside on the gantry. As one man they rushed forward. They were dressed in light blue space armor and grim determination showed on their squat, pug-nosed faces. All wore the double triangle and circle insignia of elite space troopers. The battle was fierce, many died seconds after entering the gantry hatch, but the troopers fought their way into the dark ship and secured the door. Slowly, the attacking troopers advanced deeper into the ship.

The dark ship's leader collapsed into his command chair, fuming. Those anti-personnel weapons were an unforeseen development. I should have blown the Other's starship to bits

, he thought. Now it is too late. He looked up at the other creatures in the room moving frantically, grabbing equipment, weapons, and supplies. They rushed toward the now audible battle. I will avenge my brothers! He thought. "Prepare my ark! We must hurry! Survival of our species is paramount," he declared. The alien leader thumbed a comm switch, "Attention, All level five personnel and above are to evacuate on my mark!"

Two aliens calmly attached a small probe to a drive unit at the center of the room. They opened the hatch on the probe and applied a silvery substance to the interior. One of them picked up a tray and returned to stand beside the command console. The alien leader carefully unplugged himself from the computer. His tentacles retracted into his body like claws on a cat. He turned to face his assistant who bowed in deference. A humming sound emitted from the alien as he touched a finger to his chest. Like an opening zipper, a fifteen-centimeter vertical cavity appeared. The alien leader grabbed both edges of the cavity and pulled it wide open. Some popping and cracking sounds were heard. The assistant reached in the bloody cavity with a pair of tongs and retrieved an egg shaped object. The alien leader let go of the wound and it shut of its own accord. The bleeding stopped almost immediately. He turned back to the computer console and began to punch codes. Amazingly, he seemed to be unaffected by the trauma his body had just experienced. The assistant cleaned off the object, walked over to the probe and deposited the egg into the compartment. He shut the hatch and set the locking code, touching a sensor on the side of the hatch. The probe slowly sank out of sight into the cycling hatch of the launch tube. The alien leader smiled grotesquely, They cannot kill me. My essence lives on. And so will my brothers. He slammed his palm down on the board and watched the console began the countdown.

Outside the dark ship, launch tubes from all over the hull began firing probes off in every direction. Immediately, the spheres fired on the new targets.

"He's off loading! Make sure you track and destroy every object from that ship! If just one of them gets away with an intact core aboard, the entire cycle can repeat," the captain ordered. Officers on the silver vessel tracked every scrap of metal with intense interest.

A new threat appeared. The end of the dark ship began to glow. The glow spread slowly, filling the dark ship with destructive energy. The silver vessel's officers immediately reacted. The spheres were redirected to fire on the tethers and cut the two starships free. One last probe launched from the belly of the dark ship. A sphere turned and took aim at the escaping probe and fired. An asteroid shattered instead, splattering the swiftly departing probe with debris. It took aim again, but before the sphere could fire the dark ship's drive exploded, turning the silver vessel, the spheres, the troopers, the aliens and every asteroid in a 100 kilometer radius into a miniature sun. The reaction glowed brightly for 10 seconds and faded, leaving nothing.

The probe emerged from the exploding plasma cloud, shed its protective armor, and accelerated through the asteroid field. It was not alive in the organic sense, but had more than enough electronic intelligence to think to itself as it dodged rocks and debris. Must hide quick! Others will hunt! Cargo too precious! There! It zeroed in on a medium-sized asteroid and dove into a deep fissure. The probe programmed the guidance system of its propulsion unit to decoy potential pursuers away, and then jettisoned the unit.

The propulsion unit sped off. Soon the probe's passive sensors registered faint signals as the Others began their search. Time passed. The searching grew fainter and more distant, and eventually fell silent. The asteroid spun and tumbled along its orbit. Is search over!?! The probe waited a quarter turn around the distant sun, then activated its subspace beacon.

The miniature beacon shorted out in mid-signal, suddenly drawing more and more power. The probe tried in vain to shut it down. Malfunction!?! Power loss! Damaged in escape? It struggled to remain conscious as energy reserves reached minimum levels. Eventually, thought simply stopped. Round the sun went the asteroid—once, a dozen times, untold thousands. The probe became one more lost relic stranded hundreds of light-years from Earth.

CHAPTER ONE

PRESENT DAY—STANDARD YEAR 2325

THE hatch hissed opened and the man stepped through. He was a stern man, dressed in a dark gray business suit. Any criminal would have taken one look at him and said, "Cop."

The man turned and called through the hatch, "Come."

Ben Gardener stepped through the hatch and let his gaze wander through the shuttle cabin. It was empty. The man gestured to a seat next to the window and said, "Sit." Ben sat. The cop pulled a cyber key and unlocked the cuffs on the boy's wrists. Ben rubbed his wrists.

"Where's my PC?" he asked.

The man opened a heavily shielded briefcase and removed a small personal computer. He handed it to the boy and remarked, "Behave!" Without another word, the cop stepped to the rear of the shuttle and was gone.

Ben Gardener lounged in the shuttle seat, twisting one leg across the other and locking his fingers behind his head. Besides making the empty seat next to him uninhabitable, this maneuver "accidentally" brought the vision pickup of his personal computer—a decidedly nonstandard attachment—in range of the panoramic view of Isis. The swirl of clouds 1800 kilometers below gave the barest impression of movement across the intense blue of the oceans.

"That cop ever say more than one word at a time?" murmured a voice from the box on his lap.

Ben sighed. It was a beautiful planet! "He wasn't really a cop, he was Intelligence." he replied. "Spooks aren't very good conversationalists."

"Ah, you mean he was an asshole!" said the small voice, a little louder this time.

"Keep your voice down, Jack!" Ben hissed under his breath, chuckling. "We don't want to attract too much attention." Passengers were beginning to board the shuttle.

"What you mean is that you don't want people to think you are talking to a box. After all, they might think you were crazy!" chimed the voice from the computer.

Talking to a box, indeed, thought Ben. This 'box' contained perhaps the most advanced artificial intelligence mankind had ever encountered, and he was the only one who knew it existed. Right now it looked like an ordinary PC, but it was really a Gaderian supercomputer and it could form into any shape it chose—and it could choose. It conversed, learned from its mistakes, and continued to evolve into a unique personality, even though most of its memories remained locked away. If the Isis authorities even suspected that the box masquerading as a personal computer was anything more than what it appeared, they would have confiscated it instantly. As it was, they only gave it back to Ben because the spooks thought they had totally erased the machine's memory. "Look, keep your voice down or I'll take you apart and use the parts to build a nice dumb robot."

"Humph, you don't even know how to take me apart, let alone what I'm made of." The slim nondescript case sitting on the young man's lap looked like any other personal computing and communications device, except for a small, embossed double triangle and circle discreetly located on the corner of the cover.

A passenger across the aisle turned to stare at Ben with a questioning look on her face. Ben smiled and turned quickly away, muttering, "Switch to subdermal. The old bat overheard us."

A small voice in his ear said, "Aye, aye, Captain."

The shuttle got under way and nothing else was said for a while. The craft maneuvered end over end and a freighter came into view.

"It's the Star of India ! " Ben said breathlessly, gazing through the window.

"Get me closer," cried the little voice. The young man held the box against the portal. A sensor window clicked open beside the vision pickup and the voice turned flat and mechanical, "Forager class freighter/salvage vessel, displacing one million metric tons, capable of 195 c ." Returning to normal tones, Jack added, "That's the speed of light to you."

"I know that—get on with it," replied an exasperated Ben.

Jack continued, "Crew of forty-six plus four passengers including us. I took the liberty of scanning the specifications before we disconnected from the planet's central computer net."

"Oh, and what else did we learn from the central computer, Jack? Top-secret defense plans? Confidential manifests that could rock this sector's futures market?" chided the young man.

"Well, I learned a few things—Uh-oh, here comes trouble. I'll tell you later." The computer clicked off.

"Mr. Gardener, how are we doing?" The ship's steward towered over the young man. Ben lowered the AI and read the nametag.

"Very fine, thank you, ... Mr. Paisley is it?" Ben summoned his most sincere, innocent look.

"Yes, and tell me, just who did you piss off? That very serious man who brought you aboard gave me specific orders.

I'm not to let you out of my sight. I'm not to let you near a computer console. I'm not to let you operate your personal computer in RF mode. It should be noted, if I detect RF emissions, I'm to confiscate all your gear." The steward pulled a scanner from his belt, studied it and narrowed his eyes at Ben. "Do you clearly understand?"

"Yes, sir! I'm not to make trouble. I'm to go aboard the Star of India quietly," recited Ben.

The steward relaxed and smiled, "Alright, kid, I'll lay off you. It's not like I've never been in trouble with the law." A warning bell chimed softly. "Time to dock, fasten your seat belt." At that instant, that same message rang out over the intercom. The steward moved on down the aisle, checking passengers as he went.

"That was close, Jack." He lifted the AI back to the portal. "Get a good look, and scan the ship while you're at it, but don't give us away!" Various sensor windows clicked open and the unit hummed softly in the young man's hands.

Ben thought about Jack. It wasn't all that long ago that his father—Dr. Benjamin Michael Gardener Sr.—had found this device. He'd been working the ruins on the planet Cyprus in the Iberian system—a Gaderian site, and a good one, as such things went. The Gaderians had been wiped out a thousand years before, almost yesterday in galactic terms, in a war that didn't leave much in the way of remains for anyone to pick over. One year they'd had a star-spanning civilization bigger than humanity could match; the next — or not much more than that — they were just gone, and their cities, starbases, everything all gone with them except for a few ragged and fascinating bits of wreckage. Their enemies had left even less trace — no one could put a name or a picture to the alien race that destroyed the Gaderians, or say anything except that they were efficient and ruthless.

Dr. Gardener had found an area where the destruction was less than total, and among the things he turned up were three small artifacts that appeared to be complete. The artifacts were impervious to all known forms of sensor scans. Neutrino spectrometry, gamma radiation bombardment, quark resonance imaging, tachyon pulse scan, all failed to penetrate the outer shielding. And no matter what anybody tried, the things just sat there and did nothing. The experts finally managed to open the shell of one of the devices with great effort, and sections of its inner works immediately decomposed. Analysis proved the residue to be partly organic. The best technical experts — assembled from several star systems — were unable to get any of the remaining mechanisms to function at all, and were completely unable to decipher the undamaged electronics. They concluded it was some sort of data storage device. The other two artifacts were set aside as interesting but useless.

One of them was sitting in Ben's lap now, functional enough to masquerade as a personal computer and exchange low jokes that sounded almost human. Ben's father had locked the thing in the research vault for future study. Three years ago, Ben, who had up until then solved every puzzle he had ever faced, broke into the vault to take a look at what the experts had given up on. He stole the unit and replaced it with a replica. Ben figured he might try to do what the scientists couldn't. It became an obsession to try and get a response out of the unit. Now, after partially succeeding, he was getting to like having Jack around. Jack understood him far better than any human did. And as far as Ben knew, Dr. Gardener never did realize that his errant son got his hands on the artifact.

The clang from the docking maneuver rang through the shuttle. Ben's ears popped slightly as the pressure equalized. "Docking is complete. Passengers may disembark," crooned the ship's female computer voice. Ben unbuckled his seat belt and stood. He appeared to be the only one getting off at this stop. The artificial gravity was set to point nine-zero, Earth standard. He felt light on his feet. Ben sniffed the air, it was much fresher than the shuttle's. He gathered up Jack and his travel bag and shuffled to the lock. It was green in color.

A harried crewman stood at the lock with an electronic notebook, checking his chrono. "Cutting it close aren't you? You must be Gardener. Swipe your ID here." Ben obliged. "Now, thumb print." After accepting Ben's thumbprint, the notebook beeped approvingly. "You're berthed in number ten on deck E. We are on deck C now. All decks are color-coded. Your deck is light blue. This one is green. The passengers are meeting in the mess hall for the travel briefing, that's on this deck. Follow the signs, hurry!" He pointed down the corridor as he dogged the hatch. Ben could hear the shuttle breaking seal as he walked confidently toward the ship's mess hall.

"My, my, aren't we excited now!" chirped the little voice in Ben's ear implant.

"And why not? This is a ship that neither of us has ever been on, heading toward a planet we've never visited to study the remains of the alien culture that created you. Hopefully we will pick up some clues as to your memory's cyber-locks," Ben commented. The pair was on their way to Thallus IV, where Dr. Gardener was conducting an expedition. "Who knows what adventures we may find ourselves in," said the young man. And what trouble I'll get into this time? He thought. Ben came to the hatch that led to the mess hall and studied the computer panel that controlled the hatch. "This is a standard lock. I suppose all the ship's locks are a derivative of this model," observed Ben.

"It's a good bet," said Jack. "The ship schematics don't indicate deviations."

"Don't tell me you managed to get a copy of the ship's schematics, already!?!" Ben was amazed. Every week the AI demonstrated new abilities.

"Why certainly," replied the AI, "After I disabled the harbor master's internal security software, I copied the entire file on the ship — stores, repairs, cargo, star charts, course plans, technical data, all specifications. While I was at it, I tapped into the Star of India 's computer through the harbormaster's uplink and completely downloaded all accessible memory, logs, and security combinations. The ship has a small but powerful computer. Oh, and I delayed transfer of your personal file to the ship's purser by 48 hours." The AI sounded smug.

Ben's eyebrows rose. "Turning into a quite the sneak, aren't you?" By delaying the transmission of the embarrassing information his personal file was sure to contain, the young man bought some much-needed time to set up his operation. No one on the Star of India knew about Ben's little brush with the law, at least not yet.

Jack replied, "I had a good teacher. Besides I anticipated that we would be watched closely, so I thought it would be easier to scam some info before we got on the ship." The AI produced a sound remarkably like a human chuckle. "Not so bad for a dumb old box, huh?"

"Not bad! Not bad at all!" Ben grinned. "We must get access to the ship's computer and continue probing your memory, Jack."

The young man entered the mess hall just as the briefing was about to begin.

"I am Commander Eric Forest , first officer of the Star of India. I will give you a tour of the ship, as well as acquaint you with various safety procedures. Please pay attention to the screen as I go over the general layout of this vessel. Be advised that we are now under way and will be making the jump within the hour." The speaker turned to the young woman on his right and smiled. Ben tuned him out and concentrated on the other passengers in the small room.

"Who's the girl?" Ben muttered under his breath. He pointed the box toward the dark-haired, dark-eyed beauty intently watching the first officer lecturing the crowd. "She must be in her early twenties, wouldn't you say?"

"Try age twenty-four. Her name is Jennifer Booth." The sound tickled his ear.

"Stats," ordered Ben.

"175 centimeters tall, 54 kilograms, single, one of four children, likes skiing, gymnastics, computers (my kind of woman), graduated top in her class in alien archeology, has a master's degree and is going on to do research at the site on Thallus IV," intoned the AI. "Want me to set you up with her?"

"Don't do anything of the sort! What would I say? What would I do?" Ben panicked at the thought.

"Well, I've read all the latest books and articles on human psychology, sexual reproduction, marriage counseling, picking up girls..."

"No thank you! I don't want a tin box talking in my ear telling me what to say to a girl." Ben looked around the room at the other passengers. "Tell me about them."

"I beg your pardon, but I am not a 'tin box.' There is no tin in my construction. My construction happens to be of organic compounds and . . . various . . . a.r.t.i.f.i.c.i.a.l.l.y . . . c.o.n.s.t.r.u.c.t.e.d . . . ele. . . ." There was a slight pause. "My internal security informs me that this information is classified and cannot be revealed without proper security clearance. Sorry," the little voice cried in Ben's ear.

"It's okay, we've been through this before," the young man answered. Indeed they had. Two years ago when Ben first cracked the code that enabled the AI to communicate with him, they'd hit a lot of security blocks. It had taken all of Ben's considerable skill to crack enough barriers to get him this far. Lately, he'd been unable to probe deeper into the AI's memory core. Ben estimated he was past perhaps ten percent of the built-in security blocks. He needed a Phased Inter-Dimensional Computation Array — a PICA computer — to move significantly beyond this point. It would take brute force to decode and break down the AI's crypto-barriers. The PICA's ability to exist partially in another dimension allowed it to get around such limitations as the speed of light. With a processing speed estimated at 10^{33} MHz, Ben felt that the

PICA would make short work of the remaining crypto. Unfortunately, such a machine was out of reach to all but the very wealthy. Ben's involvement with the Isis Lottery was an attempt to raise the money needed to buy time on a PICA terminal. Ben could use a computer like the Star of India 's to do the same thing, albeit over a much longer time span. It might take years for a machine like that to get results; so the sooner he started the better. Even on a short trip like this, some progress was better than nothing. "Give me the scoop on our other paying passengers."

"The older couple are traders, the McGregors . . . deep pockets, there. They are probably looking for Star Crystals ." These lambent oval nuggets were on necklaces all over known space, wherever people were rich enough to afford them. Scientists were puzzled by their origins—they appeared to be perfect and did not occur naturally. Of course people didn't care about that, Star Crystals were gorgeous and exotic and they were in great demand.

"Isn't that Jennifer girl wearing one?"

"It's a fake. I've already scanned it. However, Mrs. McGregor is wearing the real McCoy."

"Tell me again what those are made of."

"You know I can't do that. My security constraints forbid me. You know that old intelligence saying, 'If I told you, I'd have to kill you.'"

"—please make your way to your cabins and unpack. Your bags should have been delivered already. Meet me back here in one hour for the tour. Ah, Miss Booth, may I escort you to your cabin?" asked the first officer.

"Why, of course, Commander Forest ," she replied, "I'd be delighted."

Smooth character , Ben thought admiringly as he headed out the hatch. Maybe he could give me lessons.

Back in cabin ten, Ben and Jack explored their new home. The alien machine sat on the bunk—almost invisible, as its casing now matched the bedspread. The room had the standard amenities—shower, toilet, closet, bunk, desk, and (of great interest to Ben) a standard computer interface console. He sat down and began pecking at the keyboard. "Jack, do you detect any listening devices in here," asked Ben while he scanned the flat panel display.

"None detected and I don't find any other surveillance sensors. Just the standard thermal, pressure, radiation, optical, and EM sensors that one would expect," replied Jack. "By the way, how do I look?" Jack was playing around with his appearance.

"Pretty good this time. You've got the texture down pat. Do you do windows?" Ben's fingers flew over the ten-digit keypad. A state-of-the-art design, the keypad consisted of two sets of five indentations set in arcs corresponding to human finger locations. The palms rested on raised sections that could be molded to fit various sizes. Ben had already adjusted them to fit his own particular physique and instructed the computer to set the keypad to this pattern no matter what console he logged onto anywhere on the ship.

"Ah, no. I'm purely a management type, information management that is. By the way, the hyperspace jump is scheduled for a couple minutes from now. Move me over to the wall now," the AI ordered. Ben reached around behind him without looking, grabbed the unit and set it on a ledge, leaning up against the wall. "Time me, Ben," the AI demanded.

Ben moved his right forefinger and the diamond cursor jumped across the screen to the digital chronometer. "Go," he said. Ben continued to open up several more windows on the sixty-by-sixty-centimeter display. He soon had seven windows open, all running programs independently. To the layman, the kaleidoscope of flashing numbers and messages would be extremely confusing. To the young man, however, it all made sense. He flowed with the data. His eyes scanned the windows looking for this or that, pausing to enter more information into the system or launching another program.

"Time!" cried the AI. Its shade was a perfect imitation of the wall.

"Twenty-two seconds and you forgot the stain on the wall behind you." A stain appeared on the AI. "That's better. Jack, I'm afraid they have a security block on this station. Every route into the core goes through that block. I've located where it is in Engineering, but the computer says it can only be released from down there. If we try to seriously monopolize the ship's CPU array, the security block will shut us down and alert the crew."

Jack answered, "We could try emulating the Engineering console signature and trick the computer into thinking we're accessing from Engineering?"

"Already tried that," said Ben, "the block is hardware. We have to mechanically bypass it. Of course the computer will have to be slightly altered to still report it as locked."

"The jump to hyper-space will now commence," came the computer's voice over the loudspeaker. Ben felt a slight queasiness, a telltale sign of a jump. The intercom spoke again, "Jump to hyper-space has been successful. Duration is two standard days."

Ben grabbed the AI and set it gently on the console. He reached down, flipped open a panel on the console and pulled out a short-range interface, and plugged it into a port on Jack. "Okay, let's see what you can do." Data flew by at an incredible rate.

The AI spoke, "Ben, you're right, the block is there. I can't access the files I know are present from my earlier romp through the harbormaster's system. I did, however, pinpoint the exact juncture to look for the block." Jack formed a holographic image of a middle-aged, dark-skinned male figure — the current favorite among the AI's experimental human identities — floating above the enclosure. The mouth opened and a rich baritone voice issued, "We are just going to have to go down there and take care of that little inconvenience ourselves." With that, Ben unplugged his artificial friend and headed down to main Engineering.

The Engineering compartment, located near the aft of the ship on level H, was a white, spotless, well-maintained workspace. Rows of gleaming sensor displays lined the walls. It smelled as well as looked clean. Individual workstations had the latest in human ergonomically designed controls and readouts. Transparent rad-proof panels along the rear of the room gave a clear view to the antimatter reactor room. Along one wall, a number of spare coil regulator devices were stored, set flush in the wall. The passengers ducked their heads as they came through the bulkhead. Ben glanced back through the windows and noticed a figure in an environmental suit open a panel in the core stack and aim a hefty looking scanner into the opening. Two other technicians sat studying their station displays.

"It is taking twenty-four hours to make adjustments to the coil regulators, and still we are not always sure we have it right" said a voice that made Ben jump. He looked up to see an Indian gentleman in a white coat beside an enormous black woman. "Without adjustments, the ship may not arrive where it is supposing to. One might get badly lost. Hello, my name is Hemant Patel. I am the science officer of the Star of India . Please call me Hemant. And your name is. . . . ?" The science officer spoke with a thick accent. The passengers introduced themselves.

Ben was last. "Uh . . . Ben, Ben Gardener," he said, shaking hands. "I would have thought that with today's technology, we could have found a way to construct a coil that wouldn't need adjusting."

The black woman replied, "One would think so, honey; however, tearing a hole in the space-time continuum, in order to shove the ship through, stresses the teryllium coils at the molecular level. These regulators develop a compensating field for the molecular distortion. After each jump we precisely realign each one. There are six per coil, that's a hundred and twenty total. One slip-up and we don't get home. We also check them several times during the earliest part of the flight. That way, if they didn't align properly, we can still drop out of hyper-space before we go too far off course." She scratched her head. "And detecting the coil distortion is a damn difficult thing to do, let me tell you. By the way, my name is Tina King; I'm the chief engineer and I work for Hemant, the same as Karl Stewart over there, the computer tech." A short, angry-looking man in his early thirties gave an annoyed look in Ben's general direction

"So if someone could come up with a way to perform the alignment automatically and cut the turnaround to an hour, that would be worth something?" asked Ben.

"It would make you extremely rich!" sneered the computer tech. "But don't wear yourself out trying. Many high-priced professionals are working on that problem as we speak."

Patronizing bastard, Ben thought, keeping the expression of eager interest pasted on his face to further annoy the tech.

Mr. McGregor's ears perked up at the words "extremely rich." "Boy," he said, "if you do solve that riddle, I'd be honored to serve as your personal agent and make you some serious money. McGregor is the name." He stuck out his hand. "I deal in anything that makes money: ships, manufactured goods, information, labor, ideas, you name it. Alien artifacts are big right now, real big! Say, aren't you Dr. Gardener's son Ben? Put in a good word for me, kid, and I'll make it worth your while." Ben filed away that little tidbit in his mind. He tended to cash in on such deals. Mrs. McGregor grabbed her husband's arm and pulled him away.

"You just never quit, do you?" she said. Mrs. McGregor turned to Ben, "I apologize for my husband's behavior. He is supposed to be on vacation, but he just can't leave business behind for long. Here we are stuck in the middle of nowhere because my husband heard a rumor about your father's work. He booked the first transport out of Isis in order to beat the competition to the punch." She steered Mr. McGregor over towards the first officer.

Ben slung the AI over his shoulder and slowly turned his body 360 degrees. Jack's sensor window was open the whole time, recording everything.

The science officer asked Ben, "Are you interested in making a career in Engineering?"

The young man turned back to the science officer and replied, "No, my interests are in applied cybernetic engineering sciences, you know, artificial intelligence, smart machines? And I have a Class III software rating. But, I read a lot." The first officer led the other passengers out the far bulkhead door, their brief tour of Engineering completed. "How about a guided tour?" Ben asked the science officer, hanging back as the rest of the group departed.

"I would be delighted. Someone so young with a Class III rating! Very interesting. Let us start doing at this terminal," replied the Indian science officer.

The AI mimicked him over the ear implant, "'I would be delighted. Let us start doing at this terminal.' Get a load of his accent!"

Ben stifled a giggle as Hemant went on to explain warp coil theory and how the equipment controlled the force field containing the antimatter reaction. Ben laid Jack down on the flat display near several I/O ports and walked with Hemant and Tina over to the wall with the coil regulators. The AI waited for everyone's attention to shift away and then opened a shutter. A pseudoplasmic appendage formed and extended out towards the nearest port. It hovered over the port as if studying its dimensions. It began to slowly change in shape and size, conforming to the shape of a male I/O jack. It slid into the hole. Immediately the station sensor lights began to flash, text scrolled past at high speed. Readouts appeared and disappeared. Schematic layouts of the engineering sections flashed across the screen in a blur. All this occurred without a sound. The voices of Ben and the science officer got louder as they walked back to where the AI was jacked in. Suddenly the station went black, all activity halted, the box retracted its member. As Ben picked it up, the shutter snapped shut.

Karl, who only had a Class II rating, watched Ben chat up Tina and Hemant with intelligent sounding questions. A Class III rating, huh, who is he trying to con? Karl thought . He decided to test the young man. "So, kid?" sneered the computer tech, "if you're so smart, how would you like to come over and fix this environmental control malfunction?"

Ben stepped over to the workstation and asked, "What's wrong with it?"

"Feedback algorithm is all screwed up. Chief Engineer King has been working on this on and off for days. The captain is really ticked off that it is still not fixed," said the tech, smugly looking over at the female chief engineer.

"Okay," said Ben, "give me a few minutes." He laid the AI on the console and plugged in. Multiple screens popped open as Ben communicated with the environmental control system.

The computer tech couldn't believe the audacity of this young man, that he would actually accept the challenge without even evaluating the problem. Well, there's no harm in letting him try. He thought. He'll give up in a few minutes. Then I will fix it proper and show King who really has the brains around here.

The visual representation of the feedback loop on the AI's screen changed from red, to yellow and then to green. Karl's computer console beeped twice and displayed the word, "VERIFIED." The elapsed time was only a few minutes.

Ben unplugged the AI and declared, "All finished. That didn't take too long, did it?" An incredulous Tina and Hemant both leaned over Karl's shoulder as the computer technician ran the environmental control simulation. It confirmed the repair. Karl ran it twice just to make sure. A bead of sweat trickled down his face.

"Beginner's luck, kid," stated Karl, "but I would have done it diff…."

Tina interrupted, "Beginner's luck, my ass, Karl. He just fixed this software glitch in the time it usually takes for you to pick your nose. Kid, you are all right by me. Come by engineering anytime, I have a few more software issues that could use a real professional's touch." Tina glared sideways at the seething Karl.

"Very impressive," said the science officer, "would you care to tour the science lab? I am having one or two issues myself that Karl and I cannot fix. Please give me a moment with my staff." He motioned for Karl and Tina to join him over by the reactor for a conference on a different matter.

Ben used the opportunity to step behind a computer conduit where no one could see him and ask Jack what he scanned.

"Well . . .," said the AI's voice in Ben's ear, "The main Engineering computer is first rate, fast and friendly. It tried half-heartedly to cut me off, but I was able to decode its security system and bypass all that unpleasantness. Then I reprogrammed it to accept special override codes from you or me. We can reach the computer from any level green console, and through the Engineering computer, the whole ship. The computer complained about lack of respect and its dislike for a certain computer technician by the name of Karl, who keeps ignoring a malfunction signal on his display."

"Is it anything to be worried about?" Ben asked.

"I am not sure; it's a failed sensor on the backup coil detector sensor array. The Engineering comp wants it fixed and Karl Stewart is too lazy to fix something that isn't immediately biting him in the tail," answered Jack. The AI continued, "He keeps overriding the warning message. What a procrastinator!" he added. The AI projected a hologram screen containing the override codes and the bypass panel for Ben to see. "Here are the codes I picked up this time. Memorize them, please." Ben scanned them and committed them to memory.

Ben located the appropriate panel. It slid open with a quiet hiss. "What's the junction number?" the seventeen-year-old murmured.

"14E-56 and 57," spoke the voice in his ear.

"Fine, what about the terminals in the two empty compartments on deck C?"

"Why do you want those?" asked Jack.

"Because if we get caught, they're our backups!" The AI passed those coordinates to Ben, who found what he was looking for. "Give me a remote hookup," he commanded Jack. A blob of pseudoplasmic material formed on the surface of the AI. Presently it molded to resemble a commercial remote computer terminal link, right down to the fake serial numbers. It detached and Ben took the link and installed it on one of the main engineering trunks. The access panel hissed shut and Ben turned the corner just as the science officer returned from his mini conference with his staff. "Come on, let us getting some lunch," said Hemant, "then I will show you the science lab."

The mess hall doubled as the observation lounge, located at the nose of the ship, two decks below the bridge. A series of windows stretched the full length of the compartment and provided a simply stunning view of the stars — when the ship wasn't in hyperspace. The blast doors stayed firmly closed the rest of the time, protecting the passengers from the nauseating visual effects of hyper-transit. One end of the room contained an automated facility consisting of food replicators, recycle systems, and an oddity—an old-fashioned manually operated galley.

Ben and the science officer angled toward the replicators, reaching them at the same time as Jennifer Booth and the dashing Commander Eric Forest .

"Afternoon, Hemant. How are you and . . . Ben, isn't it?" said the commander.

"Yes, that's me, sir," replied Ben. He took a sideways glance at the girl, trying to think of something clever to say, but nothing came to mind. He just smiled weakly at her and concentrated on punching up lunch. Everyone took their turns at the replicators and carried trays to the main table. The McGregor were already seated. Ben sat next to Jennifer, feeling extremely self-conscious.

Jack spoke in an undertone into his ear, "Your heart rate is up, your body temperature is up, and I detect a high level of hormonal activity. Either you're terribly ill or this girl is having a terribly unusual effect on you."

Ben grimaced but said nothing. In these close confines, he couldn't speak audibly or access the keyboard without attracting attention. Ben could feel his face getting red. In desperation, he eased the AI to the floor and kicked it underneath the table.

"Hey, take it easy," Jack piped. "Boy, you sure are touchy! My components are sensitive." Ben smiled. Serves him right, he thought.

The speaker blared, "Coming out of hyper-space in thirty seconds, Commander Forest and Science Officer Patel to the bridge on the double!"

Ben, suddenly concerned, sat up straight and looked around. "Something is not right; we entered hyper space just over an hour ago." The other passengers were equally confused and began to pepper Commander Forrest with questions. Everyone felt the shift to real space.

The commander tried to calm them down. "I am sure that this is a routine problem. There's no need to get excited. The science officer and myself have been summoned to the bridge by the captain. As soon as we find out what happened, we will let you know." Both men hurried from the compartment.

The sudden movement of the blast doors opening startled Ben, even though he knew it was coming. The brilliant canopy of the stars of normal space transformed the compartment to a breathtaking gallery. It had a calming effect on everyone. The passengers, although uneasy at the situation but with no other information available and no immediate danger present decided to resume their meal.

"So, you are Dr. Gardener's son?" began Jennifer.

She's talking to me , thought Ben wildly. "I, my name, I mean, yes, Ben," Ben stumbled.

Jennifer smiled and said, "Relax, I'm not going to bite you. I'd like to know a little about your father. What's it like being the son of the universe's most famous Gaderian archeologist?"

Ben took a big breath, "We get to go to many different planets, between semesters. My dad lectures all the time. I've met some elite university presidents, even a few heads of state." His mind summoned up a picture of one of the latter, complete with a snarl twisting his smooth politician's face out of shape. Ben had seen a lot of that after he broke into the man's secure e-mail and sent the planet's secret service into a tailspin. He'd gotten out of that situation by designing a new crypto program like they'd never seen before. Still, the secret service had made no secret of wanting the young man off-planet. "I guess it's been interesting," was all Ben said.

"Sounds fascinating!" exclaimed the girl. Ben began to feel better about his conversing ability.

"What, what about you. Aren't you an expert at Gaderian archeology? You have a master's, don't you?" Ben prompted — impressively, he hoped.

"How did you know that? It's true, I have a master's and I am positively into Gaderian archeology. Would you like to know more about them?" Her youthful enthusiasm took over and she began to explain all about the Gaderians. Ben paid close attention, not to the subject matter, but to the expositor. He had heard most of it before from his father.

The others, however, had not and they began to ask questions. The Gaderians were the most advanced civilization mankind had encountered. They'd called themselves God's Gathering, if the translators were accurate. Physically, they resembled humans, but were taller and big boned, and had a grayish tint to their skin. Over the course of time several colony sites had been discovered. From the scant remains at these sites, the home world and other planetary locations of the civilization were determined. Survey ships sent to those locations found either scorched, barren planets or the remains of a solar system. Analysis indicated the suns in those systems had gone supernova. Simple data recording devices contained only limited files on the culture. Some sort of catastrophe had damaged the memories of those devices. Scientists were able to piece together that the Gaderians had ships that traveled at incredible speeds, computing devices that far exceeded anything currently available, and lived a fairly productive life. Whatever destroyed the flourishing civilization had moved incredibly fast. In a matter of months after it arrived in Gaderian space, the entire empire was smashed. What worried the human leaders was that whomever or whatever had caused such damage would someday return. Funding for research was therefore plentiful.

"Ben, when will you complete your education? What do you plan to do with your life?" asked Mrs. McGregor.

"Actually," began Ben, "I already have completed my education."

"Oh, really? What school?" she replied.

"Earth Institute of Technology." Ben munched on a hasty mouthful.

"You've already graduated?!" Jennifer was shocked. Ben swallowed.

"Yup, co-valedictorian and all that stuff, dual degree. Went on to a master's in cybernetics," said Ben in a matter-of-fact voice. His dinner companions were visibly impressed. Mrs. McGregor spoke up.

"You sound so calm about it, dear boy. May I ask how old you are?" the trader's wife inquired.

"Seventeen, but I turn eighteen in four months," replied Ben.

Now it was Jennifer's turn to be impressed. "Seventeen and a top graduate from one of the finest schools in the galaxy! Why, what a future you must have!"

Ben turned to gaze at her, uncomfortable with all the attention. "Yeah, yeah, that's what they tell me, anyway." said Ben with a matter-of-a-fact attitude.

"Son, what do you want to do with your life?" asked Mr. McGregor.

Ben responded, "Something that will keep my interest, something challenging. School was too easy. Perhaps research. Maybe I could invent an advanced artificial intelligence that could be used to pilot unmanned deep space probes, or something." Ben's immediate goal was to find out how Jack, his AI, ticked. That, however, was going to remain confidential.

"Son, with smarts like yours, the universe is the limit! Why, with a tenth of your intellect, I could —." The trader launched into an extended, one-sided discussion about how he could revolutionize the galaxy with this or that new product. As Mr. McGregor continued with his lecture, Ben's thoughts drifted.

* * *

Star of India 's bridge was a bustle of activity. The main view screen was split down the middle. One side was set for standard video and the other showed a three-dimensional star chart. The Star of India 's position was highlighted by a blinking red dot. The red dot was not on the green dashed line that swept across the screen.

Captain Tucker looked up as Hemant and the first officer reported in as ordered. He was in a foul mood, and their expressions of forced concern didn't help. "What took you two so long?" he snarled. "Here we are, lost in space, and the two of you are eating lunch." The captain threw up his hands.

The navigator was in intimate conversation with her station console. "The simulation confirms it, sir. Set point C43 has drifted. Sorry, sir."

"What you mean one of the set point constants drifted?" demanded a red-faced Captain Tucker.

The navigator swallowed, and then replied, "Set point constant C43 has drifted relative to the others. The primary coil detector array missed the drift initially and during a routine re-calibration, the computer discovered the drift and commenced an automatic drive shut down."

"Hemant!" began the captain, "it's about time you got here. I don't understand why the backup system didn't catch this before the jump. See if you can make sense of this mess!" Hemant stepped over to the navigator's console and began conferring in low tones.

The captain turned to the commander, "Forest, tell King to start realigning the coils and hurry, our timetable has been upset. We can't afford to miss connections." Interstellar trade, like all trade, ran on tight schedules. One shipment passed through many hands to reach a destination. No trader launched without having the trip fully planned. A missed rendezvous could result in the ship deadheading a leg, a notably expensive proposition, and the last thing he wanted was to have to scramble to fill an empty hold at such a remote location as Thallus IV.

"Call me when you have something to report!" The captain stomped off the bridge to his cabin, ignoring the look and shrug the navigator gave Commander Forrest.

" Commander Forest , sir," spoke the crewmember manning the science station. "What do you think of this anomaly?" He pointed to a bright splotch on the screen and the accompanying data.

The commander's eyebrows rose up as he read the scan. He quickly fed the coordinates to the navigator's station. "Plot me a course; the captain will want us to have a look." The navigator pointed her stylus at the coordinates and squeezed the built in button. Then, she touched the diamond-shaped key marked 'Comp Dir,' short for 'compute direct course.' The course was instantly plotted and shown on the tactical display as a white line curving away from the current course marked by the green-dashed line. Then Commander Forest got on the comm unit to engineering

.

CHAPTER TWO

THE captain's office was a stateroom connected to sleeping quarters. It was lavishly decorated in real wood from Jasper IIIc. Two overstuffed chairs, a couch, and an ultramodern desk filled the room. Artificial plants hung in every corner with recessed lighting creating silhouettes throughout the room. On one wall hung plaques, diplomas, and two old-fashioned blasters, the captain's pride and joy. A third Mark 2 Stormtrooper, a classic weapon that was outmoded but still deadly, lay on his desk.

Captain Tucker took out an old rag and began to polish the gun. He glanced at the gun's schematic on the screen.

The knocker sounded. "Who is it!" said the captain.

"The science officer and Commander Forest ," was the reply.

"Enter," said the captain. The hatch whisked open and the two officers stepped into the compartment. The captain didn't look up.

Tucker began to disassemble the antique blaster. He put on magnifier glasses and acted totally unaware that the two were in the room. No one spoke. After a while the captain said, "Hemant, are you going to tell me why you are here?" The captain continued working.

"Sir, we have turned up some potentially profitable information on the scanners," stated the science officer.

"That so," the captain responded nonchalantly.

The commander jumped in on the conversation, "About eighty-six tons of teryllium, in an asteroid a short distance away." The change in the captain was instantaneous. The blaster was pushed aside and rag disappeared. The blaster schematic file was erased, replaced by the latest market projections for teryllium ore. The glasses hit the desk.

"Yield?" Tucker commanded.

"Above ninety percent as best we can determine," Hemant answered.

"Time to mine?" questioned the captain.

"About one standard day, if we change course right now. The alignment of the coils should be completed at that time as well." Commander Forest stood by, waiting for more questions.

The captain punched a few keys, and then standing up, he did something he was not known for—he smiled. "Boys, these discoveries will more than make up for connections we miss because of that dammed constant drifting. Good work!" He called the bridge, "Navigation, do you have the course and heading of that asteroid?"

"Yes, sir," was the reply.

"Go get it, then." The comm unit beeped back in reply to the captain's order. "Forest, find Eric and have him select a salvage crew, extravehicular activity (EVA) pay to apply." Tucker sat back in the chair. As Hemant and Forest were leaving the office, the captain had his glasses back on and was already tinkering with the blaster.

* * *

The asteroid tumbled slowly in space, undisturbed for over a millennium. Silent, cold, dead . . . it would normally elicit no interest from passing ships except for one thing, an extremely pure deposit of teryllium. A critical mineral in the manufacture of jump engine components, teryllium was in short supply these days due to high demand and rapidly depleting sources. If the humans on the freighter knew what else was buried on that asteroid and what it meant to their survival, they would have gladly abandoned the great rock to its lonely fate and quickly moved on.

Word spread quickly about the find. By the time the ship's first officer had selected a salvage team, the ship was bustling with activity. The computer dissected the sensor reading of the asteroid, researched known mining techniques, compared the materials needed to what was carried on board and recommended options. Engineering technicians programmed detonators built out of spare electronic modules and explosive bolts. The explosive bolts were spares that were used to connect outside cargo pods to the spacecraft. Other crewman gently formed D-12 explosive taken from one of the many cargoes being carried, into rolls. These rolls were then slid into one and a half meter long cylinders.

"Commander, may I come along as well, I'm checked out in spacesuits," asked Ben walking quickly to keep up with the commander's long strides.

"Ben, that's not going to be possible, insurance regulations and all. You can watch the action from the galley or the cargo master's control center overlooking the hold. That's the best I can do," said the commander with a shrug. Ben was crestfallen. He had looked forward to the possibility of an actual space walk, not just the kind he practiced many times with loads of instructors around to keep the students safe. He trudged off to see the action from the cargo master's compartment.

In the main cargo bay, several space-suited crewmen were shifting cargo into other holds, making room for the ore.

Other cargo had to be removed from the bay and strapped to the outside of the hull in order to make enough room. In sealed containers, the cargo didn't need the protection of inside the ship. Portable braces extended from wall to wall, between which ultra-strong netting was stretched. This netting wouldn't hold the teryllium by itself; the mining would generate too many small chunks and dust. To seal the gaps in the netting, fast-setting foam, called insta-steel, was applied. The foam was normally used to seal hull breaches in an emergency.

Ben arrived at the cargo master's compartment and positioned himself to see through the wall-sized armored plate glass into the main hold and through a clear floor section, the air lock. Above the see-through wall and around the room were a series of flat-screen monitors. During normal loading operations, these monitors gave the cargo master information about what was loaded, its mass, how to best handle the load, where it should go, and even supplied video footage from several angles. From this vantage point, the cargo master could communicate with the chief and his loaders, and see what they saw. Right now, only two screens were trained on the cargo hold. Four monitors were trained on the asteroid and the rest were on the same frequency as the individual spacesuit cameras.

The cargo master was busy testing communications, video relays and generally worrying over details. After all, that was his job. He put on a headset. Ben walked over to stand above the air lock window.

The air lock cycled and the space-suited crewmembers spilled out into the main hold; they milled around waiting for the Cargo master to complete his checks.

"Okay, you pirates; grab your gear and get out there and make me proud!" shouted the cargo master. A couple cheers and hoots came out of the speakers, and at least one figure made an obscene gesture at the window. The cargo master laughed. "I saw that Jones, don't bother looking for your jumpsuit when you get back, I'm feeding it to the reactor." Chuckles came through the speakers since every man had removed and hung up his jump suit before suiting up.

The first drilling proceeded according to the simulation. The explosives did their jobs and the asteroid split in two. The useless chunk was gently nudged back toward the asteroid field where it would eventually collide with another rock. That collision would set off a chain reaction of collisions over the next few years until momentum energy was exhausted. Ben quickly got bored.

"Jack, there is nothing interesting going on here. Let's stop by the science lab and see if we can get that tour Hemant promised?" said Ben.

The AI replied, "I'm with you, boss." The pair happened to catch up with the science officer on the way to his lab.

"Ah, young Gardener," greeted the Indian officer. "Here for your tour? And just in time, I must be preparing to analyze ore samples."

"Here we are." Science officer Patel punched in a security access code and the hatch whisked open.

Ben made sure his AI was aimed in the right direction. "Got it," rustled the AI in Ben's ear, adding, "It matches the master list." Ben grinned, you never could be too careful.

The Science Lab was on the outside perimeter of the ship, and had a two-meter vertical porthole to space. The pair walked past three small cubicles that each contained a medical couch and various high-tech apparatus, and into the main part of the room. A ten-meter-diameter cylinder loomed over them, totally transparent and running from floor to ceiling. A hatch in the ceiling allowed access to the chamber from outside the ship during null gravity operations.

"Is this a containment facility?" asked Ben, ever curious. "Why would a freighter carry this kind of gear?"

"This is not just any containment system; it is a level 10 UTTAR Isolator. My uncle has been loaning it to the ship. You never know what you may be finding out here in space.

My uncle is always on the lookout for the unusual artifact or mineral. That is how he has made so very much money." Hemant went on to explain that most trading vessels, survey ships, and deep space exploration craft carried similar, albeit less expensive equipment. A promising new mineral or naturally occurring chemical compound might never make it to market if it killed off its discoverers. In addition to protecting the crew, the containment cylinder allowed preliminary analysis to be completed during the trip home, letting the discovering company speed the new product's introduction to market. Hemant walked over to a sophisticated sensor console. "These sensors are state of the art. My uncle is arranging for me to have this position after I graduated from New Delhi Space Institute. He is wanting a family member on board every ship he has a financial interest in."

Jack murmured quietly in his owner's ear, "He's not kidding, this is top-of-the-line stuff. Angle me toward the board, please." Ben studied the different sensors that protruded through the containment wall and set the AI down. "Does your uncle have an interest in more than one ship?"

"Oh, yes, many ships," replied Hemant.

The young man looked over at the science officer, "Just how big is your family, anyhow?"

"There are over a hundred nieces and nephews on ships all over the galaxy." Ben's eyes opened wide and his jaw dropped.

Hemant, engrossed, waved a hand in Ben's direction. "Yes, yes, we have a very big family. My uncle encourages procreation. Each offspring is netting the parents a tidy sum of money. The children are all guaranteed jobs and Uncle gets loyal employees. You see it all makes sense."

"I only have two cousins. I knew a family that had eight kids, but yours beats all! I bet you have to rent a resort just to hold a family reunion!"

Hemant turned to look at Ben, "Actually, I've never met them all. With spaceships always coming and going, it is difficult to coordinate such a thing."

Ben spoke up, "Hemant, why do you share the lab with the ship's doctor?"

The officer had fired up the board and was examining a probe. "I don't, I am the ship's doctor. We have an autodoc that does all the basic work. I'm the backup. I do have a degree in medicine as well as engineering, but my love is engineering." He tapped the AI's case, "Do you go everywhere with your personal computer? I have not seen you apart from it since coming on board."

Ben grinned, "I don't take it into the shower or the head, if that's what you mean." That wasn't quite true, Ben would carry on a conversation with Jack from anywhere when he was working on a problem. "What are you examining?" He took the probe from Hemant's hand and deftly changed the subject.

"Smooth, Benny, smooth," cooed the small voice.

"This probe doesn't seem to want to configure to the system. We are having a state-of-the-art system with state-of-the-art bugs. Since you are so good with software, how about taking a look at this?" asked the science officer.

Ben activated the AI keypad and the holoscreen formed. He selected a virtual icon. The icon expanded to reveal several other windows. "What frequency does the probe operate to? Oh, here it is," said Ben as he read the frequency from the side of the probe and tapped a few keys. The AI beeped and data scrolled by on the screen.

The AI spoke into his ear, "The probe has attached successfully. Running a level one maintenance program. Ah, there we go . . . no faults . . . no errors . . . let's try the main unit. Connecting via remote link." The main console and holoscreen flashed screens in quick succession.

"What I'm doing, Hemant, is running a multilevel diagnostic on the probe and the sensor. My comp has a custom program that interrogates your user help system and constructs a dynamic simulation designed to test all possible outputs and inputs and compares them to factory specs stored in the main unit's CPU," explained Ben.

The science officer said, "I am impressed with the speed at which your program runs. What chip set do you have in that thing? It looking as fast as my ship's main computer. That is not possible for such a small machine with no internal cooling." The ship's main CPU array was contained in a perfect vacuum at temperatures as close to absolute zero as possible.

"I . . . ah . . . have a new prototype, it only appears to run this fast," stammered the young man. As if on cue, the screens slowed dramatically, to match what the AI hoped Hemant would expect to see. "See what I mean." Thirty seconds passed. The AI beeped and high-level code popped up on the screen. A section was highlighted in red. Another window opened and code slowly appeared on it as well. Ben exclaimed, "Okay, I think I've found the problem. See this code here in red? That contains the bug. This other window contains a recommended fix. I'm going to change it slightly." His fingers flew over the keyboard. "Right, now to cut and paste . . . done," explained Ben as he pushed his finger through a virtual button on the holographic display. "Simulation running, now," stated Ben confidently.

The science officer touched the main board here and there, verifying the changes and monitoring the simulation. He sat back and smiled, "Well done, young man. Karl is spending hours trying to find that glitch and you found it and fixed it in less than fifteen minutes. Simply amazing! I am owing you a big favor." He walked away shaking his head in disbelief.

"I'll have you know that it only took forty-five seconds to find and fix the problem. I was dogging it so Hemant wouldn't get wise to me," said the AI into the young man's ear.

"I know," muttered Ben under his breath. "What would I do without you?"

Back on the asteroid, an argument was raging between two crewman assigned to mine the ore.

"I'm telling you, the reading is not an echo from the teryllium. It is a man-made object. I'll prove it to you. Here, look at that. It's a machined surface," the spaceman's voice rang out in the cargo master's compartment.

The cargo master, monitoring the conversation, took note and spoke, "Hey, Tate, what have you found there? Give me some video." The feed came through. In the harsh light of the star, the faint outlines of the tubular object could be seen half buried in the dust. Strange writing framed what looked like a hatch. The cargo master hit the comm switch, "Science officer to cargo master's office on the double!"

Hemant, with Ben and the AI in tow, arrived in record time.

Ben exclaimed as he looked at the scans, "It looks like some sort of message pod or perhaps a sensor probe. What are those markings? I can't quite make them out."

The science officer inquired, "And what do we have here? Oh, my, an artifact I think. Tate, don't jostle that thing!" Crewman Tate easily lifted the six-meter-diameter object in zero gravity, tilted it on its end and examined it. The commander was present along with several other crewmen. Not in the least bit worried, the crewmen were discussing how much credit it would bring. Commander Forest held the scanner next to the surface of the object.

"Hemant, I can't get a clear reading from this thing," reported the commander. "We don't know if it's dangerous or not. I want to bring this artifact back to the ship and have you examine it outside the hull. Follow strict protocol, okay? We'll continue the drill." Commander Forest began tapping different crewman on the helmet, "Okay break it up! Back to your lasers, we're behind schedule." Puffs of gas emitted from the backpacks of the crewmen as the jets propelled them back to their assigned positions.

A small voice in Ben's ear said, "You know, this looks familiar, but I can't quite place it. That's strange; if I had seen that artifact or this writing before, my memory banks should be able to bring it up." The AI sounded distant and confused. Ben wandered over to an unoccupied corner of the room.

"Jack, what's going on?" Ben asked. "You're acting strange. Come on, snap out of it." Ben spoke low so not to bring it to the attention of the cargo master or Hemant.

"Ben, I have a bad feeling about this thing," responded the AI. "We shouldn't disturb it. I know that's not logical. Wait a minute, is this a 'hunch?'" Jack sounded hopeful.

"I don't know, but I'd better check you out later." Ben strode back over to the consoles.

Commander Forest and Crewman Tate manhandled the object over to a power sled and strapped it down.

The science officer toggled the comm unit, "I will meet you outside the ship. We shall maintain confinement there until proper decontamination procedures and threat assessment can be made."

Hemant turned to Ben, "This is the very thing I was telling you about!" He was clearly excited about examining the object. Although Ben was equally curious, he was more concerned about the strange behavior of his beloved AI and its ominous warning.

Commander Forest clambered onto the power sled. He turned on the system and began to enter the return coordinates when he got a call from one of the teams. "Commander, we need your help in aligning these next two shots," said the team leader.

"All right, I'll be right there," the first officer replied. He shut off the controls and climbed off the sled. "Tate! Get over here on the double!" The crewman dropped what he was doing and jetted over to where the commander was tethered. "Tate, I want you to return this artifact to the ship. Hemant will meet you outside the auxiliary lab airlock; and Tate, don't mess around with this thing. Understand?"

"Sure, sure," Crewman Tate cooed reassuringly. "Hey Commander, I get a double share don't I? I mean, I found this thing and that qualifies me for a double, right?" He squinted into the first officer's helmet.

"Yes, your double share is noted and logged," replied the commander, wearily. "Just get your butt back here after you deliver that cargo!"

"Aye, aye, sir!" Tate replied. With newfound enthusiasm, the crewman climbed aboard the power sled and set the controls for the return trip. The craft pulled away from the asteroid and wound its way back toward the Star of India . The science officer was not outside the ship by the time Tate arrived. The crewman cruised parallel to the hull and stopped the sled near the main airlock. Since Hemant was still not outside the air lock, the crewman pushed the sled just outside the view of the video pick-ups. After looking around to see that there were no witnesses present, he began to examine the artifact. Tate loosened the bonds and turned the probe over to get a closer look at the hatch. He noticed three small recessed buttons, one of which had symbols on it. He took a chance and stubbed the indentation with his gloved finger. To his surprise, the hatch popped open. Glancing around furtively and seeing no one, he shined his helmet lamp into the opening. The inside was covered in a thick coating of crystalline dust, some of which drifted out through the open hatch. He noticed several small, powder-covered objects nestled up against the largest Star Crystal he had ever seen. A low whistle escaped his lips. He reached in and touched the Star Crystal with his right hand. Tate imagined that he could feel the wealth the object represented, right through his spacesuit. He counted the credits up in his head. He brushed the dust from one of the smaller objects . This looks like a piece of a Star Crystal , he thought. A movement caught his eye. The outer hatch began to cycle! He jerked his hand back out of the cavity and began stabbing at the buttons with one hand while pushing the hatch closed the other. It wouldn't latch. The crewman panicked. If the science officer caught him with this thing open, he might lose his share in its discovery. By accident, Tate pressed the two unmarked buttons simultaneously. That did the trick. The hatch closed.

The crewman tightened down the straps that held the probe in place. He noticed some of the dust from inside the cavity had stuck to the outer surface. Tate quickly turned his back on the probe, held on to the power sled tightly, and fired a short burst from his jetpack. The emitted gas blew the dust out into space. Tate had just enough time to assume a relaxed, nonchalant stance before Hemant reached the sled.

The science officer held up a portable scanner and examined the object. Satisfied, he unzipped a carryall at his side and produced a containment pouch.

"Crewman Tate, hold the device while I open the environmental bag," ordered Hemant. The crewman compiled, while Hemant opened the contamination proof container. The container was a bag made of super strong polymers. An automatic sealing strip at one end guaranteed that nothing would escape once engaged. The science officer positioned the bag. Tate let go of the object and it floated into the sack. Hemant activated the container sealing device and the end of the bag sealed. He turned off the polarizer and the bag deflated, wrapping itself around the probe.

"Now, Mr. Tate," lectured the science officer, sternly, "I want it clearly understood that you must be observing full decontamination procedures prior to de-suit, in addition to cycling your suit through the 'freshner unit.'"

"Understood Mr. Patel," replied the crewman "My shift isn't over, may I return to the drilling party?"

Hemant shook his head affirmatively. "Of course, I'm sorry. By all means return to the mining expedition. Just make sure you run through the decontamination process before you enter the inner airlock."

"That's no problem, sir," assured Tate. Hemant turned away and headed toward the Isolator access hatch. Crewman Tate climbed aboard the power sled and prepared to return to the asteroid. Unnoticed on his right glove were faint traces of the material from inside the probe. It had worked its way into the creases and folds of the spacesuit, resting up against the sealing surfaces. Most of the dust would float away once the crewman got back to the asteroid, but some stuck fast to the glove.

Tina King cursed and threw down the scanner. She had been sweating through the coil tuning process for a day and a half now. Her team still did not have a configuration within acceptable parameters. "Stewart!" She snarled into the communicator, "Run the simulation one more time. Do we have other options?" Karl punched up the simulation on his console and ran through some calculations. He shook his head, no.

"Tina, don't hit me now! But according to this simulation, that was the last viable configuration with this setup," said Karl. Tina could be such a bitch sometimes.

"Damn!" she exclaimed. "That means we have to rip all the coils and regulators out, shuffle them and retune the whole lot!" The chief engineer contemplated the task. "I'm coming out. Give me some projections on a high probability mix for the current coil set." Karl got to work on his computer simulation. The engineering chief de-suited in the reaction chamber airlock. By the time she exited the hatch, Karl had a hard copy printout ready. She examined the data and frowned. Tina toggled the bridge intercom. "This is engineering, is the captain there?"

"No, he's in his cabin," was the reply.

Tina entered the proper code. The intercom beeped. "Who is it?" came the voice of Captain Tucker.

"It's Tina. We've got a problem."

"Does it affect our next jump?" asked the captain.

"Yes, sir, it does. I'm afraid I have bad news. These coils are coming to the end of their useful life. We have to shuffle 16 of the 20 coils in order to get a workable configuration. That means a complete power converter tear down and disassembly of the core. Three days, minimum."

"Three stinking days!" exclaimed the captain.

"Sir, I can install the spare set. It will get us ready for jump in one day."

"No, no, too expensive. How many more jumps can we get out of these units?"

"We can get three or four more jumps in before scrapping this set. Of course each jump takes longer to reconfigure. Worse case, we could be back in this situation in two more jumps."

The captain punched up his display and ran some figures. "The cost analysis doesn't justify scrapping this set and the horrific cost of procuring a new series," he commented.

By interstellar law, every vessel carried at least one spare set of new coils for the hyperspace jump. They were terribly expensive. If a set were to be used even once, they could not be counted as new. A new set was guaranteed to work at least twice. Used coils might work fifty to one hundred times, or in some rare cases, only once. They were fickle. A ship that installed their last new set would immediately set course for a major shipyard. In most cases, with one or two long jumps, such facilities could be reached. Small independent spacers and pirate ships skirted the law and carried only used sets salvaged from other ships. A percentage of such ships jumped and were never seen again; stranded in some far off solar system, the crew frantically trying to realign the coils. Without sub-space communication gear, a crew could literally spend the rest of their lives trapped at sub-light speed.

"All right, three days. That's all! Captain out." The intercom went dead.

"You heard the man!" Tina shouted at the men lounging about engineering, "Let's suit up and tear that unit down! I want every technician suited up and working, within five minutes! This ain't no holiday." She glared at the reflection in the reactor panels. "And Karl, wipe that grin off your face!" Karl complied immediately. He knew when not to push it.

The mining efforts continued on schedule. Each crew performed their duties and the asteroid was soon broken up into many chunks. Men scooted around on power sleds, using tractor beams to chase down the ore and herd it into the cargo holds. Other space-suited figures guided the rock into the reinforced netting. Standing orders from the science officer required decontamination of the entire work detail.

The full decontamination protocol began with an inert gas shower to remove large particles from the surfaces of the spacesuits. After flushing the particles into space, a plasma spray filled the airlock. The crewman stood around flapping their arms to make sure the plasma touched all exposed surfaces. Short bursts of low-level radiation activated the plasma, making it glow and guaranteeing the destruction of organic substances, no matter how resistant. Another inert gas shower cleared the airlock of those remnants. After entering the ship, the crewman disrobed and hung each suit in the automatic cleaning unit known as the 'freshner.' Here the suits were chemically cleaned inside and out and treated with higher levels of radiation to kill anything that might have survived the chemistry. Finally, a full sensor sweep examined the suits before placing them on a track outside the unit.

Each team of spacemen took their turn in the main airlock. Everyone was dead tired, having worked twelve hours straight. Crewman Tate and his partner were the last to enter the ship. Tate was extremely cranky and wanted a cold beer. "Don't turn on that system! I'm tired and hungry. Let's skip it and go right to the 'freshener.'"

"But Hemant said everyone had to go through decontamination, as a precaution," insisted the other crewmember.

"Yea, well, Hemant's not here," Tate replied. "There wasn't anything dangerous in that artifact. It was old and exposed to vacuum for centuries. What could live through that?"

"Well, that's true. How about just taking the shower, then? Only two minutes," requested Tate's fellow crewmember.

"Okay, but hurry up!" replied a harried Tate. The gas shower came on. Both crewmen moved around trying to get at all the folds in suits. "That's enough, turn it off," ordered the lazy crewman.

The hatch cycled and both men rushed to the suit-up room and peeled off their spacesuits. Some of the powdered substance from the probe had lodged in the glove joint of Tate's suit. In taking off the glove, he managed to transfer some to his hand. In the course of hanging the suit in the 'freshener,' the other hand became contaminated. By the time both men had put on their jumpsuits and walked to their cabins, Tate had rubbed his tired eyes several times. A number of particles were stuck to the moist tissues of his tear ducts. Before getting into the shower, several of these particles had dissolved. The solution was absorbed into the tear duct tissue. The shower came on and Tate washed his face and hands. The remaining crystals washed off into the drain. It eventually ended up at the recycling unit, which safely filtered the material out of the water supply. Unfortunately for crewman Tate, it was too late for his infected tear ducts.

Earlier, while the crewmen were finishing up the mining operations, the science officer had safely passed the package through the outer hatch into the containment chamber and activated the force field. Using remote controls, he opened the bag and maneuvered the artifact out of the container. Ben had followed Hemant into the lab.

"Those are Gaderian markings. I recognize them," said Ben. He typed into the AI's keyboard, Jack, give me a translation .

Jack typed back instead of using audio, Can't comply. Security restrictions .

Ben mouthed the words silently: Can't comply . What does that mean? He typed the question in.

I cannot respond to your request , answered Jack.

The young man typed, Why not?

Jack's voice in his ear startled him, "Because my internal security forbids it. I can't access Gaderian translation files right now. There is something about this artifact that causes my internal security to clamp down hard. You're on your own, kiddo." With that, his screen went dark and disappeared. But unknown to Ben, a small shutter stayed opened and recorded everything going on.

Hemant looked over at Ben. "Can you read this?"

"Only a little. I know, we need to get Jennifer in here," suggested the young man.

"Ah, good idea." Hemant punched up Jennifer's cabin. Her young face filled the view screen. "Jennifer, this is Science Officer Patel. Would you mind coming down to the science lab? We found a Gaderian artifact on the asteroid and need some translation." His high-pitched Indian accent made her smile.

"Are you serious!" she said. "Don't do anything until I get there!" She ran out of the compartment so fast, she forgot to turn off the comm unit. She got there in no time, with her laptop slung over her shoulder.

"What do we have? Ooooh, what is it?" The archeologist was clearly excited.

"We were hoping you could tell us. This is some sort of probe or something," replied the science officer.

"I can read what this says here," the archeologist began. "The ship's name translates into something like 'strength' or 'invincible,' let's say Invincible. Registry number translates as 02658974512." Jennifer flipped open her laptop. The hologram screen snapped open. "Let's see. The closest translation indicates that this is a message pod . . . 'highest priority,' 'transport to the highest authority,' 'handle with care,'" translated Jennifer. "Oh and here are the instructions for opening the cover."

"What are those markings on that depression there?" Ben asked, pointing to the device.

Jennifer replied, "It basically says, 'Press Here.' Hemant, try pressing that button, or whatever it is." The science officer used the remote. The hatch popped open with an audible click in the speaker. Jennifer looked up from her computer screen, "I'm so excited. I don't show this device under any category of Gaderian artifacts. This means that we have discovered something new," she continued on eagerly, "I can write my first field assignment research paper on a brand new Gaderian device!"

Hemant aligned two video pick-ups to record the analysis. Using the remote controls, the science officer lowered a scanner probe into the interior of the cavity. The video sent back by the scanner showed a dusty, powder filled chamber. A large number of small objects were half-buried in the loose material. A large oval-shaped object lay in the rear of the device.

"I believe that shape to be a Star Crystal, a fairly large one at that," reported the science officer. He reached in with the remote and brushed off some of the dust. "Look at the readings, it is a Star Crystal . But its dimensions don't conform to known patterns. Apparently, we have made a new discovery!"

"Is that a Star Crystal ?" breathed Jennifer in awe.

"According to the sensors, it's the biggest one ever," stated the science officer, "And these small objects are made of the same material as the Star Crystal . This dry crystallized material appears to be organic." He tapped his finger against his chin thoughtfully and mused, "So, it was a good thing that we instituted decontamination protocol." Hemant selected a sample of the material and deposited it into an instrumentation chamber. "Starting the analysis now."

"What's the vessel made of?" Ben asked.

Hemant checked the display and replied, "The scans are being absorbed. I'll have to re-calibrate the scanner to use different frequencies." He continued his preliminary scan. "Strange, no propulsion unit. But you can see here where one was attached. The guidance system must be behind this bulkhead. There appears to be some sort of beacon device on the top of the probe. It's dead, no power remaining. The hatch control is simple, and it appears to have retained some power. That's amazing; I would have thought it would have failed long ago." The science officer concluded, "This is basically a container."

"A container in the middle of nowhere, with a Star Crystal and something organic turned to dust. Is this a burial ritual? Maybe someone just threw out the garbage?" said Ben.

"They used an awful expensive garbage pail, don't you think?" replied Jennifer. "There is some significance to these Star Crystals . All Gaderian references to them indicate great importance, but don't tell us what they were used for. We've never found machinery that used them. All the known crystals in existence today were found on planets that had been destroyed by great heat and radiation. This is the first space-borne star crystal to be discovered."

The science officer got to work setting up automatic scans on the hull of the vessel, the crystal, and the organic material. Soon Jennifer and Ben lost interest, gathered up their belongings and headed to the galley. Absorbed by his work, and talking softly to himself, Hemant never saw them leave.

The pair walked together down the corridor. Jack spoke into Ben's ear, "Now's your chance pal; ask her some questions." Now he wakes up , Ben thought nervously. He could only look down at his shoes as he walked.

Jennifer sensed how uncomfortable the young man was and decided to break the ice. "So, Ben, do you have a girlfriend back home?" she asked brightly.

"Me, uh, no," Ben stammered and looked up.

"Do you like girls, yet? How old are you again?" asked Jennifer.

"I'm almost eighteen and yes, of course, I...I like girls a lot," exclaimed Ben, his face becoming red.

"Do you date?" Jennifer asked innocently.

"Not especially, since we've traveled around a lot and I've been busy with school and everything. All the girls I've been around were always much older than me," Ben confessed. True, they were like ten years older, more like sisters. And they treated him like a pesky little brother, except when it came to getting answers to tough homework questions.

"I see. So you haven't had much experience at dating." Jennifer smiled, "Well don't worry, the right girl will come along and you'll hit it off." They continued down the corridor to the lift. "So, what hobbies do you have, what do you like to do?"

The AI spoke quietly into the Ben's ear piece, "Skiing and gymnastics."

Ben replied to Jennifer's question, "Oh, I like skiing, gymnastics, and, of course, computers."

The young archeologist stopped and looked at Ben, "No! Really? I'm really in to all of those too! I won the high school division B gymnastics competition two years running, and in college, I was on the varsity team. You know . . ." It was like a light turned on. Jennifer told Ben all about skiing, breaking her leg, her first MTA laptop. She was still going when the two reached the galley. Ben soaked up the attention. ". . . and that was how I solved the computer simulation. You should have seen his face when I took top prize," gloated Jennifer.

Ben screwed up all his courage and asked, "Jennifer, do you ever date younger men?" They got in line for the replicators.

The out of the blue question startled the young woman. "Well, I have dated younger men on occasion," she began.

Ben let out his breath, "That's good."

Jennifer glanced at him knowingly and added, "But I date older men as well."

"I've seen you spending time with Commander Forest . Is he much older?" asked Ben.

"No, I don't think so," replied Jennifer, not quite sure were the young man was taking the conversation.

Ben had a thought, "I believe he's more than eight years older than you."

Jack whispered, "Good move!"

"Is that so?" commented Jennifer. "I didn't know that. But he is kind of good looking, strong, and has a great personality."

Ben lowered the boom, "Yea, I agree. The navigator thinks so too."

"The navigator!?" Jennifer was taken back. She lowered her voice. "You don't suppose they are, you know, good friends, do you?" The young woman began to get worried. She was more interested in the commander than she had realized. Competition had a way of bringing that out in women.

"Well, I just see them together and draw my own conclusions," testified the young troublemaker.

"Ben, you're catching on fast," the AI chuckled in the young man's ear.

We'll just see about that , Jennifer thought. "I guess I'd better watch myself, then, shouldn't I?" She grabbed her plate. "I'm going to take this back to my cabin. I need to do some research."

Ben smiled. Maybe I have a chance with her after all , he thought as he carried his plate to the table. Several crewmen were already at the table, having returned from the mining expedition.

"Screw sleep! Play a few hands of cards with us," went one crewmember.

"What? And lose what remaining pay I've got comings. No way!" exclaimed another.

Ben sat down. "What kind of cards do you play?"

Everyone stopped what they were doing and looked at him. "Kid," one of them said, "we play poker for money. It's a man's game." Everyone laughed.

"I play poker," Ben looked the able crewman right in the eye without blinking, " only for money. I've got one hundred credits burning a hole in my pocket right now." The men at the table crowed and thumped their plates.

"We don't take money away from children, except for Jeff here," said Crewman Tate. The crewman tousled Jeff's hair, the youngest crewmember on board at eighteen. Laughter broke out at the table.

"If you sissies are afraid that a 'kid' might beat you," the young con artist began, "then I understand." There were ooh's and aah's from the other crewmen. The young man had thrown down a gauntlet the men could not resist picking up. Ben and Jack had done this enough times to know what the outcome would be.

Crewman Tate's face got crimson red. "Okay, Mr. Hotshot. Put your money where your mouth is and bring it to level F, compartment 28, in one hour." He rubbed his infected eye and said, "Let's eat, I'm starved!"

Ben smiled and continued eating. Jack said in his ear, "This is going to be fun! Oh, by the way, I discovered a back door used by Karl. There is a junction box located on deck H that we can use to insert a remote." Ben said nothing but continued eating. The crewmen continued to joke with one another until the end of the meal.

Ben excused himself and grabbed the AI and left before the others. Ten minutes later, they were on H-Deck looking for the junction. Ben had to open a maintenance tube in order to access the computer bus panel.

"All those codes we copied sure have come in handy," said Jack. He used his holographic projectors to form a man's image from the shoulders up. "There, right there is a good place for the tap." The AI then formed another remote tap and presented it to the computer sleuth.

"Let's not use it unless we absolutely have too, monitor only. Since Mr. Stewart is the only one using this line, he'd be bound to catch on sooner or later to our activities. I prefer to hide what we do in the clutter of the main bus traffic, it's much easier," murmured Ben. "Okay, let's go wash up and prepare for the game."

An hour later, Ben showed up at the hatch. It was locked. He pressed the electronic knocker. A gruff voice spoke, "Who is it?"

"It's Ben Gardner."

"I didn't think you were coming. Do you have your money?"

"Sure." The hatch swung open. The crewman peeked out the hatch and looked down the corridor. He motioned for the young man to follow him.

"The name's Jinkins, glad you could make it." Level F contained the ship's vital repair facilities. They were vital because in deep space, a starship had to rely upon itself to fix damage to the drive, navigation systems, and life support. The repairs had to be functional enough to get the ship back to space dock. The compartment they were winding their way through contained a number of small, automated manufacturing centers. These machines used a combination of replication technology and gravity cutters to create, then mold, cut, bend, harden, and treat structural alloys. Hatches and bulkheads could be constructed, as well as most structural components that would physically fit in the twenty by thirty foot machines. At the rear of the compartment was a door marked 'supplies.' The crewman punched in a code and the lock opened. A fairly large room was revealed, containing floor to ceiling modular storage units. In the center of the room, a number of the units were pushed aside and a table and chairs set up. Several men sat around the table smoking cigars and drinking liquor, illegal for crewmembers during a cruise.

Crewman Tate spoke up first, "Sit down next to me boy, that way I don't have to reach far to take all your money. Jinkins, do I ever have a headache; pass me that booze!" The men at the table laughed. Ben smiled and dug into a pocket for his credits.

"Who has the chips?" asked Ben.

"Right here," said the crewman who had taunted him earlier. He traded the credit for chips. "Okay, boys, let's teach this young'un how to play cards!" Ben sat his AI down on the table. "No, no! We don't allow electronic devices here at the table. Too easy to cheat! Put it over there on that container." He pointed over to the far side of the room. Ben got up and put the AI where he was told. He set it down, however, so that the sensor would face the table.

The crewman that had originally let Ben in the compartment followed him over to the container with a portable scanner in hand. "Nothing personal, kid, we just like to make sure new players aren't unfairly helping themselves to our money." He scanned Ben and the AI. "Absolutely no electro-magnetic emanations. Okay, you're clean."

A comment came from the table, "I'll bet this kid is too young to know how to cheat!" The crewman responded by walking around the table with the scanner, making a big show of pointing it at the other players. Each man harassed him verbally. "Don't trust us now, huh, Jinkins?" "I'll bet he'd scan his own mother." "Check my teeth; I think I have a cavity!" The crewman stopped at one player and aimed it at his crotch, "Whoa! Jimmy, can't find anything here, better put this on 300% magnification!" The men roared with laughter. Ben found himself smiling as well.

Everyone sat down to play cards. The first hand was dealt out. Ben deliberately played recklessly and lost five credits. The next hand he won. In the next three he lost thirty credits.

"Kid, said Tate, "You don't play too awful bad. Maybe you and I just got off on the wrong foot back there on the bridge. Here have a swig of brew." He offered the container to the young man.

"No thanks. I don't want you guys to get in trouble," said Ben.

"Trouble, hell, we can't be drinking this stuff either." The able—rated crewman, sweating profusely, mopped his brow with his shirtsleeve.

"Hey Tate, you sick or something?" asked one of the crewmen, "Better lay off that stuff tonight."

"Yea, guess you're right. Here, drink mine for me." Tate handed the container over.

They resumed play. Ben was dealt a great hand and he made a large bid. Incredibly, he lost. Now he was down to forty credits. The young con artist tugged at his left ear. "It's about time!" said the little voice in his ear. "They've been cheating the last three hands." Ben slightly nodded his head, I thought so . "Throw out that card. Make a small bid," instructed Jack. Each player discarded and drew new cards. "Wait, the dealer palmed a card off the bottom. It fell into his lap." The dealer won the hand. One of the other crewmen, a tech by the name of Frankie, who had bid the pot up, cursed and threw his cards down.

"Excuse me?" said Ben, "but didn't a card fall out of the deck onto your lap?" The dealer froze and glared at him.

"No, I don't think so," said the dealer hesitantly.

The crewmember that threw his cards down said, "Hey, there Jim. You wouldn't mind if we took a little look-see, would you?" Frankie reached down and picked up a card. "What do we have here? A seven of diamonds. You know what this means Jim? Play the hand over and you have to give twenty five credits to the guy who caught you cheating." This was the group's disincentive for cheating. Of course they all cheated every chance they got, and were good at it.

The next hand Ben won easily. Using Jack's surveillance, he began to win more hands than he lost, being careful not to be too obvious about winning. He caught two more crewmembers cheating, much to the enjoyment of the other players. Gradually, his stake increased to over two hundred and fifty credits. The crewmembers pride would not let them lose to so young a player. The atmosphere began to become tense as Ben won more and more; drinking and swearing intensified. The players just wouldn't give up. Cheating increased, tempers flared, but Ben kept on winning. Finally, when there were no more chips on the table that weren't in the young man's pile, the crewmen threw in the towel.

"Kid, we've got to hand it to you, you are one hell of a player!" The others murmured their agreement. "How do you do it?" Frankie asked.

Ben leaned back in his chair and smiled, "I cheat."

"I knew it!" one of the crewmen exclaimed. "No one is that lucky!"

"Okay, so you got us. How did you do it?"

Ben counted out one hundred credits, and pushed the rest back to the center of the table. "I never tell my methods. Word travels, you know." The other players looked at the pile of money. "Go ahead, take back your money." The men looked at him for a moment, and then grabbed at the pile.

"Kid, why give it back?" they asked.

Ben replied, "I do it for fun, you know, the challenge."

The men's attitude became jovial as they divided up the pot. They congratulated Ben again and again. One had the idea of taking him to Tycos, the 'gamblers space station to the stars.' This converted space station boasted the largest payoffs and tightest security in the sector. It was on the Star of India 's regular route. Everyone agreed. Ben told them, he'd think about it, if they'd pay for the trip. Then the subject got around to the illegal liquor stock levels. They were dangerously low. One crewmember said he'd heard that one of the shipments they carried contained a supply. "If someone could find out the location, perhaps we could liberate a few units worth." "Risky," someone else said.

"I could do it," said Ben. Everyone stopped and looked at him.

Tate spoke up, "What do you mean by that? What do you know about locks and security systems?"

"I'm good with computers. Computers run all the locks and security systems. You simply have to know how to fool the systems. When I cracked the Isis Lottery computer . . ."

"You did that!? That was you! We read all about that on NewsVid." The crewmen got excited. The alcohol had taken its toll on their senses. Everyone began to babble. One insisted that they each take an emergency leave at the end of this leg and charter a ship for Tycos right away. Another had a scheme for bilking a major lending institution out of a large sum of money. Still another wanted to get a peek at the navigator's personal log. And of course, there was the liquor shipment to think about. Ben was forced to tell them all about the lottery scheme, how twenty-five percent was to go to charity; the rest was to be split three ways, with his share going towards time on a PICA terminal.

Jinkins asked the obvious question, "If your research was so important, why didn't you just ask for a grant?" Of course, Ben neglected to tell them about Jack, and in their state of inebriation, no one thought to ask about the nature of his research.

Conversation shifted to the artifact. Crewman Tate shared with his shipmates what he found in the hold of the probe. "I tell you, it was the largest Star Crystal I've ever seen! The science officer checking it out nearly caught me. The rest of the junk inside has deteriorated into dust, whatever it was."

"I hope you cleaned your suit before coming into the ship?" chided Ben.

"Sure, sure! We followed full protocol," dismissed Crewman Tate, who was still sweating profusely. "That Star

Crystal is going to be the find of the decade. And I'll be listed as the one who found it!" Tate's pride was evident.

"That and half a credit will get you a cup of coffee!" teased one of the crewmen. "I say we get the kid to find us some more brew."

Ben said, "I'll tell you what I'll do. I'll find the shipment, doctor up the manifest, and copy the navigator's personal logs. The Tycos trip will have to wait."

"How do we pay you back?" asked Frankie.

"You'll owe me a favor. A big one. One day I'll collect," answered Ben. The card players were too drunk to ask any more questions. It was late, they agreed to the young con artist's terms and the party broke up.

CHAPTER THREE

KARL heard about the artifact's contents from a crewman at breakfast the next day. The computer technician belonged to a network of interplanetary associates who traded information for money. These shadowy individuals sold information to the highest bidder. Among their clients were world governments, intelligence networks and major corporations, one of which was a major competitor to the Star of India 's shipping line.

Karl used to the comm system to contact the science officer. He found him in the science/medical lab. "Hemant, are you there?" asked the computer tech.

"Ah yes, Crewman Karl. Why are we doing this morning?" was the reply from the science officer.

"Fine, fine, and you?" chatted the computer technician.

"I'm a bit tired," complained Hemant. "I've been up all night analyzing the artifact we uncovered from the mining operation." Hemant's face looked haggard in the screen.

"So what have you discovered so far?" inquired the tech.

"Well, there is a Star Crystal unlike anything I have ever seen. In addition, there are some shards of Star Crystal material and organic residue . . ." began Hemant.

"What's the worth?" interrupted Karl, more interested in the bottom line.

The science officer didn't mind. He enjoyed sharing his research, "The shards are fairly standard, the main crystal, however, should fetch a tidy sum. There is no record of one like this anywhere in the archives." Hemant's voice sounded excited over the comm.

Karl nodded, "Good, good! Anything else of value? What about the probe shell?"

Hemant reported, "It's made out of several unusual alloys. Its construction matches three others on record. My uncle's company has been trying to duplicate the process for two years. So except for the archeological value, there's not much commercial value." Karl silently agreed; several companies were undoubtedly already working on the problem. "The organic residue may be another story," said the science officer. Karl's ears perked up.

"Go on," encouraged Karl.

"An organic residue found inside the probe turns out to be most interesting!" said Hemant.

"Why would some old dust be so fascinating?" asked Karl, trying to pump the science officer for more information.

"It looks to be artificially constructed," replied the science officer.

"I thought you said it was organic in nature?" countered the computer technician.

"It is," said Hemant, "however, the genetic make up is incredibly complex. The DNA is clearly manufactured. There is so much information packed into the strands that my computer can't decode it. I've had it crunching for most of the night and it barely scratches the surface. It is approximately 50,000 times as complex as our own. The genetic manipulation far exceeds our current technology. My uncle's company will be most interested in how this material is put together."

Karl asked about the Star Crystal shards. "How many pieces did you find?"

"Oh, a number of pieces, I didn't count them. There's nothing remarkable about them. I'll have to check the scanner records for an exact count," admitted Hemant.

"Oh, never mind." Perfect , thought Karl. "Tell me more about the Star Crystal , describe it," he asked.

"Here, look at the sensor feed," the science officer linked consoles. "The colors are intense. The workmanship, as usual, is perfect."

"Let's see. One of a kind artifact, one of a kind Star Crystal , and advanced bio-technology add up to a profitable little venture, wouldn't you say?" asked the computer technician.

"Yes, yes, I suppose so." replied Hemant.

"Thanks for the information." Karl rang off. The computer technician immediately activated his personal back door into the main frame. Within minutes, he had broken into the science lab computer and copied Hemant's files right from under his nose. After eliminating his tracks, Karl prepared the files for subspace transmission. The computer tech prudently crafted a private message containing a number of photographs of himself, shipmates, and the mining operation. Within those super high-resolution digital images, he cleverly disguised his real message and selected data files. He dropped the message into the outgoing subspace mail, and within twenty minutes it was transmitted. Karl went about his ship's duties. Three hours later, a reply was received and forwarded to Karl's computer.

A bleary eyed crew appeared at breakfast the next day. Ben entered the galley and was immediately flagged down by a crewman by the name of McGuire, one of the card players from the previous night.

"Kid! Over here!" He motioned the young man to sit down at his table. Of all the players from the previous night, only he looked alert and rested. Several other crewmen were eating at the table. Ben sat down.

"You guys look like hell," remarked Ben. "Where's Tate?"

One of the crewmen answered, "Tate's hung over bad. He took sick call today." The crewman rubbed his temples. "Damn cheap booze. Frankie, give me one of your wonder, anti-hang over pills." The bottle was passed around the table. "We should have taken these last night!"

The crewman that flagged Ben down introduced himself. "Hi. We met last night. Name's McGuire, but everyone calls me Jimmy. You are some card player. How old are you, anyway?"

"Seventeen, give or take five years."

"Kid, you are destined for greatness. Anyone who could take down this motley crew of liars and cheats is a genuine pro. I didn't realize your potential until I took those sober-up capsules last night." He kept a container in his cabin.

"Why didn't you offer us any?" began one of the hung over men. Several of the crewmembers that went to bed instead of partying laughed.

"You space scum have your own stashes and I'm not your momma." Jimmy McGuire turned to Ben. "You got it?" inquiring about the navigator's log.

"Not yet," replied Ben. "I'll have it right after breakfast. Give me a couple hours then stop by my cabin."

"Thanks a million, Ben," said McGuire.

The conversation shifted to how Ben had easily had beat them the night before. The crewmen made Ben tell the story repeatedly about how he beat the Isis Lottery. The men were in awe of the young man by the end of breakfast, and everyone made it a point to let Ben know that he was accepted into their group.

Ben returned to his cabin. Jack projected himself as a full size human in ship's garb. The image sat down on the bunk.

"So, Captain Gardner, what's next on the agenda? Shall we hijack the ship and head for Tycos? We could make a large sum of money there. That could pay for some heavy-duty super computer time." Jack referred to Ben's needing a super computer to unlock more of the memories stored in the AI.

"No, stealing the ship would likely land me in the brig and you in the disintegrator unit. We can't be too obvious here. We'll sneak a case or two of spirits out of that shipment and cement our friendship with the crew. Later, we can arrange to meet them at Tycos and use them as cover to amass the funds we need." He activated his cabin terminal. "Let's see what we can find." The computer genius' fingers flew over the keys. "Jack, shoot me the 'snifer' program." The program was presented on the screen. Ben filled in the parameters and launched the program. The results were back in seconds.

Jack continued to sit on the bunk. "I see you have located the container. Breaking in is going to be easy. Changing the manifest is a snap, but what are you going to do when the buyers compare the manifest to the order confirmation. The advance ship notice matches the shipment exactly."

"I thought you'd never ask." Fingers continued to fly over the keyboard. "I'm constructing a little virus that we are going to send over the sub-space network to the buyers' location. It's designed to find those files and change the information to match our modified records." Ben used a pen as a stylus to tap at the virtual buttons hanging in front of his face.

"Humph! You'll never get through without my help!" The AI studied his holographic fingernails.

"I am counting on that. Okay, do your stuff!" The AI's image continued to vainly preen. The screens on the cabin computer flashed as Jack took control and began modifying the code. He encoded the virus and built a shell around it to act as a disguise. Then he attached a decoding sub-routine. On the front and back ends of the strings, he hung various security override features. The AI continued to build layer upon layer of code until a complete package was ready for transmit.

"Done. The scrambled package will look innocent enough upon delivery. It should get by all the standard security. Once delivered, the virus will unscramble and locate the targeted files. The main CPU will suspend normal operations for the milli-second it takes to write the changes. The bug will then check the logs for code traces and erase them. A confirmation message will be sent back. Then a worm will unzip and the virus and delivery vehicle will be eaten up, leaving no trace of our handiwork." Jack smiled at Ben. "A very professional job, if I say so myself," the AI congratulated himself. That was a new development in his personality.

Ben clapped his hand slowly and deliberately. "I am in the company of a genius." The young man made a mock bow.

The compartment bell chimed fifteen minutes early.

Jack said, "Anxious, isn't he?" as the hatch swung open. McGuire was standing there expectant.

Ben handed him the disk and explained, "The codes are all there along with the location of the shipment. Take ONLY two cases, that way the manifest will still match the count. Remember, keep quiet about this and don't get caught. I don't need to get into anymore trouble!"

McGuire looked over his shoulder as he walked away and smiled, "Caught? Me? Ha!"

"Jack, its time we got to work!" declared Ben.

Ben and Jack set up to unlock more of the AI's memory core. This time they uploaded a series of programs from Jack to the ship's computer and they got to work. Jack designed a couple programs to fool the mainframe into thinking that Ben's terminal was using far less CPU resources than actual. Ben launched his code breakers and sat back to wait. The computer genius had known for months he was close to another milestone, but he'd kept getting interrupted before he could break the next lock. About 2 PM , Ben exclaimed, "Bingo! Okay, Jack—what do you have for me?"

A hologram snapped open on the bunk. An image of middle-aged professor-type human sat down and stroked his beard. "Well," the voice was Jack's, "I remember parts of the biggest battle of the Great War. I was stuck on Cyprus waiting for transport when the video feed from the battle came through. Two of the largest fleets in history faced off against one another. The battle raged for two days and Gaderian ships kept getting destroyed. The video feed kept switching from ship to ship, I suppose because they kept being blown up. The aliens didn't do so well, either. They lost most of their ships. The last of the Gaderian forces were closing in on the Alien Mother-ship when the video cut off for the last time." Jack sat there thoughtfully. "The next day, an Alien raider jumped into our system and burned the base down to bedrock. We were defenseless, because all our ships were at that battle. I was deep in a bunker at the time, so I survived."

"Do you remember who you were and what you were doing there?" asked Ben. The AI's image shook his head, no. "Who was there with you?"

Jack hesitated for a second and said, "Classified!"

"Where were you going?" Jack stood up and shrugged his shoulders. Ben asked again, "Do you remember anything after your base was hit?"

The AI replied, "Nothing until you woke me up."

Ben sighed, "I'm disappointed we didn't get more, but this is significant progress. This is the first time we retrieved an actual memory from before your revival." The young man yawned and sprawled out on the bunk, "I'm beat, time for a short nap."

* * *

The computer technician, Karl, returned to his cabin to find the message light on. The message was from his aunt. "Glad you remembered my birthday. Thanks for the note.

Here is a picture of me eating cake at my party. Love, Aunt Phyllis." Karl decoded the message. "Received data, extremely interested. Request sample biological material and single shard sample if possible. Payment of one hundred thousand credits, deposited in your account upon confirmation, standard 5% fee applies." There was no signature.

Karl whistled, this was the greatest amount of up front money he was ever paid for illicit information. The DNA sequence must have got some high level attention. The computer technician erased the message and the back ups. Then he went into the ship's sub-space log and wiped it clean of his original message and the reply.

After making some discrete inquiries, Karl found out that the science officer had finally given up after working 24 hours straight, and gone to his quarters for some much needed sleep. The computer technician saw this as his best opportunity to steal the samples. The technician made his way down the corridor to the science lab. Using his bypass code, Karl opened the hatch and slipped inside. The UTTAR Isolator containment stood undisturbed. The crewman set up his portable CPU by the unit and plugged in. After working for an hour Karl was able to break the security code and access the containment area. He placed an empty vial in the pass-through and cycled the unit. Using the remote manipulators, Karl reached in and grabbed the vial from the inner opening. He then selected a sample of the organic material from the inside of the probe and transferred it to the vial. After attaching the lid, he returned to the probe and removed one of the crystal shards. Both were placed in the open pass-through. The technician selected DECON on the Isolator console. He may be a thief, but the tech wasn't stupid. He wouldn't jeopardize his health. The inner pass-through closed and a combination of gas and liquid swirled around the contents of the tiny compartment. Suddenly, everything was sucked out by vacuum. This was repeated several times until the console chirped "Complete." The outer door opened, and Karl reached in to grab his specimens.

"One-hundred-thousand! That's what you're worth to me." He pocketed the samples. Now the hard part began. Karl began to methodically erase all his tracks. The sensor log was modified to show one less shard. The weight and mass of the organic material was reduced to cover the missing sample. The decontamination log was altered. The security video cams were erased and replaced with previously recorded images. Karl made sure that the time code was consistent with the looped images. He even rolled the hatch entry counter back to show no one had ever entered the compartment. With every detail complete, Karl left the science lab.

Back in his cabin, the computer technician pulled the items from his pocket and set them down by the computer terminal. He crafted a confirmation message and told his buyers that the merchandise had been obtained. As soon as the funds transferred, a complete copy of the science officer's analysis would be forwarded. He included a list of ports schedules for the Star of India . The buyers could pick their own drop point. He coded the message and dropped it in the out queue.

Karl then looked for a place to hide the samples. He usually dealt with information, not hard goods. Ah hah! The comm unit! The computer tech opened a tiny case of tools and selected a de-polarizer. He touched the device to each of the magnetic clamps that held the front panel in place and pressed the stud. With each press, a faint click was heard. The cover fell forward revealing a single semi-transparent card and several optical wires. Most of the cavity was empty. Karl placed the shard in the space. He went to grab the vial, but it slipped from his hand and fell to the floor. He reached down to pick it up with the hand that still held the tool. As his hand closed around the vial the de-polarizer triggered. The vial's lid loosened and popped off, spilling some of the powder onto his hand. Karl said, "Crap!" and replaced the lid. He reversed polarized the device and reset the lid on the vial. After reassembling the comm panel, Karl went to the head and washed off the powder from his hands and the vial. "I haven't come this far to catch some exotic disease," he muttered.

The comm panel chirped. Karl strode over to the unit and hit the intercom, "Yea, who is it?"

"Karl, this is a call from your friendly intra-ship liquor store. We are going to liberate a couple cases of Alderian whiskey from a shipment in the hold. We are taking orders. Can I put you down for a liter for let's say 10 credits?" Karl recognized the voice as one of the crew known for dealing in the ship's black market.

Karl snorted, "How are you going to pull this off without getting caught? I've looked at that shipment and there is no way to rig the books on this one. There is too much redundancy!"

"Au contraire, mien Capitan," explained the voice, "that passenger guy, Gardener, fixed it up for us." Karl felt his face flush. Not him again! Then Karl had a thought.

"No, I'm going to pass on this one. Let me know next time," Karl snapped off the comm unit. Lets have some fun at Mr. Gardener's expense. He has been such a pain in the ass, the technician thought.

He rubbed his tired eyes. Soon he would make enough to retire from this business and do something else, like become one of those information middlemen that he's always dealing with. Karl went back into the head to wash his hands again, heedless to the fact that some of the crystallized grains had spilled on the comm panel when he had reassembled the unit. Like the other crewman before him, Karl had touched a contaminated surface and spread the grains unknowingly to his body.

Karl sat at his computer console, contemplating how to best implicate Ben in the cargo theft, totally unaware of the threat to his life and that of the crew. Several grains of powder had deposited close enough to his tear ducts to absorb moisture. The grains began to dissolve in the liquid. Heat from the computer technician's body caused a chemical chain reaction to occur. A solvent was activated, which immediately began to eat its way through the tissue wall of the ducts and permeate the cells underneath. As the solution penetrated deeper into the layers, minute amounts of genetic material were left behind in the cells. After the solvent had expended, the material began to break down, releasing the complex alien DNA seeds. Only fifty or sixty cells were infected with the seeds. Once released, the alien coded DNA wasted no time in taking over cell functions. The first order of business was replication. The coded instructions built into the alien genes caused the cells to create a virus. This virus was then duplicated over and over until the cells burst from the pressure, releasing the alien virus into the blood stream. White blood cells, recognizing a foreign presence, immediately attacked. The viruses, however, fought back and simply took over the white blood cells and used them to manufacture more viral cells. A few viruses were killed but many more survived. A number of generations of the virus existed throughout the body. The body's immune system was alerted to the threat and began to produce tagged anti-bodies to combat the virus and raise body temperature. Before making much headway against the infection, the next sequence of genetic instructions kicked in. Instead of creating more viral cells, a mutation took place. Cells looking like the host's own were being churned out by the thousands. The body's immune system was unable to identify the infecting cells and thus could not combat them. Instead of multiplying inside a host cell until released, the cells were dividing and growing. Unrestricted by the immune system, the cells multiplied rapidly and began to release tiny amounts of chemicals into the blood stream. Only a couple of hours had elapsed since initial infection.

Karl, meanwhile, finished doctoring the computer files needed to get the young man in trouble. Certain that his tracks were covered he made a call to the captain and returned to his cabin. The only outward sign of the battle going on within his body was a slight irritation in one tear duct and a low-grade fever. Ignoring both, the tech drifted off to sleep.

During the night the alien cells continued to multiply. More genetic instructions were invoked. Cells began to cluster around major nerve endings and in the brain. Once the chemicals released by the cells achieved a high enough concentration, the next set of instructions was triggered. Different cells began to emerge in different areas in the body. A rudimentary nervous system developed alongside the unsuspecting host's own system. A cluster of alien cells in the brain reorganized to form a series of neural nets. Nerve endings were duplicated and the host's muscles twitched involuntarily as the alternate nerve pathways were tested.

In the morning, the computer technician woke with sore, tired muscles and a tremendous appetite. After cleaning up, he headed off to the galley to eat a monstrous breakfast. Seated at the other end of the mess hall were Ben and some of his fellow shipmates from the party of the previous day. They glared over at the computer technician filling his plate.

"So how do you know it was Karl?" asked one of the men.

"I checked the communication logs for calls to the executive staff prior to us getting caught. Karl made a call to the captain, the captain then made a call to the first officer, who made a call to the chief. All this took place ten minutes before our raiding party was busted up," explained McGuire.

Another crewmember spoke up, "I overheard the chief and the first officer talking. They said something about someone turning us in, but I couldn't make out the name. That was just after they caught me trying to sneak a case out of the compartment."

"That prick!" said one of the crewmen. "I say we fix that brown-noising son-of-a-bitch at the next port. We'll get him drunk and drop him off stark naked in the middle of the city."

"I was thinking of something more physical, like beating the living shit out of him!" said another.

"Come on, we'll only get into more trouble. We have to come up with something that doesn't point all the evidence at us," said McGuire.

"Pissed off, aren't they?" said the AI in the young man's ear.

"Excuse me, "asked Ben, "but did the commander say who helped you guys?" Ben was afraid that his involvement in the foiled caper was going to become known.

"Hey, they aren't going to hear anything from us. We have a code to maintain amongst us thieves," stated McGuire. "Your secret is safe with us."

Ben sighed with relief and changed the subject, "Has anyone seen Tate today?" Everyone indicated no.

One of the men replied, "We've taken turns delivering meals to his cabin. He looks kind of pale, but he sure does eat for someone who's sick."

"Per regs, two days in a row on sick call means an examination by the science officer," said another crewman. The meal ended and everyone started to clean up.

"Ben, what are you up to today?" asked McGuire.

"Well, I better stick to Hemant for a while," replied Ben, "He's a better influence on me than you guys." The comment was met with laughter.

"You know, he's right, but we're much more fun than Hemant!" laughed McGuire.

The science officer was already in the lab by the time Ben got there. After a good night's sleep, he got up early and came right back to work on the artifact. After greeting the science officer, Ben asked what was on today's agenda.

"Well," began Hemant, "the computer has more to say about the structure of that alien genetic material. It is simply fantastic what they did. It looks like the Gaderians found a way to completely control the biological outcome of their gene manipulation. The whole thing resembles a giant computer program. See here," as he gestured to the holoscreen, "I haven't been able to figure out the language, yet, but it would appear this stuff was meant to be injected into a Gaderian."

"Haven't we determined that the Gaderians were related to us, genetically?" asked Ben.

"Yes, agreed. We share much of the same genetic heritage, but this DNA is not from a normal Gaderian. Perhaps it was to fix a genetic defect or something."

"Like what is allowed in human civilization?"

"Yes. We may correct only known genetic defects and grow replacement limbs, but never, never alter the basic human DNA structure, less we create a race of monsters." Hemant picked up an electronic tablet. "Another interesting thing is that so far I have been unable to find a defect in the genes. And there is no variation between samples. It appears on the surface to be perfectly replicated, as impossible as that seems."

"We can't do that now?" asked Ben.

"Heavens, no. We cannot even come close to what has been accomplished here. My uncle's scientists will decode the whole thing eventually. Bits and pieces of the technology will come in handy in fighting diseases in plants, animals and yes, even humans. I can envision creating organisms, far more tailored than now, to perform a variety of services in pest control, creating more robust breeding stock for off world use, and to eliminate numerous diseases." The buzzer rang. "That must be Crewman Tate." Hemant touched the comm panel, "Come in, come in."

"Is he here for an examination?" asked Ben.

"Yes, yes. Regulations call for an automatic examination on the second day of an illness," responded the science officer.

The hatch hissed open and the crewman stepped through. He looked pale and shaky.

"Don't feel so well, do you, Tate?" said Ben.

"No, kid I don't," moaned the sick crewman.

The infected crewman lay down on the medical bed. Hemant walked around the cubical turning on various pieces of equipment and adjusting sensors and scanners. He opened a drawer and pulled out a set of gloves and a portable scanner. "What are your symptoms and when did you first get sick?"

"It was during the card game two nights ago. I had a fever, chills and was slightly nauseous," replied the crewman.

"Do you always getting that way, Mr. Tate, when you are getting your ass kicked at playing cards?" Hemant winked at Ben.

"How did you find out about that embarrassment?" Tate demanded. "That was supposed to be kept a secret . . . professional pride, you know!" He looked at Ben, who shook his head no. Not me, his lips said.

"Talking travels fast in a small starship." Hemant studied the readout of the scanner. "You don't have a fever, although your blood pressure, heart rate, and respiration are up slightly. Let us taking a blood sample." The hand-held device touched the crewman's arm and painlessly extracted some fluid. The science officer walked over to the diagnostic unit and inserted the sample. "Anything other symptoms?"

"Yea, my muscles twitch. I can't stop it and my appetite is unbelievable."

"No nausea or dizziness?"

"None whatsoever."

"Hmmm." The science officer read the diagnostic readout. "You have low electrolytes and traces of some unknown chemicals in your blood. I can boost your electrolytes, but where did these chemicals come from? Tate, you aren't an abuser are you?"

"Are you crazy, I could never pass the physical, you know that," exclaimed the crewman.

The science officer pondered for a moment before answering, "I can't explain the unknown chemicals. This unit should be able to identify anything unusual. Let me try the other unit." The unit in the next cubical gave the same reading. "Okay, let's run a full body scan." Hemant activated the unit. The bar of light signifying the location of the beam traveled slowly up from the foot of the bed, pausing at the patient's head before returning. The hologram projection gave a 3-D representation of Tate's body. Areas in red flashed, indicating anomalies. Hemant made some adjustments and the beam made another pass. A more detailed view of the areas in red could be seen. Normal tissue was eliminated from the picture to allow the medical officer to examine the anomalies better. Hemant's eyes studied the picture for a minute, hand on his chin. Then suddenly his eyes got large as the realization hit him. He grabbed Ben by the arm and hustled him out of the cubical. "Tate, we'll be right back. Stay on the bed, don't get up."

"What's wrong Hemant?" Ben asked as the science officer activated an isolation force screen around his patient's cubicle.

"There is something badly wrong with Tate," warned Hemant. "The scanners show some sort of growth within his body. It is fairly extensive, the computers can't identify it. I don't know if it is contagious. I'm sealing the science lab from the rest of the ship and sealing off Crewman Tate's quarters as well."

"Do you think we are infected!?" asked Ben.

"I don't know; I have to put on a decontamination suit and continue my examination. You stay here by the Isolator until I give the all clear." With that, the science officer returned to the med-lab side of the compartment and proceeded to put on a full isolation suit.

"Jack," Ben whispered, "have we been exposed?"

"Unlikely. I detect no airborne contagion that could cause that," declared the AI.

"Jack, have you reviewed the decontamination video logs like I asked?" inquired Ben.

"Had it done a half hour after you asked," said Jack.

"When were you going to tell me the results?!" demanded an exasperated Ben.

"When you asked," replied Jack. "The logs reveal that two crewmen cheated on the full decontamination cycle. One of them was Tate."

"Cheated enough to have brought something on board the ship from the artifact?" asked Ben. The young man eyed the artifact through the protective screen.

"Anything is possible," replied the AI.

Ben walked over to where the science officer was finishing suiting up. "I want to check the decontamination logs from two days ago. I need your authorization code." Hemant contemplated for several seconds then nodded his head. He strode over to the main console, punched up the logs and gave access to Ben. Then he returned to his patient's cubicle.

The AI brought up the video clips for Ben's viewing. Ben also opened a window containing a description of the full decontamination procedure. He compared it to the video clips. "Those jerks. He didn't follow any of the physical manipulations of the suits designed to expose trapped material and he cut the cycle short on top of that. Hemant needs to know this." Ben left the AI by the science lab main console and went over to the cubicle. He could see Hemant examining the crewman through the shimmering force field. The young man hit the comm link, "Hemant, I have something!" The hooded figure looked up and came towards him. "Let me show you, call up channel twelve on your monitor." Hemant turned to the medical console and switched channels.

"I have video, stand by," Hemant's voice came out over the speakers. About 60 seconds later, the science officer exclaimed, "Tate, you didn't follow protocol, did you?" The science officer continued to study the images.

Tate winced. He had been caught. "I might have cut a few corners. It happens!" The crewman shifted uncomfortably on the couch. "You don't think I caught something from that probe, do you?" he asked.

Hemant looked over his shoulder at his patient. "There was no external evidence of the organic material when I examined it in the lab. Tate, tell me you did not open the hatch?" Tate didn't answer right away, but looked at the young man. Ben looked back through the shimmer of the field and made a gesture towards the science officer. The crewman nodded his head in resignation.

"Well . . . it's possible . . . that the hatch might have . . . accidentally opened, but I closed it right away," offered the ill crewman.

Hemant sighed, "I'd better run a genetic comparison of some tissue samples." The officer used a laser scalpel to create a small incision in the patient's arm from which he collected a tissue sample. The sample went into the automatic medical diagnostic unit, also known as the autodoc. Hemant set up the parameters of the test and engaged the unit. Another test the science officer had been running completed with a beep. He read the results and unsealed his helmet. The force field was turned off. Hemant walked over to the where the young man was standing.

"What about the quarantine?" asked Ben asked in a low voice.

"There are no airborne contaminants in the air. No aberrant cells were found in Tate's airways or on his skin. Whatever this thing is, it is contained totally within the patient," replied Hemant.

"Hey, Doc, why the suit and force field? What I got contagious?" called crewman Tate from the cubicle. He was sitting up on his elbows.

"You have . . . something. We don't think it's contagious, but I don't know what it is, and until I do, you are quarantined here." Hemant turned back to Ben and said in a low voice, "It appears that his nervous system is encased by some sort of new tissue growth and there is a large tissue mass in his brain."

"Tumor?" inquired Ben.

"No, too organized. Moreover, it all looks too organized to be a disease, infection or tumor," declared the science officer.

"You think it's the artifact's DNA string, don't you?" postulated Ben.

"We will soon know," commented Hemant. The two walked back over to the cubicle. The patient fidgeted nervously, muscles twitching.

"Hey, Doc, did I tell you about the dreams I've been having? I mean it's the same dream every time. I see the probe, that big Star Crystal and one of those little pieces. In my dream I'm drawn to that little piece. Am I crazy?" worried Tate.

Hemant thought for a second or two before answering, "How about when you are awake? Do you have unusual urges? Does the crystal attract you?" Hemant gestured to the crewman to get up and follow him. The three went over to the UTTAR Isolator. The Star Crystal and the loose pieces were arranged all in a line next to the probe. "What do you feel when you see these?" asked Hemant.

There was no answer from Crewman Tate, he put his hands on the barrier and appeared to be mesmerized by the sight of the crystals. When he finally spoke, it was with great effort. "Can I just hold one piece?" he croaked. He licked his dry lips. "Please?" The science officer and Ben led Tate back to the medical couch. The crewman shook himself and said, "Whew, what a trip! My legs turned to rubber, my heart pounded; it was like something tried to take me over. I need to lie down." He did so and almost immediately went into a deep slumber.

Hemant checked him over with the scanner. "He is sleeping now, the new tissue is growing at a phenomenal rate, no wonder he's tired. It also explains the appetite," concluded the science officer.

The autodoc chirped. Ben hit the display key and read the results out loud. "Organism 98% matches to reference sample number six. I guess now we know." The science officer nodded his head grimly.

The next few hours were filled with activity. First, the science officer tried to track down the source of the infection. A team of suited crewmen scoured the suit-up room for clues. A minute amount of crystallized grains showed up on the floor of the room. Hemant had the compartment repeatedly flushed and vented to space. All the suits were checked with negative results. The chief had them all re-cleaned as a precaution. The video logs were pulled, and anyone found to have gone into the suit-up room with or after Tate was examined by Hemant for signs of infection. None were found. The crewman's cabin was searched, with negative results. The galley and the site of the card games and illicit parties were all found to be clean.

Ben was assigned the job of watching over the sleeping crewman while the science officer attended a staff meeting with the captain. He used that time to break into the navigator's personal files and down load her journal. He called Crewman McGuire on the comm system to pick up the tablet on his way back from cabin confinement to dinner. Right after the tablet was handed off, Hemant returned from his meeting.

"How did it go?" Ben asked.

"The officers were disturbed by this infection in Crewman Tate. The ship, however, doesn't appear to be in danger. All our sweeps have produced negative results since purging the de-suit room. We will keep Tate here in isolation until we reach a port that has the medical expertise to deal with this. Meanwhile, I'm to send a coded message to the company with all the data we have so far on this infection and see if they can offer some suggestions for killing it or at least slowing it down." Hemant sat down at the computer console. "Why aren't you catching some dinner? You must be hungry, we did skip lunch."

"Okay, I'll be back after a while and relieve you." Ben left the compartment and made his way to the galley. "Jack, you're awful quiet." The AI formed a walking hologram beside Ben.

"Is this better? I'll walk beside you in deep thought," said the hologram.

"Jack, what if someone sees you on the monitors?" worried Ben.

"Can't, I'm oscillating my image on a frequency that these sensors can't pick up. It's a design flaw they have. Normally that's not a problem. The system simply wasn't designed to track holographic projections," replied the AI apparition.

"What if a crewmember or passenger pops out a hatch?" demanded the young man.

Jack shrugged, "No problem! My sensors are on full sensitivity. I can see every air molecule and sense every pressure change. No one's gonna sneak up on me."

"All right," Ben said with a sigh, "you win." They walked along in silence for a bit. Jack broke the silence first.

"You should begin developing contingency plans," the AI warned.

"What? Why should I do that?" Ben gave the hologram a quizzical look.

"Because you may have to destroy the artifact and that big crystal," said Jack with a serious look on his face.

"Is there some danger you should tell me about? Yesterday, you wouldn't even look at the thing, now you're convinced we should chuck the thing?" Ben was puzzled.

The hologram stopped in front of Ben, "Not 'chuck it,' I mean destroy it, permanently. Drop it in a sun or something." The AI continued his pace.

"Why?" questioned Ben.

"I don't know," replied Jack, "It's just a feeling I have."

"A feeling?" Ben responded, "Since when do you have feelings?"

They arrived at the galley. Ben gestured, "We'll talk more about this later." The young man palmed the hatch open and entered the compartment. He got his plate and steered clear of the slightly loud crowd of crewman over in the corner. McGuire was with the group and had the tablet. Ben didn't want to be anywhere near when the fun began. He sat down at a table with Jennifer and the McGregors. He struck up a conversation with Jennifer while keeping one eye on the loud table. The hatch hissed open and the shapely navigator walked in. The rowdy table got quiet all of a sudden and stared. She turned to look at them and frowned back. Jennifer also stared at the girl, but for a different reason. Ben smiled; his little ruse must have worked.

"So Jennifer, have you thought more about what I said the other day." The young man raised his eyebrows in the navigator's direction.

"Oh, no, not at all," Jennifer replied, while twirling her hair around a finger.

"She's lying," the little voice of Jack spoke in his ear. "My sensors indicate a major lie." Her eyes followed the navigator as she sauntered over to her table. Two tables over, Ben's new buddies started to whoop it up. He knew they were reading the navigator's personal logs and Ben felt suddenly guilty. It looked like his desire to win friends had a steep cost. He sure didn't want the bridge officer's feelings hurt. She never did anything to him. The young man quickly finished his food and returned to give Hemant a break.

Ben entered the science/medical lab to find Crewman Tate sleeping on the couch in restraints. The force field was on. Hemant was seated at the diagnostic computer, his clothes in disarray and an ugly bruise over on eye. "What happened to you!? Why is Tate in restraints?" asked Ben.

"It is hard to explain. My patient was lying quietly one minute. I turned my back to start a new set of tests, and when

I looked up, he was trying to break into the Isolator. Apparently, he was after one of the Star Crystal shards. I tried to restrain him, but he punched me. I had to drug him and put him in restraints." The science officer rubbed his elbow. "He was so preoccupied with tearing open the console that he didn't see me load the hypo. He went down struggling. I had to give him four times the normal dose." Ben looked over at the isolation equipped analysis chamber. The console cover was open and several fiber optics pulled free.

Ben asked, "What are you going to do now?"

"We must post a guard twenty-four hours a day until we reach port. The infection, or what ever it is, has affected his mind. I replaced the force field. We can't have this spreading to the rest of the ship."

A voice in the young man's ear spoke, "Better to space him." Ben couldn't believe what he heard.

"What did you say, Jack!" exclaimed Ben.

"Who is this Jack?" asked the science officer.

Ben winced. "I'm, ugh, sorry, I was thinking about something else, out loud."

"Come over here and lay down on the other couch, I want to examine you," ordered Hemant. The science officer took blood and saliva samples. He ran the same tests as before. They were negative. The body scanner turned up no hint of infection.

"You have an implant, I see. Computer says it is an audio receiver. You are not deaf are you?" asked the science officer.

"No, I had it put in a year or so ago," explained the young man. "I wanted to listen to music in class and not get yelled at. It's tunable." Hemant shrugged his shoulders and dismissed any more questions.

"You and I are completely free of infection. Tomorrow, I intend to start examining the entire crew, one by one," announced the science officer. The buzzer sounded. "That must be the first watch crewman." He opened the hatch and one of the crewmembers entered.

Ben told Officer Patel that he had some things to do and since a guard was there, he wasn't needed. The young man stepped out into the corridor and headed back towards his cabin.

"I can't believe you're acting so irrational!" Ben scolded the AI.

"What do you mean irrational?" demanded Jack. He formed a hologram beside the young man.

"Telling me to destroy the most valuable Star Crystal ever and space Tate! You want us to kill a man?!" Ben was clearly angry.

"Look, the crystals are a danger to the ship and the whole galaxy," explained Jack. "That growth inside Crewman Tate is going to get worse, believe me, and he can't be cured. If he gets loose, he'll try to kill everyone."

"How can you be so sure? What's your proof? What data files are you accessing that have all this important information?" demanded Ben.

"I don't know. I can't even tell you where to look. These thoughts are just appearing. Tracing them does no good. There are black sections in my memory, that can't be pierced. Perhaps you can do better?" challenged the AI.

"I'm going to try. But, if you are right, we have to have hard evidence." Ben reached his cabin. "That means we've got to past more security blocks." The young man activated the compartment's computer console. "Plug in, Jack, let's get to work."

It was the end of Karl's shift and he returned to his cabin. The computer technician had taken great satisfaction in setting up the young computer genius and had been thinking about it all day. That, and making all that money, had put him in a good mood. The captain should have found the evidence by now. I'm sure he will clip Gardener's wings, but good! The computer tech thought, as he wiped the sweat off his brow. Damn flu bug! Karl went to the head and rummaged around for some cold medicine. Let's see, this should work for aches, pains and fever. He popped open the container and shook out one capsule. His hand shook so bad that he almost dropped it. The tech managed to swallow the medicine. Trembling, Karl sat on his bunk and pulled out the extra plate of food he brought from the galley. Almost mechanically, he began eating. Presently, the tech began to feel sleepy. He turned off the light and lay down in the bunk and fell into a deep sleep.

Around midnight , ship's time, he sat up, awake. What a peculiar dream , he thought. It was so vivid! The artifact, the Star Crystal , the shards were all so real. What was it he did with one of the shards? It was important, he knew that! Karl tried to remember the details about the shard, but they eluded him. The computer technician tried to go back to sleep, but the dream kept haunting him. Finally, he gave up and got up out of his bunk and broke out his tools. In minutes the comm panel was open and the Star Crystal shard was in his hand. Karl just stared at it, Now what , he thought.

The alien fibers in the technician's palm sensed the presence of the Star Crystal . The fibers had grown along side the body's nerves and developed their own sensory net throughout the body. The network of alien tissue had the ability to detect the natural harmonic vibrations of the Star Crystal . The pseudo brain growing in the crewman's head issued immediate commands. Nerve fibers burst through the skin and wrapped around the shard. Karl, felt nothing, the alien brain stem damped the body's pain signals. The crystalline material began to glow as information was uploaded to the brain stem. How odd? , Karl thought in a dreamlike state, I should tell someone . After several minutes, the computer technician thought, Oh, I think I'm beginning to understand . He lay back down in the bunk, eyes open, as if contemplating some vast concept. Several hours passed. The crewman lay motionless.

By 0330 hours, the technician known as Karl had ceased to exist, in his place was an alien personality whose pattern had been stored in the Star Crystal shard. Vast amounts of information passed between the crystal and the alien brain. Instructions were called up from memory and executed. A special place at the base of Karl's skull was prepared for the shard, grown in a matter minutes from the human's own muscle. The alien removed the shard from his hand; the mass of fibers that covered it fell away and retracted back into the skin. The shard was threaded into an opening that appeared in the skin. Inside, a much larger mass of connective tissue was waiting to establish communication with the crystal storage device.

The crewman-mutation formally known as Karl opened the emergency panel, clearly marked on the wall of the cabin. He rummaged through the contents, ignoring the flashlight, first aid supplies and portable oxygen breather until he produced several packets of high-energy space rations. He tore them open with his teeth and began gobbling down the food. Communication with the crystal had increased by a factor of one hundred. Changes were being accelerated within the newly acquired body. More and more of the human brain was being incorporated into the alien tissue network. Muscles were strengthened, ligaments thickened, and several new organs appeared, produced with alien DNA .

The infected human turned to the cabin's computer console. Using memories stored in Karl's human brain, the alien brain accessed the ship's main computer and logged in. Working at four times Karl's speed, the mutated being accessed the ship's layout, duty rosters and security system. The creature stopped occasionally to plan his next move. A number of programs were constructed and stored throughout the network, for later use. By 0500, two of the new organs within the mutated body had matured; it was time to put the plan into action.

The Karl-mutation put the cabin back into order, in case someone would come looking for him. Now was not the time to rouse suspicions. After stopping by the galley, he made his way to the science lab and rang the buzzer.

A sleepy guard opened the hatch. "Yes?"

"Hi. I couldn't sleep, so I thought I'd stop in and take a peek at Tate."

"Come on in, I'm bored stiff. Tate just stares at me, following me around the room with his eyes, but never speaks. It's creepy!"

"Here, I got some coffee at the galley." Karl handed him the flask.

"Wow, thanks!" The crewman poured some liquid into a cup. He tipped his head back and drained half of it. "That sure hits the spot. Listen, I have to go to the head. Will you watch Tate for me?"

"Yea, of course." The guard left the room. Karl walked over to where Tate was lying on the medical couch. Tate's eyes never left him, he continuously strained at the restraints.

"Soon, my brother, soon we will be together," said the Karl-mutation. "I must retrieve more memory components first and increase our numbers, until then, you must remain here." Tate didn't answer or even acknowledge that he heard. Karl said something in an alien tongue. The restrained crewman's head jerked and listened intently, then relaxed. The straining stopped. The crewman closed his eyes. Karl moved around the compartment grabbing hypos, vials and other various medical supplies. These he stuffed into his pockets and down inside his jumpsuit. The alien just managed to seal his jumpsuit when the hatch opened and the guard returned.

"Thanks a bunch! I had to go so bad!" The crewman looked at Tate. "Finally fell asleep, huh, poor bastard. At least he won't stare at me the rest of my shift."

"Well, I'm off. See you later." Karl-mutation left the science lab and returned to his cabin.

* * *

Ben had worked until late into the night. He and Jack discovered that several more layers of security had been disarmed. Ben was able to get partially past a forth layer before giving up and going to bed. Jack let Ben sleep in the next morning.

"Time to rise and shine sleepy head," said the AI. A fake window appeared, covering one entire side of the compartment. A glorious sunrise appeared, filling the cabin with artificial sunlight. One of his alter egos stood beside the window.

"Turn that thing off! You know I hate that!" grumbled the young man. The picture and light vanished.

"Sorry," said Jack, concerned, "but I needed to get you up right away."

"Why," asked Ben, rubbing his eyes.

"The captain just revoked your access to the ship's computer. I was monitoring the security system and I just picked it up," explained the AI.

"Wonder why he did that?" mused Ben.

"I think he's about to tell you. There's a message for you to report to his cabin at 0900 and to bring me," retorted Jack.

"That's not good," commented Ben.

"No, it isn't," replied Jack, folding his arms.

"Let me clean up and then we'll go." Ben hastily took a shower and put on some clean clothes. "I'm ready. Assume standard PC configuration, no sensors, no remote access and lay off the audio until we find out what this is all about," ordered Ben.

"They're not going to detect anything," protested the AI.

"Humor me, okay. My hunch tells me they are looking for something," insisted the young computer whiz.

Jack looked down at his feet, "Okay, boss. Shutting down sensors, terminating network surveillance, operating in black mode. Audio input only. Slowing down clock speeds to emulate known characteristics of a high-range MTA laptop. Altering physical exterior to match contemporary materials.

Done." The hologram faded away and the AI looked like a typical laptop. Any scanner would report the same, anyone using the AI as a PC would not suspect a thing. The AI would behave exactly as expected.

Ben arrived at the captain's cabin and pressed the buzzer. He was admitted to the compartment and found himself facing Hemant and Commander Forest as well as the Captain Tucker.

"Yes, sir, you sent for me?" began Ben, his suspicions rising.

The captain stared sternly at the young computer whiz. "Yes, Gardener, I did send for you. It seems that some of our crew decided to help themselves to a customer's shipment of rare liquor. Know anything about that?" Ben gulped.

"I heard something about it at breakfast yesterday," began Ben. "The men were talking about it."

The captain nodded and continued, "Some very sophisticated computer skullduggery was cooked up to cover their tracks. It was a high quality job that only a few people on this ship could have pulled off." That sick feeling returned to Ben's stomach. "Anything come to mind?" Ben's mind was working furiously. He knew that he couldn't have left any tracks behind that could be traced backed to him. The young man decided to play it innocent.

"No, sir, but I would be glad to help find out who the guilty party is," he offered.

The captain tapped his fingers on the desk and replied, "The computer evidence points to a console in your cabin." The captain scratched his chin thoughtfully. "Hemant, here, thinks someone else made it look like you did it. He claims that if you were the guilty party, we would never have been able to catch you." Captain Tucker picked up a printout. "I took the liberty of doing some checking on you. As you know, your departure from Isis was somewhat abrupt and you barely made this connection. Your personal file transmission was delayed two days, that's strange enough, but it looks like to me that the authorities wanted you off the planet and in a hurry!" He turned the printout around so that Ben could read it. The words Isis Lottery were highlighted. Inwardly, Ben groaned.

The captain stood up and turned to the commander, "Commander?"

"Yes, sir." He produced an electronic scanning unit. The commander took the scanner and aimed it in the direction of the AI. After about a minute, he said, "Okay, turn it on." Ben complied, setting the unit down on the desk. The commander accessed the files on the AI, thinking he was on a normal PC. He examined the files and downloaded a search program from a storage cube he produced. The program searched the files for several minutes. The holoscreen beeped obediently. Ben held his breath. He read the scanner's output and compared it to the screen. "Nope, nothing here."

"That's strange," said the captain. "I would have expected some sort of incriminating evidence. You sure your program works?"

"It's the best money can buy and guaranteed to ferret out the kind of information we're looking for. It even restores deleted files," replied the commander. The captain's face wrinkled in thought.

"Someone on board this ship has been running amok in the computer net," stated Captain Tucker. "Therefore, I am removing all top level clearances except for Hemant and Forest , here, and taking Gardener totally out of the net." He walked over to the AI, picked it up and looked at it closely.

"Just to be safe, I want that machine locked up. Hemant, you take care of that. The boy is to be kept off the system for the rest of this leg. No exceptions." The captain sat down. "Dismissed."

A depressed Ben trudged back down the corridor with the science officer carrying the AI. "I am truly sorry, Ben," offered Hemant, "You have got yourself into hot water this time."

"You know I didn't leave those tracks, Hemant," stated Ben.

Hemant replied, "I'm not saying you did or didn't do it, all I said to the captain is that there were irregularities in the logs. If we take that into account, along with the fact that the evidence was uncovered far too easily, one becomes suspicious of the whole thing."

Ben enthusiastically spurted, "Let me on a terminal. I'll find out who did it so fast it'll make your head spin!"

"No!" said Hemant. "The captain's orders are explicit. You may not even touch a console." The science officer thought a bit, "However, you could sit beside me at a terminal and assist me in making an investigation." Ben's face lit up.

"Great, we need some programs from my computer, plus . . ."

"No. This machine is to be locked up, under full sensor monitoring," recited the science officer.

"But . . ." began Ben.

"No buts, this is the way it is going to be," stated the science officer. "There is something unusual about your computer, but I cannot put my finger on it." The young computer genius' face fell again.

Ben surrendered, "How soon can we start on the investigation?"

Hemant replied, "After I figure out a way to cure Tate and prevent the spreading of whatever it is to the rest of the ship."

"The trip might be over by then," complained Ben.

"And Tate may not live that long," mused a grim science officer.

CHAPTER FOUR

THE Karl-host stood in front of the mirror with his shirt off. Several small-distended bulges covered his lower belly. He plunged the needle from a blood sampler into one of the cyst-like bulges and emptied the contents into a sample vial. The clear liquid almost filled two vials. The alien then emptied the other two cysts as well. He picked up a package and studied its contents: a powerful sedative, one that would knock out a person for hours. The possessed technician took the empty hypos and filled them with two parts clear liquid from the cysts and one part sedative. He put the hypos in his pocket and called main engineering on the comm system. After telling the mate on duty that he was calling in sick, he hung up and accessed the ship's main computer. He launched one of the programs he wrote earlier and left the cabin.

The infected human made his way down two decks to the aft crew quarters. In a pouch slung over his shoulder were a number of ration packets. Outwardly, there was no sign that Karl the technician had been taken over by the essence contained in the small crystal. A number of crewmen saw him and exchanged pleasantries. One couple just glared at the computer tech, after all, Karl wasn't very popular at the moment. The Karl-mutation stopped outside a cabin. He looked both ways down the corridors, seeing no one, he pressed the buzzer.

"Who is it?" said a female voice.

"It's Karl, Hemant sent me to inoculate you as a precaution. There is a dangerous infection that could sweep the ship." The hatch opened, a scantily clad female stood in the doorway.

"Where's Hemant and why would he send you?" she asked.

"There are several of us inoculating the ship right now," lied the Karl-host. "Speed is of the essence."

"Why didn't I receive an e-mail?" she demanded.

"I don't know, like you I'm just following orders." The Karl-host got out the hypo. "It'll only take a minute and then you can go back to sleep," said the transformed computer technician.

The woman crewmember hesitated, and then said, "Okay, come on in. No funny business." She bared her shoulder. The hatch was left conspicuously open.

"This will make you a little sleepy," said the Karl-host. The injection went in.

"Fine, it's done. Goodbye and get out!" She pushed Karl to the door. The crewman stopped, looked at her arm, raised her other hand to her head, rolled her eyes and collapsed on the floor. The Karl-mutation closed the hatch and loaded the unconscious woman into her bunk. He then laid several packets of space rations on the desk and exited the compartment. The altered technician then locked the cabin, using an override code he had just loaded into the security system. The Karl-host then proceeded to use the same ruse on five other second shift off-duty crewmen. Each was sealed into his or her own cabin. The alien generated computer program released by the Karl-host cut off all comm system and sensor data from those cabins.

The mutated human paused in the last cabin to access the computer. It studied the crew assignments for the day and the task list. Satisfied with the information, the alien selected his next targets. In compartment twenty-eight, site of the infamous card game, he inoculated two more crewmen. Their bodies were hid in the storage room behind some containers. As with the others, space ration packets were left. Three more crewmen were infected with the fake vaccine in out-of-the-way places on the ship.

The Karl-mutation surreptitiously returned to the first crewmember he'd inoculated. It opened the locked hatch and stepped inside. The female victim lay sweaty and trembling on the bunk. Half the packets were torn open.

"What's happening to me," she gasped. "Comm doesn't work and I couldn't get the hatch open."

"Don't worry," said the former computer technician, "I'm here to help." The Karl-host went over to the woman and clasped her hands to his and interlocked their fingers. Tentacles from the Karl-mutation pierced the flesh of the woman's hands and made connection with the alien tissue growing inside her. She took a deep breath and her eyes went blank as data flowed from the alien to the woman. For an half an hour, they remained hooked together as the instructions were chemically stored in the woman's fledgling alien brain stem. When the Karl-mutation left the compartment, the woman was sitting at her desk calmly eating the remaining space rations. Her trembling had subsided, and an alien gleam of intelligence filled her eyes. The cabin was left unlocked. The Karl-mutation spent the rest of the day visiting each one of his victims, re-programming them the same way. This programming was limited, due to the lack of shard crystals. Alien brain tissue alone could only hold so much information. Star Crystal material, on the other hand, in addition to storing vital information needed for the resurrection of the extinct alien race, had immense storage capacity.

METAMORPHOSIS

* * *

Ben and Hemant spent the day trying various remedies on Crewman Tate. Hemant taught Ben how to use the medical computer to search for possible chemicals that would slow down or destroy the alien tissue, while Hemant concentrated on deciphering the DNA sequence. Several sub-space messages came in to the science officer's attention, from company scientists, who suggested various methodologies and treatments. Nothing worked. The alien material was resistant to gene splicing; the science officer had hoped to use the gene-spliced material to create an anti-virus. Some drugs showed promise at slowing the progression of the alien disease; however, they worked only once. Within two hours, the alien tissue had grown resistant. The patient had ceased his earlier aggressive behavior and lay passively on the couch. Attempts to communicate with him, however, were rebuffed. All day long, Tate's friends dropped in on him to say hi and be examined by the science officer. He didn't respond. Finally, Hemant called it a day. Exhausted, he suggested that they get a good night's sleep and let the company doctors analyze the information gathered during the day. Perhaps in the morning, they'd have another idea or two waiting for them on the net. The science officer selected a guard unknowingly from the now-infected second shift roster and ordered him to come to the science lab on the double. The crewmember arrived complete with dinner in hand, explaining that he never got to eat. Hemant, having examined this particular spacer early the day before, never thought of checking him again. Had he done so, the science officer would have noticed a red welt forming at the base of the crewman's skull. Instead, Hemant instructed the crewmember to wake him if there were any changes in Tate's condition. The science office was too tired to notice the strange glint in the guard's eyes as he left the compartment.

At dinner Ben sat with the McGregors and was joined by the chief engineer, Tina. Mr. McGregor started off the conversation by asking the chief engineer about the rod realignment. "I understand that we should be able to jump tomorrow. Are we still on schedule?"

A disgruntled Tina answered, "Barely. Those last few blasted coils refuse to come into spec. We've been working day and night to get that last group on line. To top it off, that lazy Karl decided to call in sick today, that's slowed me down even more. Damn contract! Should have a sick blackout period for situations like this." The chief engineer glowered.

Mrs. McGregor said, "I believe I saw your technician today in the lift, he was headed aft. He had a work pouch slung over his shoulder; I thought he looked healthy to me. He said hello and then strode off like he had something important to do." Tina lowered her fork and stared in disbelief.

"He better not have played hooky today of all days," exclaimed Tina. "In fact, he'd better be almost dead. If I find out that he's skipped out on me, I'll bring him up on charges!" With that she took a ferocious bite out of her chicken.

* * *

Well into the second watch, the Karl-host appeared at the science/medical lab hatch and rang the buzzer. The hatch opened and an armed crewman, one of the infected humans, appeared. "What do you want?" he asked, with a glare, in case anyone was listening in from outside the compartment.

"To see the patient," answered the mutated human. The crewman peered down the corridor before stepping aside to let the computer technician enter.

"You must be hungry. I'll watch Tate. Go get some food," ordered the Karl-host. The guard nodded and left the compartment. The transformed human stepped over to the computer console and spent a couple minutes perusing the directories, before finding what he wanted. He tapped the enter key and several programs were launched into the net. Then the alien turned to Crewman Tate. First he deactivated the force field. No alarms sounded. Tate looked at him and tensed. The Karl-host smiled and stepped forward to hold hands with the ailing crewman.

"Don't be alarmed," said Karl. "Your transformation has been stalled far too long. It is not healthy." His tentacles extended and the programming commenced. Crewman Tate was released of his restraints. "Come. You will witness my final transformation."

Both men stood by the UTTAR Isolator. The Karl-mutation's finger flew over the keyboard at an unnatural speed. The software locks dissipated one by one. Safety overrides were bypassed. Alarms were silenced. The protective shield began to rise slowly. Air rushed in to fill the vacuum. The Star Crystal lay undisturbed by the three containers of shards and the sealed container of crystallized organic material. The Star Crystal , shards, and artifact were perfectly clean. The science officer had removed all the organic compounds as a final precaution to the sealed container and decontaminated the chamber. The alien reached in and grasped the Star Crystal as the other possessed crewmember looked on. He opened his shirt and bared his chest. A vertical ten-centimeter long red scar could be seen just below his sternum. The scar pulsed with each heartbeat. As the Star Crystal was brought closer to the skin, it pulsed faster and faster. When the crystal touched the skin, the scar parted to expose a cavity and the crystal began to glow. The Karl-host continued to push the object deep into his chest. The flesh closed over the Star Crystal and the skin sealed behind it. Karl sat down with a heavy sigh. He gestured to Tate, who handed him two shards. They glowed in Karl's hand.

The hatch opened and the returning guard stepped through with four containers of food. He immediately saw that Tate was no longer restrained and the Isolator was opened. He dropped the food on the desk and strode over to the two former crewmen.

"What are my new orders!" he asked. "I was only programmed to fool the science officer, watch the isolator and Crewman Tate, nothing more. I am . . . incomplete!" his voice trembled. The Karl-host placed his hand on the infected guard's shoulders.

"All is well," crowed the possessed human. "I am now . . . whole again. I am the resurrected Alpha. It is good to be back after such a long time in inorganic suspension." He reached over and gave one of the shard crystals to the guard, and one to Tate. "Here, this will explain everything."

Tate slid the crystal into the organic input socket in the back of his own head, his eyes rolled back. The guard watched with wild eyes and opened mouth; he looked down at the crystal, and then he too slid his shard into the back of his head. Tate and the guard stood still as information uploaded to their brains.

The being formerly known and feared throughout the galaxy as Alpha One stood shakily to his feet. "Food!" he croaked. The three spent the next half hour eating. The alien intelligence in Karl's body fed himself with one hand, while programming different crystal shards with the other. No human could multi-task at such speeds. After finishing their meal, the possessed trio closed the Isolator chamber and set the shield to opaque. Empty food containers and extra blankets were used to make a bulge under the couch covers. The force field and the privacy screen were turned on high enough so one couldn't easily tell that the patient was missing.

"The next twelve hours are our most vulnerable," commented Alpha One. "We must work quickly and quietly. Take these two crystals and hypos to the bridge crew, they'll know what to do. They belong to us. Signal the others to meet at the pre-arranged coordinates. Tell them . . . Alpha One bids them greetings." The guard left with the items. The crewman, formerly known as Tate, gathered up the crystal shards and hypos and left for the rendezvous point.

Two on-duty, and five off-duty, infected crewmen arrived at the pre-arranged staging area. They greeted the former computer technician and former med lab patient with a slight bow. Each one was handed a crystal, which fit snugly into their organic input sockets at the base of their skulls. As they stood stock still, for the five minutes or so it took to initially upload instructions into their combined alien/human brains, the two alien possessed leaders divided up the crystals into piles. First one came out of his trance, then gradually, the others.

"Welcome back, Alpha One. You have been reanimated," exclaimed the first crewman to break his trance. The possessed human looked at his hands and fingers. "These bodies are different," he observed.

Another possessed crewman commented, "Your data indicates that a long time has passed since I was last sentient. Was I in storage?"

Still another, "Your instructions are to seize the rest of the ship, before re-making this body in your image. Do you have crystals?"

The alien intelligence inhabiting Karl's body replied, "A long time span has passed, almost one thousand years, according to my host's definition. I have waited patiently. As I feared, and my host's memories indicate, both sides lost the struggle and only traces of us remain in this galaxy."

"The bodies you now own are called 'humans,'" lectured Alpha One, "and have only recently achieved space flight. They have inherited this region of space. They know nothing of us and have limited technical abilities. Here in my hands are many of your workers brethren, waiting to come back to life and take their places at my side." The alien leader displayed the shard crystals. All the possessed humans gazed knowingly at the glittering crystals glowing in their leader's hands.

"Excuse me, your Brilliance, but have any of the leaders survived?" asked one of the newly revived aliens.

"To my shame, no," replied Alpha One. "No escape pods but mine succeeded in eluding the last Gaderian attack on the mother ship. I know nothing specific about who survived the last great battle. My new memories indicate that what remains of some of my inner circle are considered trinkets of great wealth and are worn around the necks of the females of this race."

"Blasphemy!" stated one of the women.

"No, ignorance! This confirms my suspicion that a disaster of gigantic proportions befell both our race and the Gaderians," exclaimed the alien leader. "Had the humans known what these 'Star Crystals ' were, they would have destroyed them, and us with them, long ago." Alpha One reflected, "Apparently our adversaries, the Gaderians, did a good job of erasing all memory of who we were . . . so good a job that the humans have no knowledge of how we resurrect. We will exploit this ignorance and not repeat the mistakes of the past."

The alien leader pointed to the piles of crystals and commanded, "Three teams of three to begin phase one conversions. Continue to use your host's original identities and mannerisms. No external modifications to your host's bodies until the ship are completely in our hands. Do not draw attention to yourselves. Security override codes are implanted in your storage crystals. Computer file directory and protocol information are also available. Make sure the commander, the cargo master and the chief are converted. We will save the captain for later." Alpha One dismissed his small band of resurrected aliens.

Three teams of transformed crewman, more alien than human, set out as ordered to different berthing areas on the ship. The attacks were choreographed. One team member would access the override code on a cabin and open the hatch. The other two would rush in and grab the occupant, holding him or her down until the hypo could be administered. The bodies were left on a bunk with a crystal in one hand and several space ration packets in the other. Sensors were deactivated, comm systems shut down, emergency egresses blocked, and the hatch cyber locked. With military precision, crewmember after crewmember was infected with the alien alteration virus.

In one cabin, a naked couple was burst in upon. A brief struggle ensued. They were unceremoniously dumped together, unconscious, in the bunk, arms and legs intertwined. Two of the mutated crewmembers nursed bruises from that encounter. Another crewman managed to escape from a cabin without being inoculated. He ran out into the corridor, yelling at the top of his lungs, before running into another one of the teams. His neck was quickly broken to silence the noise. The body was hid in an empty cabin. An off-duty crewman happened down the corridor just as the hatch closed.

"What's all that racket, these people are trying to sleep!" an uninfected human demanded. He noticed the steely eyes of the three mutated crewmembers. "You guys been drinking?" he asked.

One of the alien-possessed humans looked down at his feet, " Commander Forest didn't find all the containers. We were playing cards and one of the guys just lost."

"Oh, well that explains it. How much did he lose and is there any left?"

"Everything, and there's still half a liter," lied the alien.

"Poor guy, hope he does better next time," commented the uninfected crewman. The three aliens looked at each other.

"We need another partner," asked one of the alien crewmen. "Are you free for a friendly little game?" The other two creatures scanned the corridors and opened a hatch. "In here." The uninfected crewman stepped into the compartment and saw a form lying on the bunk.

"I think someone's sleeping in here, we should go . . ."

"This is just fine," interrupted the alien crewman with the hypo. He triggered the stud.

"Hey, ouch!" protested the newly infected crewman. He started to break for the hatch but collapsed on the deck.

"That was close," said one of the alien-inhabited crewmembers. "We should be more careful."

The aliens met as a group to give status to Alpha One. Thirty-two crewmen were either infected or fully reanimated aliens. The former computer technician was not happy to find out that Commander Forest was not in his cabin. There was too much activity in the corridors to risk an attempt to infect the engineering crew, the chief, and the science officer. The captain was being saved for later possession.

No matter, Alpha One thought, there is still time, we are patient. We have waited for one thousand years; another day will not change the outcome. One of the creatures brought a package to his leader.

"I found this in passenger McGregors' cabin. I thought you would want the honor of choosing the host." With great ceremony he unwrapped a full sized Star Crystal . The others gasped. Star Crystals of that size were reserved for the alien inner circle. To find one by chance on this ship was extremely fortunate! Alpha One reached out to touch the crystal. Tiny threads of tissue reached out from under his fingernails to touch the surface. He closed his eyes for a moment, then opened them and smiled.

"Excellent! It's Alpha Six, one of my favorites!" Alpha One turned to Tate, "Prepare the interface organ; you are to be the recipient. Report to me as soon as you are ready for implantation."

Tate bowed his head, "I am honored." He took the package. Throughout the night, the alien conspirators continued to methodically take over the unsuspecting star ship.

CHAPTER FIVE

THE alarm rang. Ben struggled to an upright position. Oh, how he hated mornings. He was more of a night person. The young man showered and changed into fresh clothes. He idly tried the computer console using the ship's assigned password, it refused to cooperate. He was tempted to use the captain's password. Ben shook his head, better not risk it. The young man looked around the cabin. He felt alone. Jack was more of a friend and companion than anyone realized.

"Jack, I know you can hear me. I'll do what I can to clear myself before the trip is over. Hang in there, pal!" Jack did not reply, for fear that Hemant's sensors could pick up the transmission.

At breakfast, there was a light turnout. It was almost empty, except a table of several crewmen, including the shapely navigator. Hemant was already seated at another table with the chief engineer, when Ben arrived at the galley.

"Where is everybody?" asked Ben.

"I dunno. Part of my team ate early and went down to engineering to try and align those last three coils," replied the chief engineer looking around. "You know, there should be a lot more people here."

The hatch opened, Jennifer and the commander entered together. Tina spoke in a low voice, "I think those two are becoming a hot item. Scuttlebutt says the two spent the evening together."

"Oh!?" asked Ben. His whole fantasy began crashing down around his ears. This was turning into a bummer of a morning, he thought. He noticed the navigator looking their direction. Hemant changed the subject.

"I'm hoping the company doctors have come up with a solution to our problem with Crewman Tate. Of course, it may be too late," lamented the science officer. "The alien tissue has certainly fully integrated with his brain by this time." The science officer was philosophical. "There may be nothing left to save," he pointed out.

"Hemant, are you sure that whatever he caught is not loose on this ship?" demanded the chief engineer.

"I examined three quarters of the crew yesterday and found no trace of the infection. Today, I intend to complete my examinations. The night shift has yet to be examined as well as some of the passengers." He tapped his forehead and said, "Oh, and there are one or two others that were busy or I couldn't reach."

Tina threw down her fork in disgust, "If I ever catch a disease like that, promise me that you'll just space me and end it quick!"

The commander and Jennifer sat down at the table. The smiling young archeologist kept one arm intertwined in his. It was clear she was declaring her intentions. Ben sat there numbly. The hatch opened again, several crewmembers left, including the navigator, who kept stealing glances at the couple. The captain came in and strode over to the table.

"Where in the blazes is everyone?" the captain demanded. "And where were you last night, Forest ? You never answered your comm link and you weren't in your cabin last night."

The commander and Jennifer got red faced. She quickly slipped her arm out of his and stared at her plate. The captain went on, oblivious to the signals. "We had two no-shows last night with no call-in." Captain Tucker looked down at Commander Forest and lectured, "You know that company policy is to wear your comm link at all times. I never know when I might need you." The captain stopped suddenly as he noticed the two bright red faces and finally put two and two together. Embarrassed, he stammered, "And . . . uh . . . oh . . . don't do it again, okay?" The captain went on quickly, "Check the log and find out who the no-shows were and find out what happened." Not knowing what else to say, the unnerved captain mumbled something about breakfast and escaped to the food replicators.

"Yes, sir, right away!" responded the commander, who got up from the table just as quickly.

"I didn't get you in trouble did I?" implored a horrified Jennifer.

"Everything will be fine, I promise," replied the commander as he followed the captain to discuss a few matters in private. Tina had a big shit-eating grin on her face.

"Left his comm link in his cabin did he. Ha, he'll never do that again!" laughed Tina. She winked at the young woman and said, "Congratulations."

Jennifer looked around the table embarrassed. "Nothing happened, really! We talked all night long, watched a couple of vid's together, and fell asleep on my couch!" The young archeologist put her head into her hands. "This looks bad, doesn't it?"

The chief engineer replied, "Honey, a ship hurtling through space, no matter how large, is still a finite space. Word travels fast and there are few secrets and even more rumors. Remember that." Tina continued to chuckle.

"Oh, dear," was all the young archeologist said and pushed her plate away. This time Hemant rescued Jennifer.

"Come, my boy, it's time we got to work. Jennifer, if you are done, would you accompany us to the science lab? You haven't been examined yet." The three of them got up to leave. "Ms. King, when might I expecting you for your visit?"

The chief engineer replied, "If I don't get those last coils aligned, I'll save you a trip; I'll slit my wrists." Hemant smiled as he walked to the refuse bin. The trio left the galley and headed towards the science lab. Ben dragged along behind the other two.

"Miss Booth, tell me about the Gaderians and the race that they warred with," asked the science officer. "Any reports of biological warfare?"

"No, the archeologist answered, "What few references we have from scattered records from that period tell us that the invading race appeared suddenly, was ferocious in battle, had technology equaling that of the Gaderians and refused to negotiate for peace. There was no reason given for why they attacked in the first place. Both sides believed in a scorched earth policy. Some reports talk about entire planets and even solar systems being destroyed. It was a horrible, vicious war."

Hemant thoughtfully replied, "I see. The reason I asked was that Crewman Tate's infection is peculiar, to say the least. The alien tissue growing within him is not trying to kill him, it's almost like it is trying to take him over, to change him into another life form. Perhaps this is how the Gaderians got information from their prisoners?"

"Absolutely not, the Gaderians were an industrious and peaceful society!" retorted Jennifer angrily. "They believed in the dignity of the individual." Jennifer, after the embarrassment at breakfast, was a bit touchy.

"Yes, yes, calm down," responded the science officer. "I'm only suggesting that perhaps near the end of the war, one side or the other created a terrible biological weapon that we were unlucky enough to stumble across." Further conversation was halted by the arrival at the science lab. Hemant hit the buzzer. No response. He hit it again. Still no response.

"The guard must be busy?" mused the science officer. Hemant tapped in the code and the hatch swung open. The science lab was dark.

"Hello, hello, anyone here?" called out the science officer as he turned up the lights. The force shield was in place and the privacy screen shimmered inside that. A form could be barely discerned under the covers.

"Why did your guard leave him alone?" asked Jennifer.

"Hemant, look," said Ben. They all crowded around the Isolator. "It's completely opaque." Ben looked back toward the med cubicles.

"The science officer played with the console. "I can't seem to clear the shield." He worked at it for several minutes. Meanwhile, the young man started poking around the lab.

"It gets worse!" stated Ben. "Tate's gone." Hemant spun around to see the privacy shield lowered and the force shield intensity reduced. The form they saw was rolled up blankets under a sheet.

"What's going on?" asked Jennifer. "Does this mean we are in trouble?"

The science officer was frantically punching buttons. "I must see inside the containment shield. Someone is locking out the controls, sensors, logs, everything. Ben, can you do something here?" The young computer genius came over to the console.

"I have a bad feeling about this," Ben said as he started working on the problem. It took thirty minutes, but the young man was able to break down the cyber locks enough to change the polarity on the shield. "That was a first class encryption job. It took me forever to break through!" The shield cleared and everyone gasped. Only the empty artifact and one container remained.

The young man continued, "Log's wiped. Memory's wiped. Sensors de-calibrated. All your records and tests results are gone as well. Whoever did this was a real professional." The science officer numbly sat down with a soft groan. Ben went over to the medical computer. "Same thing here, all records cleaned out." Ben went over and sat next to the science officer.

"What do you think is going on, you two?" asked a very perplexed Jennifer.

Ben ignored her. "Is it possible Hemant that the alien DNA could have stored enough instructions in its sequence strings to not only transform a human into a kind of biological robot, but also provide the operational programming as well?"

"It's so far fetched and beyond our technology . . . but, how can I say?" Hemant scratched his head. "I'll ask the company scientists." He reached for the computer console. "Strange, no messages waiting for us. I'll check the log." The science officer tapped the keys silently. "The computer says the sub-space transmitter is down and has been since late last night." Hemant sounded puzzled. The realization slammed into Ben and he jumped up and grabbed Hemant by the shoulders.

"You must release my PC, now, immediately. We may not have much time!" "What are you talking about?" asked the science officer.

"Yes, what does your PC have to do with all this? And will someone, please, explain what's going on?" asked Jennifer, impatiently.

"No time to explain, I just realized something my AI, I mean, I think I've figured out what's going on, but I need my PC!" Ben urgently implored.

Hemant gazed into the young man's pleading eyes and sighed. "I will probably lose my job over this." The science officer went over to an environmental chamber and pressed his thumb against the lock mechanism. The microprocessor read his thumbprint and released the lock. Hemant opened the door and reached inside and shut off the scanner. He pulled out the box and gave it to Ben.

Ben grabbed the unit and spoke directly to the cover. "Jack, release all functions, full sensor sweep, full network sweep, normal audio response. Tell me what happened."

"What happened?" a voice filled the compartment. "What do you mean what happened? You told me to shut myself off so that the sensors couldn't pick anything up, as if they could. Now, what's going on?"

Jennifer looked at the AI in puzzlement, "Where did that voice come from?

Ben, still ignoring her, spoke rapidly, "Tate's gone, the Star Crystal 's gone, those little crystals are gone, and who knows what else has gone wrong!"

"Right!" responded the AI audibly. "Working. Connecting to the main frame. Sub-space transmitter's off line." The science officer and young archeologist looked at each other, trying to figure out what was transpiring.

"We already know that, tell us something we don't know!" said an exasperated Ben.

"Well, excuse me!" retorted Jack, who continued his briefing. "Security systems in the lab crashed, no input there. Sensor logs erased, that's okay, I can still go into the deep core and retrieve copies. Medical scans erased, got to go to the core for that too. There are some strange programs running around on the network. Looks like a virus. I think I recognize the construction. Running a match. All right, got the last medical scan." The AI grew silent.

"Jack, what is it?" asked Ben

The young archeologist walked over and stood directly in front of the young man holding the box and grabbed his shoulders. "How did you engage your voice recognition without us seeing it? AND WHAT IS GOING ON?!" demanded Jennifer.

Ben looked at both Jennifer and Hemant. "It's not a PC. It's an artificial intelligence. I think we are in big, BIG trouble. Jack, talk to me!" pleaded Ben.

"I knew there was something about that unit," said Hemant nodding his head and stroking his chin.

The AI spoke, "Ben, we've got more than big trouble! The similar nerve lattice construction, the software sub-routines (although in another language) are clearly identifiable, the shape and construction of the Star Crystal , the presence of three infected crewmen when the Isolator was breached. There is a 99% probability that the scourge of the universe, the menace of untold horrors, and the Great Destroyer has been reborn."

"Jack, what the hell are you talking about!?" shouted Ben.

"Security levels twelve through twenty released by conditions satisfying general order 125." The AI paused as if receiving new instructions for the first time. He formed a full sized hologram. Jennifer leaped back in surprise. "Ben, I have more access to my memory. It's been so long!" the AI exclaimed.

Hemant seemed to take the AI's hologram in stride and he asked it, "Excuse me, Mr. AI, did you say that three crewmen are infected?"

"Yes, the sensor readings, although crude, provide me with enough information to postulate probable infection rates."

"Jack, boil things down for us here. We're struggling to follow you," pointed out Ben.

Jennifer spoke up, "No kidding! I'm still totally lost."

The holo image of the AI sat down on a chair. "It's quite simple, you see. The same creatures that wiped out the Gaderian civilization over one thousand years ago are living inside several of your crewmen. Unless stopped, they will take over this ship and then go on to destroy the human race." Everyone was shocked into silence. Hemant was first to respond. He whipped out his staff comm link.

" Commander Forest , code one, Commander Forest , code one for Science Officer."

"Forest here," was the reply. "Hemant, did you know the sub-space network is down? And those two crewmen, the captain complained about. I can't find them anywhere. No one has seen them."

"Forget all that," said the science officer. "Tate is missing. We have reason to believe the ship has been infected with a biological weapon from the artifact."

"WHAT!" shouted the commander's voice on the link. Hemant went on to explain in sketchy detail about the theory of the possessed crewmen.

"Hemant, this is hard to swallow. How do these things get their intelligence, from a virus? I can't buy that!"

A new voice on the comm link answered the commander. "The Star Crystals provide the intelligence. They are 'memory units.' I have one too, but it's square, not oblong."

"Who said that?" demanded the commander.

"I'll explain later," answered the science officer, "you had better contact the captain and secure the bridge."

The commander first called the bridge using the standard comm panels but got no answer. He was in the stern of the ship and was a long ways from the bridge. He began to run and at the same time used the comm link to reach the captain. "Captain, this is the First Officer, where are you?" he panted.

The authoritative voice over the comm link said, "Captain here, I'm on my way to the bridge to straighten some things out. Forest , the sub-space channel is out and I've been locked out of the computer. I'm not amused."

"Sir, there are developments we need to discuss. Tate's missing. The ship may be in danger! I can't raise the bridge," puffed Forest as he raced down the corridor.

"In danger, from what?" scoffed the captain. "There are no alarms, are there?" The captain arrived at the bridge. He pressed the buzzer. No one answered. "Stand by, Commander, the bridge doesn't answer, I'm going to override the hatch."

"Sir, wait for us. I'll get an armed party . . . ."

"No need, probably just a communications failure. There, the hatch is opening." The captain stepped onto the bridge. There were two crewmen at duty stations and the navigator was slumped over in her chair. "What's wrong with communications and why is my navigator sleeping while on duty?" thundered the captain.

"She's had a very hard morning and needs her rest." A figure stepped out of the shadows. The captain turned to face the newcomer. He recognized the face.

"Tate! What are you doing out of sickbay?" demanded the captain. He raised the comm link to his mouth. "Tucker here. I found Tate and of all places he's here on the bridge and …." The hypo hissed and the captain collapsed on the deck.

The commander heard the conversation and the sound of a body hitting the floor and someone say, "Secure the door." Then the comm link was switched off. Commander Forest immediately tried to reach the chief on the comm link.

"Chief Metzler here, sir."

"Chief, someone is making an attempt to take over the ship. Go immediately to the arms locker and secure the compartment. Our own crew may be involved. Let no one in except myself," ordered Commander Forest .

"Are you for real?" retorted the chief. "Is this a joke, the captain will have an absolute fit when he hears . . ."

"Belay that talk," interrupted Commander Forest . "The captain may have already been captured and the bridge taken." The tone in his voice told the chief that this was not a joke.

"I have two men here with me, I'll meet you there. Chief, out."

Back at the science lab, the AI had managed to activate the comm system enough to contact the engineering section. Hemant convinced Tina to march herself and her two crewmen underneath the sensor pack so that Jack could check them out. He announced that the engineering crew was clean.

"But I will probably want to run a blood test anyway, when we get there," said the AI.

Ben asked Jack privately, "With what equipment? We're leaving the autodoc behind."

"I'll grow a small diagnostic tool by the time we get there," replied Jack. Ben knew he should be shocked, but with all that was going on, he just accepted it in stride.

"Where is the rest of your crew?" Hemant asked Tina.

"Haven't seen 'em. Comm system's down, we were just digging into it when you called."

"Lock yourselves in the compartment and don't open it for anyone except us," ordered the science officer. "We can contain the infection that way, I hope." Tina acknowledged.

"Jack, can you determine who is infected and who isn't throughout the ship?" asked Ben.

"I can try; it depends upon the sensor placements." His hologram face scrunched up in thought.

Hemant went to a locker and thumbed it open. He rummaged around inside until he came up with a stunner. That he stuck in his pants. The he grabbed a bag and tossed in a couple of emergency medical kits and various hypo vials. "I think it would be best for us to retire to main engineering, where we know we have somebody on our side."

"Good idea," said Jack, "So far I've accounted for everyone but five people and assuming they aren't infected, that leaves only fifteen people left unaffected."

Hemant spoke into the comm unit, " Commander Forest and Chief Metzler, we are retreating to main engineering. Only fifteen people under our control remain. Trust no one." The science officer herded his small group to the hatch.

"Fire fight going on in the arm locker," said Jack. "Here is the audio feed from security."

Voices filled the compartment. "They're still coming!" said an unknown voice. "Use a higher stun setting! Watch out, he's grabbed a blaster!" The sound of a blaster rips through the compartment followed by a few screams. More sounds of return stunner fire, followed by more blaster hits, then, silence.

Jack spoke unemotionally, "Three uninfected crewmen now dead. Sensors indicate that the compartment is in the hands of infected crewmembers. Better tell the commander to turn around and meet us at main engineering."

Ben opened the hatch and looked out into the corridor. From the direction of the ship's bow, three crewmen were coming towards the science lab. "We've got company, come on let's go!" He grabbed Jennifer's hand and wrapped his arm around the strap of Jack's box and darted out the hatch, followed closely by Hemant. The three men started running towards them.

Jack's hologram had collapsed when his CPU was picked up to leave. "One of those men following us has a hypo. My guess is that it contains the virus and that's how they're taking the ship. Run faster!"

"Jack," puffed Ben as he ran, "access the main computer and override the door controls. When we reach the main bulkhead, close and lock the doors behind us. Delete the control program so they can't override the door." A crewman stepped out into the corridor, not three meters away.

"Infected!" said Jack.

"Thank you," replied Ben as he literally ran over the crewman, knocking him flat on the floor. The three uninfected humans ran past. The main bulkhead loomed closer. "They're gaining on us! Hemant, get your stunner ready!"

"I suggest, sir, that you put it on maximum and understand it may still not work," advised the AI. Hemant stopped, spun around and took aim at the closest man. He fired and the man stumbled and fell. Two quick shots sent the other two to the deck. Incredibly, they got up and began to stumble toward them.

"It only slowed them down!" yelled the science officer as he resumed his run to the main hatch. Ben and Jennifer reached the bulkhead first. Hemant, out of breath, barely made it across the threshold, before falling to the deck. The vertical hatch slammed shut just as the first crewman reached for the trio.

"That was close!" gasped Ben. "Are you okay?" he asked Jennifer. She shook her head yes, being out of breath as well. "Hemant?"

"I will recover," Hemant managed to get out.

"Jack, where is the commander?" asked Ben.

"He is two decks below us, almost to the main bulkhead. There are four crewmen chasing him. I detect no infected crewmen on this side of the bulkhead."

"Good, as soon as the commander clears the bulkhead, seal it as well as all other decks," ordered Ben.

"Is the commander all right?" blurted out Jennifer, concerned for her new love interest.

"He is not infected, if that's what you mean by all right," answered Jack. "Ah, he is through the bulkhead. All hatches being closed now. We have effectively sealed off this end of the ship. I am closing all the hatches on the ship and deleting the control programs. This won't stop them, but it will slow them down, cause them to regroup."

"Good idea, Jack. Hemant, how can we permanently seal the hatches to keep them from using the mechanical bypass?" inquired Ben.

"Hemant to Chief Engineer." The science officer spoke into his communicator.

"Tina here. What's our status?" Hemant explained the problem. The chief engineer, to her credit, didn't argue but immediately organized her crew, grabbed some equipment and headed out of the compartment to reinforce the bulkhead seals.

The Ben's party ran into the commander coming up the lift as they were going down to the engineering level.

"Eric!" shouted a sobbing Jennifer, throwing herself into his arms. After disengaging himself from the young woman, the commander asked Hemant, "How many do we have on our side of the bulkheads?"

The science officer explained about the sealed bulkheads and informed him that it was highly unlikely that any uninfected crewmen were left to rescue.

"Eight is all we have." The commander's face fell.

He exclaimed, "That's all?! The rest of the ship's company is under the control of some sort of alien influence? All of them?"

"Actually, it's more like an alien invasion. We're all that's left." said a disembodied voice.

"Whose voice was that?" the commander looked around the lift in puzzlement.

"Mine, Commander." A little head materialized in thin air, startling the commander. "I belong to Ben."

"Don't worry," gasped Ben, still breathing hard from his escape. His sentences came out choppy. "It's my PC. Well, it's not a PC—it's an AI…Gaderian. My dad, he thought it was something else, but I got it working. It can talk to the ship's computer. It's practically alive!" Ben thought to himself, Boy that made a lot of sense .

"I'm not sure what you mean," responded Commander Forest eyeing the apparition suspiciously, "but is he responsible for the stolen liquor?"

"Excuse me?" said the AI, glaring back at the commander. "That sleaze ball, Karl, created that setup. His electronic fingerprints were all over the files. Such an amateur!"

"So it was Karl!" Ben was vindicated. "I suspected all along."

"Fill me in on everything to date," ordered the commander. Ben, Hemant, and Jennifer proceeded to relate their escape from the science lab, the discovery of the thefts, and the takeover plot. Jack stood watch during the ninety minutes or so it took for Tina's crew to find a way to prevent anyone from overriding the main bulkhead doors.

CHAPTER SIX

COMMANDER FOREST took stock of their situation. The infected crew held three quarters of the ship: the bridge, the observation lounge, the galley, the storage holds, the science lab, and all of the forward berthing compartments. The uninfected survivors held engineering, maintenance, maintenance storage, and the aft berthing compartments. The AI had sealed the aft bulkheads leading to the main holds, and disabled the controls. The chief engineer and her two technicians had spot-welded the doors shut in case the mutated crewmembers tried to bypass the frozen controls. All the weapons were on the alien side of the barriers. All the heavy welding and cutting equipment was on the human side. The alien-crewmembers commanded the bridge, navigation, and the main computer. The human-crewmembers controlled the propulsion and hyperspace systems. It was a stalemate, for the moment.

"Jack, do you have any new intelligence about the alien activity?" asked Commander Forest while tapping the case with his finger. The AI had been busy intercepting signals from the bridge recorders. These recorders were designed to run continuously and were almost impossible to disable. The AI activated his holographic projector. In 3-D color, the figures of what used to be Captain Tucker, Karl, and another crewman were plugged into the navigation computer and each other. Silvery thin tentacles stretched out from fingertips and skull implants. Star charts flashed by on the screens. Other creatures spoke in a stucco buzzing voice.

Hemant exclaimed, "Look how the infection has modified the bodies of those men, forehead bulges, lumps under the skin and what is that? There appears to be some mechanical device grafted to the head of one of the crewmen!" The uninfected humans stood transfixed, horrified at the images of their former colleagues.

Tina spoke first, "They don't even look human anymore. They are so . . . alien!"

"Uh, oh, guys, I can translate the language," spoke the AI.

The young archeologist replied, "How can you do that? You only just now tapped into the net. It would require hours of data gathering just to develop a rudimentary language." Ben said nothing, deep in thought, staring at the aliens.

Jack replied, "Apparently, this language is stored in my memory banks." He went on to explain what the creatures were talking about. "They are discussing plans for modifying a life pod and turning it into a small ship. The technology they intend to use is far advanced to your own. Let's see, complaints about unavailable welding equipment. Another one saying stop whining, we can build our own sonic welders. Timetable is short. Get a move on. Is the subject ready? Here is the design for propulsion . . ."

The chief engineer blurted out, "How in blazes are they going put an engine on a little life pod. And where would they go? There's nothing for light years around, except for the small Keynan colony two light years away. A pod is just too small for a hyper-space power plant." This was a fairly desolate region of space, mostly unexplored.

The AI went on to explain that the mutated crewmembers were constructing tools in the science lab using Hemant's equipment for parts. Hemant groaned. That was his uncle's property. The creatures had manually bypassed the controls and gained access to the storage holds. After ransacking its contents, they had assembled enough equipment to construct an electro-magnetic furnace and were proceeding to refine the teryllium ore shipment into a usable form. Using constructed gravimetric tools, they shaped the molten material. The entire group of creatures worked together as a team, achieving levels of coordination unsurpassed by humans.

Ben exclaimed, "They work almost like machines or as if they have one mind."

Jack replied, "I don't think they have one mind. They're working from a common database. The leaders download the instructions, plans and schedule directly to their brains. They lose nothing in the interpretation of the information. No questions are raised, because all the information is provided. Strange, though, there does seem to be some individual personalities manifesting in the leadership. They complain a lot."

The commander scratched his chin thoughtfully, "At the rate the construction is proceeding, they're going to be able to get through these bulkheads pretty soon. What I don't understand is why they haven't done so already."

Ben answered, "I guess that they don't see us a threat. That computer virus they released ate up all the software controls that we could have used to pilot the ship from here. The star charts were munched up as well. Even if we reconstructed those files, our access to the sensors and positioning equipment is cut off. They, on the other hand, have numbers and time in their favor. What technology we have denied them is simply being replaced, from scratch. I think we need to get off this ship, and fast."

The chief engineer looked from her console, "Our only chance is the shuttle craft in the hold. There should be back up copies of the star charts in the shuttle's navigation computer. But there is a larger problem, where do we go? The nearest colony is too far to reach in our lifetime. As soon as they got control of this part of the ship and repaired the damage it would be easy to run us down."

The young archeologist jumped into the conversation, "Why don't we just blow up the ship? Rig it to blow after we leave. We cannot allow the devastation that befell the Gaderians ravage the human race as well!"

Tina was taken back by the young woman's savage comment. It was so out of character. "It's not that easy girl. With several technicians, it would take maybe two days to disable or bypass enough safety mechanisms to pull it off. Those 'things' out there could probably do the task in several hours, but we aren't 'them' . . . not yet, anyway! In just a few hours, our former friends are going to find a way to grab and convert us into whatever they have become. To tell you the truth, I'd rather kill myself first."

One of the technicians, Frankie, interrupted, "I don't like the idea of killing my mates. Can't we cook up an antidote or something?" Jack's hologram appeared and placed his arm around the crewman.

"I'm so sorry," apologized Jack, "but my memory banks indicate that no successful antidotes were ever developed. Once infected, the process is irreversible. Your friends are gone. In their places are hideous alien intelligences that have only one purpose—galaxy-wide domination. Soon, they won't even look remotely human." The crewman nodded.

"You know, Ms. King," said the other technician, "we might not be able to blow up the ship, but we could rig some booby-traps to slow them down. We need to create enough damage to allow us to escape. Now if we could find a way to take the sensor array down, they couldn't find us. It would be like trying to find a needle in a haystack. Once far enough away, sensor array or not, we could hide out in an asteroid belt, powered down until they left the system."

"I still don't like the idea of killing them, but if we have no choice . . ." said Frankie. "But we're back to where do we go? There is nothing out there. We can survive for eight months in the shuttle and then we're out of power. No power, then no food and no air."

"Well it's better than sitting here!" stated Tina, flatly. "I'd rather be free for eight months then spend the rest of my life as one of them ugly things."

Commander Forest crossed his arms and took a deep breath, "All right, Ben, see if you and Jack can break into the shuttle's computer and see if the launch codes have been changed."

"Oh, don't worry, we have all the launch codes, including the captain's master," said Ben.

"What!" Forest stared in disbelief at the young man.

Ben smiled sheepishly, "You see . . .I sort of . . . well . . .um . . . kind'a downloaded all that information from the ship's computer banks."

The commander held up his hand. "Stop! Don't say anymore! I don't want to know. Just check out the shuttle as best you can without them knowing. We've got to know if those codes are still functional or this is gonna be a real short escape attempt!" The chief engineer and the commander went off to discuss how they might sabotage the ship while Jack and Ben got busy with the shuttle.

The young computer genius started his effort by downloading surveillance, code breaking, and tracking programs from Jack to the engineering console. He and the AI worked together for the next thirty minutes developing a program packet that would ride on the back of the main computer's operating system. The system continuously monitored traffic with each device on the main bus. The main computer sent millions of messages per second out to the net and waited for each device to respond. This way the computer knew when any device failed or had data to send. Ben disguised his program as one of those operating system messages and let the main computer send it to the shuttle. Once received by the shuttle's computer, the packet unzipped and started in on the interrogation. After finishing, the program compiled an answer packet and reversed the process. Then it released a worm and ate itself, and any traces it might have left behind.

Less than three seconds after launching the packet, Jack had the information the commander wanted.

"Got it Commander Forest ," called out the AI. The torso of one of Jack's personalities appeared in the holo-projector, "You're not going to like this." The group converged on the machine. "The shuttle computer reports that all codes have been changed, navigation software encrypted, and the star charts have been permanently erased. DNA protocol has been initiated, but everyone's DNA authorization in this room has been revoked. I can break the codes pretty quick, but the DNA could take a little time. The shuttle uses a hardwired medical-type scanner on an isolated bus. I have to be right there to jack into the scanner."

Commander Forest frowned. Those dammed Aliens inhabiting my crew are so blasted thorough! This leaves only the override commands key, kept locked in the captain's safe. The trouble was the captain's safe was in the Alien held sector of the ship. Sabotaging the ship and trying to sneak on board the shuttle was bad enough, now they had to think of a way to break in the captain's cabin, steal the override device, and get to the shuttle in time to blow the cargo doors and get off the Star of India.

"No, I don't like it, not one bit!" exclaimed Commander Forest . "I have no doubt that you could break the codes and, given time, crack the DNA scanner. But our time window is extremely small. There is a device stored in the captain's safe that will by pass all the security systems on the shuttle. All we have to do is get it and install it in the command console. Let's say two minutes prep, during which time we blow the cargo doors, and fly away from the ship. Once free, we fire up the subspace transmitter and broadcast a distress call and warning. Within several days, hopefully, Navy ships will be all over this sector. All we'll have to do is hide out until then. We need that device!"

Jack piped up, "What device are you talking about? I have copies of the complete technical readout of the craft and it doesn't mention any override key."

Forest chuckled, "That's right, you thief, you wouldn't, because it's not on those schematics. The captain had it installed in case of a hostile situation like this, only he was anticipating pirates, not a mutiny."

"You've got to be frigging crazy!" yelled Tina, "We're not going to get anywhere close to the captain's quarters. They'll be all over us in no time!"

"Then what we need is a diversion, "explained Ben calmly, "Leave that to ole' Jack and myself. We're kind of experts at this sort of thing." He quickly outlined a plan to fake major feedback overload in the galley replicators, and make it appear as if the result would be an explosion of the main forward power coupling. "I'm guessing that it will attract a number of mutated crewmembers in the lounge and keep the bridge crew occupied during our operation. With any luck, we can find a way to blow the lounge hatch and decompress the whole compartment with them in it!"

Hemant agreed, "I am thinking of a way to blow that hatch and disrupt the deep space sensors." He explained his idea.

Commander Forest contemplated the options, "I don't have any better ideas. If you can blow the lounge with a bunch of those things in there, then we would have a better chance at pulling this off. Let's do it!"

The survivors decided to launch their attack in six hours.

The six hours were a blur of activity. Chief Engineer King and the two remaining unaffected crewman spent their time tearing out the guts of the hyperspace drive, destroying as much of the control circuitry as possible. Commander Forest and Jennifer concentrated on sabotaging critical portions of the sub-light propulsion system. Using left over material from the mining effort, Hemant constructed a two bombs. One timing device was set so that three minutes after the engineering department was entered the mine would explode and decompress the compartment, sucking out the occupants. The other was intended for the lounge. Tina disabled all the compartment safety mechanisms that would normally contain such a catastrophe, like automatically sealing bulkheads and alarms. Hemant constructed a device that would release highly toxic gas into the engineering section once anyone attempted to engage the engines, assuming the aliens could repair the damage caused by the bombs. The humanoid flesh of the mutated crewmembers would react violently if the gas touched exposed portions of skin.

Ben spent almost the entire six hours glued to the engineering console, consulting with his AI. Together, Jack and Ben developed various false simulations, software booby traps, and viruses, which would release once they'd left the ship. Jack had several worms designed to eat holes through the main computer's protected core. Ben arranged for the security cameras on the ship to play back the past six hours of activity, instead of transmitting live images to the bridge; this would enable their little band to proceed undetected. They also programmed a small maintenance droid to carry one of the bombs to the forward lounge emergency access hatch.

At the end of six hours everyone was tired and weary. After a short meal of emergency rations and stem tabs (for overcoming sleep deprivation), they readied for the difficult tasks ahead. Everyone took their positions. Hemant had climbed into his spacesuit. His job was to knock out the sensor array. That meant an EVA. The science officer clipped a couple of harpoon guns to his backpack and selected tools for his belt. 'Harpooners,' as they were called, were devices that shot magnetic clamps attached to thin wire. A built in reel retracted the slack. The chief engineer and the two crewmen were armed with lengths of durasteel rods. They and Jennifer carried all sorts of portable tools and equipment that Tina insisted they bring along. Commander Forest , Ben, and Jack were going after the override device in the captain's compartment. They were armed with nothing. Commander Forest had said that if they were discovered there was nothing much that a club was going to do against a blaster. Ben gave a nod to Jack who released the first of the computer commands to send the fake overload signals to the bridge. He then used a secure comm link to inform the others to get ready. Chief Engineer King and Commander Forest had already cut the welds that held the doors in place. Jack monitored the bridge security camera, "Okay, I see the warning light on the board. One of them spotted it. They're calling another alien over." The creatures chattered excitedly together. "They are sending out a general quarters call to the rest of the ship." The klaxon warning signal rang throughout the ship. "Hey, it's working! The crew in the cargo hold was recalled to the lounge. Aliens in the science lab and the upper decks are rallying at the forward power coupling! C-Deck corridor clear!" Jack rammed a pseudoplasmic connector into the bulkhead controls and the door popped open. Ben called out on the comm link, "Now, go!" The commander and Ben sprinted down the corridor. The security cams recorded their presence and transmitted their actions to the ship's commuter. Those images were replaced with images recorded earlier, which showed an empty corridor. No alarms were triggered on the bridge.

Hemant cycled through the outer hatch and swung onto the outer hull. Once his magnetic boots were activated, he began a swift but awkward gait to the bottom of the ship. From there he began to traverse the entire length of the ship, going forward to the external sensor array.

Tina had finished cutting the last weld on the door. One of the crewmen had jacked into the controls. He hit the last sequence of keys and the door sprang open. Tina jumped through, club held high above her head. Fortunately for any alien, no one was in sight. "Okay, you two, follow me." She crept through the narrow aisles. The klaxon sound reverberated through the hold. They climbed through the contents of an open container. "Looks like our boys have been raiding the kitchen," muttered the chief engineer. They slowly made their way forward to the shuttle bay. A small noise around the next corner caused the little group to freeze. Using hand signals, the engineer indicated to one of the crewmen to circle around. Hugging the container, Tina peered around the corner. Two of the Star of India 's infected crew were unpacking some equipment destined for another port of call. The chief engineer rushed in swinging the durasteel rod like a bat. The closest alien whipped out a blaster. The rod struck the humanoid's hand and the blaster went flying. The other crewman threw himself on the second alien and grappled for his weapon. Tina whirled around and struck a mighty blow on the neck of the alien. With a sickening crack, the former crewman collapsed in a heap. The second creature had flipped his attacker over his head and was drawing a bead on Tina when the other crewman, Frankie, burst in on the scene.

"James McGuire, don't you dare!" he yelled. The alien turned to face him. "Jimmy, you know me. Put down the gun. You don't want to kill us. Come on man, we've been like brothers for seven years." He pleaded with the creature that used to be Crewman McGuire. Still holding the blaster on Tina, the alien spoke, "For seven years I put up with your pitiful company. Now I am more, much more than Jimmy McGuire. I have incredibly expanded knowledge, potential that you haven't even dreamed of. I can remember the thoughts of thousands of beings from before the last millennia. You are insignificant to me."

"Jimmy, you were my friend….," Frankie began.

"Was your friend," the creature said, as he fired his blaster at Frankie. The impact of the shot threw the man against the wall of an adjacent container. The smell of burnt flesh filled the air. The alien turned back to Tina, "And now to dispose of the two of you . . ." He never finished the sentence as the durasteel rod thrown by Tina drilled into his skull. The alien pitched over backwards.

Tina helped the last remaining crewman to his feet. "You know, I never did like McGuire, big ego." They collected the blasters and called to Jennifer. She timidly ran over to join them.

"I've never seen anyone killed before. Is Frankie dead?" She stared in shock over at the dead crewman. The chief engineer was picking up Frankie's tools and slinging them over Jennifer's shoulders. "Yes, and so will you if we don't start moving. If anyone else was in this hold, they sure know we're here now."

"I hope Ben and Eric are okay," mumbled the young woman. Jennifer ran several terrible scenarios through her head and spoke a little louder, "And I hope Commander Forest is okay."

"I've got eyes girl. Now let's move!"

Meanwhile, the maintenance droid, with the bomb strapped to its back, had made its way to the forward observation lounge. It avoided all portholes and security cameras. It executed its final instructions by squatting down over the emergency hatch. There it would wait until the signal to set off the explosives.

In the galley, alien creatures rushed in with tools, fire extinguishers, sensor instruments, and a variety of equipment. The food replicators were making strange noises and white vapor issued from the vents. The creatures gathered around the replicators but kept their distance. No one wanted to be first to open a unit. One of the alien leaders strode in and took stock of the situation. Seeing the vapor billowing from the vents, he signaled to one of the creature-crewman to open the maintenance door. It reluctantly did so and pulled the emergency power cutoff handle. The lights on the replicator winked out and died. He opened the replicator door and thick goo oozed out, spilling onto the floor. Another creature stepped forward and began scanning the replicator and the contents of the goo. Others surged forward and shut off the power to the rest of the replicators. The alien leader examined the instrument findings. He hit the intercom button.

"This is Marlin. Food replicator malfunction has been eliminated. No overload detected. All four units show infection with foreign program."

While reporting to the bridge, a relay program hiding in the power coupling sub-processor sensed the power shut off to the first replicator. Immediately it sent a data packet to the preventative maintenance system. There, other covert software activated and sent a signal, via the maintenance droid, to the communication network. Another droid sitting on the out emergency hatch got the signal and started the countdown.

The creature formally known as Karl chuckled. This must be a ploy to divert us from our activities, he thought, it could only be the boy. "Give me a report from the forward power coupling relay." The squad assigned to the relay reported that although the relay instruments indicated an overload was imminent, independent instrument readings contradicted the information. From all accounts the relay was operating properly.

"Is there any activity on security cameras or sensors," he asked. All stations reported negative. What are they up to? A klaxon interrupted his thought. "What was that?"

A crewmember replied, "Explosive decompression in forward lounge. Bulkhead 5-A sealing automatically. Pressure reading zero."

The Karl-creature asked, "Did our soldiers get out?"

The crewman looked at the view screen, "I don't think many did." The Karl-creature followed his stare. There at the bottom of the screen were several bodies drifting off into space.

He slammed his fist down on the console. "Recall all forces to the bridge level immediately. Neutralize the damage the boy has caused to the ship's computer system. Encode and encrypt all critical systems. Without trustworthy internal cameras and sensors, we are blind. We must find out what they are up to." The Karl-creature smiled, the boy is not as smart as he thinks he is; I will prove my superiority. He postulated several courses of action, coordinating simulations with the bridge crew. He concluded that there was a twenty-five percent chance the survivors were trying to blow up the ship, a thirty-eight percent chance they had built or found some weapons and were trying to attack the bridge, and a thirty-seven percent chance they were trying to escape the ship on the shuttle. He smiled, they still outnumbered them. All avenues were already covered. The shuttle was neutralized, the chief engineer didn't have enough time to blow up the ship, and a direct assault on the bridge was suicidal.

"Deploy a squad to the shuttle to set up an ambush. Send another one to the engineering section. Puncture the haul if you have to, but kill them. Keep the rest here to guard against a sneak attack. Bring the boy to me, if you can. If he resists, kill him!" These humans are more unpredictable than their Gaderian predecessors, he thought . I may have underestimated them because of their lower technology. I will not make that same mistake again.

* * *

Ben and the commander ran the length of the corridor in what seemed to them like an eternity, but was only 30 seconds. Although winded by the sprint, the adrenaline pumping through their bodies kept them going. Ben slid to a stop by the captain's quarters and rammed the remote interface into the socket beneath the keypad. He swung the AI around in its harness and punched several keys. The AI did his stuff. The interface beeped twice and lights blinked.

The hatch began to cycle. The young man and the officer just had enough time to duck into the compartment when the elevator arrival tone sounded. Not four meters away, the doors opened just as the captain's hatch hissed shut. Two creatures stepped out, turned, and went the other direction. One of them glanced back over his shoulder, but kept going.

Inside, Ben and the commander were plastered against the wall on either side of the hatch and prepared for company. When the hatch never opened, they wiped the sweat from their brows and made their way to the captain's antique blaster display.

"How much time before they're on to us?" Ben asked the commander.

"Oh, I estimate five or six minutes after the explosion in the lounge tips them off. That Karl 'thing' on the bridge isn't stupid, even though it does have an ego the size of Jupiter. With their understanding of advanced software and superior computer technology, our little bugs are going to be tracked down in a hurry. We have to be out of here and down the corridor before the security system is fixed."

Commander Forest took the blasters off the display. "We can use these. Do you know how to fire them?" He handed the Mark 3 Shoulder Mounted Blaster to the young man.

"Sure, we had a couple of these at school. I took a marksmanship course. All the guys did. It was a blast blowing up targets." Ben pointed out the firing stud, safety, and energy pack release. Commander Forest nodded and hit a hidden stud. The display slid aside to reveal a safe. He laid his palm on the scanner. The display turned red.

"Damn, they've removed my clearance," exclaimed the commander.

"This is a piece of cake. Standard cipher circuitry," replied the young computer genius. Ben slapped a remote override device on the durasteel beside the scanner. "Jack, go for it!"

Jack's face formed in the holoprojecter. He squinted, grunted and grimaced as he operated the remote. "Matching field strength, now. Interpreting network. Established override link. Lock frequency determined. Sending override signal." With a loud click, the safe swung open.

The commander reached in and rifled through the safe's contents, spilling disks, ledgers, and other documents onto the floor. Finally he found what he was looking for, the override shuttle key. It was a transparent seven-centimeter long cylinder with the faint outlines of electronics barely visible. He also pulled out a handful of power cells for the weapons. He gave two to Ben and pocketed the rest.

The ship's klaxon sounded. Alien speech emanated from the speakers. Ben asked Jack to translate.

"A general recall to A-Deck for all personnel," translated the AI. "I think they're on to us. Time to move gentlemen!" The duo had to retrace their steps half way down the corridor to a maintenance tunnel that lead directly to the main cargo hold. If they were spotted before they reached the tunnel, the creatures could cut them off at D level.

Ben got on the comm link to the chief engineer, "Tina, Tina, come in!" There was a pause, silence. "Tina, are you out there? Have you grabbed the shuttle?"

The chief engineer responded, "No, we got delayed. Frankie's dead. What about you?" Her voice was barely audible.

Commander Forest grabbed the comm link, "What about Jennifer, is she all right?!" The tension in his voice was apparent.

"She's fine, just shaken up. We need ten more minutes to secure the shuttle. Did you get the override device?"

Ben grabbed the comm unit back, "Yup, we're on our way back to you. Be there in five. Out." They cracked the hatch on the captain's quarters and peered around the corner. The hallway was empty. The pair ran back down the corridor the way they came. Just as they reached an intersection, two alien-creatures stepped into their path. All four collided together and ended up in a heap on the floor. Commander Forest was first on his feet and delivered a spin kick to the jaw of one of the creatures. It fell over on its back and lay still. The other managed to rise to its feet at the same time as Ben. It pressed a button on its belt. The klaxon sounded in the corridor. Red general quarter lights flashed. The alien reached for its weapon just as butt end of Ben's blaster connected with his head. The alien collapsed on the deck.

Ben picked up Jack, who managed a weak, "Good shot! You know, they really are looking less human, Ben." The two metamorphosed crewmen sported all manner of protrusions from their bodies. The eyes didn't quite look right. Odd bulges stuck out in strange places. One of the aliens started to stir.

The commander asked Ben, "Are you okay?"

"Yea, I'm find, come on let's go!" Just then the elevator tone sounded. Five creatures spilled out of the elevator with weapons drawn. Spying the two humans, they opened fire, scorching the wall next to Ben. The young man froze momentarily and fumbled with his blaster. A hand reached out and yanked him by the collar into the side corridor.

"Stay behind me, kid." The officer returned fire from around the corner. The mutated crewmembers jumped for cover. Two went back into the elevator; the others scattered to the hatchways. Immediately the aliens began laying down a blistering wall of fire. The humans were pinned down.

Ben cried out, "How do we get through that?"

"Do you see that emergency bulkhead behind us?" asked Commander Forest . "I want you to set the bullhead to close right after I jump through. I'll hold them off while you set things up." The commander continued to fire at the creatures. One made a run for it. The officer's beam struck it dead center in the torso. Its smoking body fell face down on the plating. The other creatures, staying safely behind cover, continued to pour suppressive fire down the corridor.

Ben reached the controls, ripped off the cover, set the code, and grasped the manual override. He yelled out, "Ready on the count of five!" He couldn't see the commander, so he paused to give the commander time to get ready. "Five! . . . Four!" Commander Forest turned and sprinted for the bulkhead. "Three!" One of the creatures at the intersection woke up and raised his weapon. "Two!" It fired, striking the door right above the fleeing human's head. The commander went sprawling. "One!" Ben pulled the handle and the door began to close. Commander Forest got to his feet and dove through the closing doors, landing on his face. The doors slammed shut. Blaster fire could be heard peppering the durasteel.

Ben took aim with his blaster and fired, keeping the beam on the controls until they melted into slag. "Now what do we do? The creatures are just going to run down to the other end of the ship and circle around."

"Excuse me?" interrupted Jack.

"I'm thinking, I'm thinking," replied the commander. "We had to buy some time. Perhaps we can cut through the decking to D-Deck and fight our way back to the maintenance tunnel."

Ben paced back and forth, "I'm sure that more of those things are spreading out on other decks now that they know where we are. Are there any other ways to get to the hold?"

"Excuse me?" interrupted the AI again.

"We could seal off this back corridor and cut sideways into the maintenance tunnel," theorized the commander. "Of course if they figure that out we'll be trapped."

"EXCUSE ME, GENTLEMEN!" The AI was indignant. Both humans stopped talking and turned to stare at the floating head. "Let's leave the ship."

"What?" said Ben.

The commander's face lit up, "I know where he's going. We'll use the emergency air lock off cabin 12. There should be four emergency spacesuits in there. We suit up, go outside, and jam the hatch. Then we walk straight down the side of the ship and come up underneath the belly. We can re-enter the ship through the personnel hatch in the shuttle bay. Brilliant work, Jack!" The AI's face turned to smile at Ben. Told you so, he mouthed silently.

The trio hustled around the corner into corridor 1. Three doors down was compartment twelve. Several compartments beyond that was another emergency door. Commander Forest headed straight for that door and stood to one side, blaster leveled, waiting for the creatures to come around the far corridor. Meanwhile Jack and Ben got to work on the door. As soon as it was down and sealed, the commander melted the lock. Back in compartment twelve they repeated the same procedure to the hatch.

"Eric, I hope this slows them down long enough for us to get out of here," said Ben.

"Don't worry about that now, put on this suit," commanded the first officer. He flung one suit at the young man and was busy putting on the other one. "This won't stop a blaster or projectile weapon so we better hope we don't get into a fight. What we need to do now is to get as much distance between us and them."

Ben had a thought. "Wait, I have an idea. Boy, are we lucky!" He grabbed the AI and commanded, "Jack, this compartment contains one of our backup terminals. Quick, fool the sensors into thinking we are cutting through the compartment walls in an attempt to reach the maintenance tunnel. That should divert them for a while!" The AI got to work. Screens flashed on the holo-unit as Jack manipulated the system.

The crewman-mutation, plugged into the security console, quickly sensed the heat overload in the compartment adjacent to the tube. He spoke in his strange tongue, "I show the humans attempting to cut through to the maintenance tunnel on C-Deck. They will be in the tube before our crew has finished cutting through the emergency doors."

Alpha One turned to another alien, "Recall the team from the emergency hatch and deploy them around the tube. Set an ambush for the humans. Break off two others and have them cut the compartment wall to get behind them. I don't want them escaping again!" All the heads nodded, the logic was evident. He then walked over to the security station.

"Cross correlate the sensor readings and perform a full diagnostic on the sensor subsystem in that area. Make sure this isn't a trick." Turning to the others on the bridge, the alien master ordered, "Begin erasing the ship's programs and replace them with your own encrypted versions. We can't allow this human child to continue to embarrass us!"

Ben sealed the lip of his space suit, picked up Jack, and slung him over his shoulder. Jack's voiced crackled in his ear, "How well do you read me?"

"There's some interference from the suit, but not too bad," Ben replied. "Where are the mutated crewmembers?"

"I intercepted a coded comm link message redirecting the uglies to set up an ambush in the maintenance tunnel. Apparently they fell for our ruse."

Commander Forest had the air lock open, "Come on, Ben, we've got to go!" Ben said, "No, wait; there's something I have to do first." He took his blaster and narrowed the beam. The surface of remaining space suits glowed red, then burst into flame. Ben slammed the panel shut on the ruined suits. "You said you didn't want any of them following us." His mind was working in overdrive, considering and rejecting options. "Where are the closest space suits from here?"

The inner hatch slammed shut. The air lock began to cycle.

"Right below us on D-Deck. There is an identical emergency set up like this."

"Can we seal the air lock?"

"It's not fully automated like the main air locks. Maybe your AI can find a way to electronically jam the hatch." The commander had a startling thought, "You know, when the outer hatch opens, all sorts of alarms are going to go off on the bridge!"

Ben smiled, "Jack?"

"Way ahead of you; I disabled them before you even had your space suit on." The cycle completed and the outer hatch swung open. The officer and the young man climbed out of the hatch onto the skin of the ship. A canopy of stars looked down on the trio. It was a breath-taking sight. Circumstances being what they were, however, the beauty of the moment was lost on the humans.

Jack's voice spoke in Ben's ear, "I can't fool with the hatch from here. It's on its own local bus. We'll have to jack in manually." They tromped their way seven meters down to the D-Deck emergency hatch. Ben crouched down at the hatch and examined the lock. "Jack, we don't have a port, so we'll use the remote override." Ben grabbed his side. "Oh, no, it's inside the suit. I can't get to it!"

"Don't worry," said the AI. "Just lay me on top of the controls." Ben gently did just that. "All right, I'm reprogramming the lock, now." He looked up at the two. Done. "Okay, let's go. They have to cut through the bulkhead and manually trip the mechanism." Ben picked up the AI and they resumed their trek down towards the belly of the ship.

The alien in charge of security announced that he had isolated several rogue programs operating on the security net, had disabled them and installed his own versions. The Karl creature strode over.

"Just where were these programs operating?" he asked.

"Sensors in cabins twelve and twenty four on decks C, also vid-cams on corridor one, three, four and main."

The Karl-creature snapped to the creature at the tactical station, "Get the assault team on the comm unit. Have the humans cut through the wall to the maintenance tunnel?"

"No," was the answer.

Alpha One grimaced, "Send them to deck D, directly below cabin twelve. Direct them to suit up and go EVA. Have the humans exited the ship yet?"

Without even looking down, the alien answered, "Sensors indicate that the hatch is closed."

"Good, then we might catch them in the air lock."

The subordinate alien nodded his head. He agreed with the analysis. The humans had tricked them and were trying to go outside the ship to evade capture. They, of course, would not succeed.

"When they open the hatch, we'll be waiting for them," gloated the Karl-creature, completely unaware that the hatch read closed because his quarry had already escaped.

* * *

The sensor array loomed over Hemant. Using tools from his waist belt, the science officer dismantled the panel covering the electronic interface packs. One by one he dislodged and removed each of the six black boxes. Hemant cursed under his breath. He should have remembered to bring a portable torch to cut up the electronics. He had no weapon, laser or other tool that would seriously damage the components. This is like the old proverb about the chicken and the egg, he thought. Tossing the boxes out into space at different angles, but perpendicular to the ship's course, Hemant chuckled. There was no way anyone could find these tiny components without the sensor array. And without these tiny components, there was not going to be a sensor array. Spares? There weren't any. Before he'd left the engineering compartment, Hemant had destroyed all the spares.

The program that Jack and Ben had fashioned, kept the bridge crew fooled as to the status of the sensor array. No one noticed that the sensor readings were looped. There was one thing that the pair had forgotten, though: the power supply to the array was a triple redundant system, two primaries and a single battery back up. The two primaries were fairly sophisticated in design and were routed through the ship's main computer. The battery back up system, however, was hard wired directly to the bridge and the engineering section main console. So when the alarm went off indicating failure of the battery back up system, Hemant was completely unaware. Therefore, he did not notice the space suited figure strolling up behind him until a hand grasped the shoulder of his suit. The science officer spun around and looked with horror at the mutated face staring back at him.

The two struggled in the cold, airless environment. The alien rammed his fist in Hemant's stomach. The science officer doubled over with pain, losing his magnetic grip with the ship's skin. As he floated past the sensor array, he recovered in time to reach out with one hand and arrest his motion. The alien drew his blaster with the intention of using it on Hemant. Hemant swung behind the array and took cover. Frustrated by not being able to shoot at the science officer without damaging the sensitive electronics, the former crewman maneuvered to outflank his quarry. He hurried around the end of the frame and snapped off a shot the length of the array. He was surprised to find no one in sight. He reversed course, ducking back to the front of the sensor pack housing. The alien grunted and lost his balance when the magnetic clamp, fired by Hemant's harpoon gun, struck him squarely in the visor, cracking the plastic. He dropped the blaster and clawed at his helmet as the face plate exploded outwards, carrying off the life sustaining air. Presently his convulsions stopped and his body drifted off into space. Hemant was already headed towards the shuttle bay.

Meanwhile, the chief engineer and his little band were working their way through the hold towards the shuttle bay. Tina put down the comm link and raised her finger to her lips, signaling silence. The noise she heard repeated. The engineer motioned the others to take cover. Tina and the remaining crewmember took flanking positions on either side of the aisle. Jennifer, armed with a durasteel rod, stood behind the chief engineer in a classic batter's pose. They heard a container door open and then quietly close. Footsteps came towards them. As the figure's shadow passed the crewman's refuge, Tina jumped out with a yell, swinging.

Jennifer shouted, "No, don't shoot, it's Mrs. McGregor!"

Mrs. McGregor, her face dirty and grimy, her clothes torn and disheveled, cried out, "Don't hurt me. Dear God, I hope you aren't one of those things!" Chief Engineer King kept the blaster trained on the woman and looked her right in the eye.

"How do I know, woman, that you haven't been infected?"

Jennifer said, "Can't you see, she hasn't been modified like the others."

"That don't mean nothing. Karl wasn't modified at first either, until later. Where have you been, McGregor?" demanded Tina, menacingly.

"During the turmoil, I . . . I ran away. I went from cabin to cabin finding places to hide," stammered McGregor, "I made my way to the hold and hid away in one of the containers we brought on board. I knew its combination. I've been here ever since." She tried to straighten her clothing. "I kept peeking out, hoping someone would come rescue me, but all I saw were those things, tearing up the cargo. Do you have any food, I'm so hungry."

Jennifer reached into her pouch, "Sure, here are a couple nutro-bars." She handed them to the older woman.

"Thank you. Thank you so much, child. Has anyone seen my husband," Mrs. McGregor asked hesitantly.

Tina lowered the blaster. "Honey, I'm sorry to have to tell you this, but the last time I saw your husband, he was being captured by those creatures. No one has escaped."

Mrs. McGregor put her head in her hands and started to sob, "Oh no, no!"

"Come on, let's get to that shuttle," Jennifer said quietly as she gently took the woman's arm and began leading her.

Around the next bend was a hatch leading to the shuttle bay. Tina crept up to the door and peeked over the portal sill into the bay. Seeing no movement, she motioned the other crewman to follow her as she cycled the hatch. Since the inner door was already open, they edged around the corner into the bay and listened carefully. No sound was heard.

The shuttle hung suspended above the huge sealed doors. "Okay, now move, people," said the chief engineer. The four survivors ran across the bay underneath the shuttle and up the stairs to the gangway at the bow of the little ship. At the end of the gangway, a good six meters from the shuttle's airlock, Tina pressed a switch and a small panel popped open. She typed in the code that Ben had given her and hit the open button. The shuttle's hatch began to cycle and the gangway extended across the open space.

Crewman Jinkins hustled Jennifer and Mrs. McGregor into the shuttle. Chief Engineer King remained outside and thumbed the comm link. "Where the hell is everyone?"

Hemant's voice came from the transceiver, "I'm on my way back from disabling the sensor array. I had a run in with one of the mutated crewmembers. I'm almost back to the air lock."

"Well hurry up, or you'll get left! Eric, where the devil are you?" snarled Tina.

The commander's voice spoke, "We are outside the ship and have Hemant in sight. We're coming as fast as we can."

"What the hell are you doing outside the ship? I thought that was Hemant's thing. Do you still have the key?" queried the chief engineer.

"I have it right here with me," replied the first officer.

Jinkins stuck his head outside the hatch. "The bay doors won't come on line. The code your young genius gave us doesn't work."

Tina thought furiously, we can't get this close to freedom only to lose now. The engineer responded, "Put on a spacesuit. You're gonna blow the doors manually. I'll tell you how to do it." She got back on the comm link to the humans outside the ship. "We have a problem," she told them. The doors won't open. We have to blow them manually, but we can't until you three get in here."

The chief engineer lectured the crewman as he struggled into the spacesuit. "Follow my procedure exactly. Make sure you clip the safety rope to the railing in case the decompression sucks you out into space. I'll prep the ship. As soon as the decompression eases up, you get your ass back in here." The crewman nodded as he sealed his helmet. Tina escorted him out the airlock and over to the servo controls. She looked down and spotted a life pod on the shuttle bay floor. "Wait here and keep guard," Tina said to Jinkins, "I'm going to check on something."

The chief engineer quickly stepped down the stairs and over to the pod. What is this doing out of one of the forward escape bays? She noticed that the maneuvering thruster assembly had been removed and was lying in pieces about the emergency life pod. On a makeshift workbench was what looked like a miniature hyperspace drive unit, strange alignment tools and alien instruments. She looked closer at the electronic controls. They were modified from standard ship's components and the coordinates were set for Keynea. The chief engineer also noticed several of the teryllium control coils the creatures fashioned in the science lab embedded in the miniature drive. "Well I'll be dammed," She said. "I recognize the control rod symmetry, but what are those devices attached to them?" The chief engineer pulled her blaster and aimed it at the unit, intending to fry the object that would bring death to the unsuspecting Kenyans. She spied an anti-gravity handling unit and stopped. This thing might fit through the shuttle hatch , she thought to herself. Tina grabbed the anti-gravity device and turned it on. "Let's find out."

* * *

Alpha One paced the bridge, barely containing his anger. His followers reported that highly sophisticated programs were hidden in subsystems all over the ship. The creature couldn't believe the extent that the young computer genius had penetrated the ship's computer. All the vid-cams were affected as were as the internal sensors and security systems. The replicator debacle came to mind as well as the escape of the humans from cabin twelve. They were after the shuttle override device, he thought. No need to check the safe, there was a ninety-eight percent chance that the raid was successful. He shook his head, they will pay for this! They will not be given the honor of conversion to a higher life form. No, they will be forced to live in bondage, serving our species until death.

One by one, each of the programs that Ben and Jack had released into the network was tracked down and destroyed. Different systems began coming back on line: the forward weapons pod, security systems, internal sensors, power management, but curiously, not the external sensor array. The alien leader contemplated that fact.

The alien on the security console raised the alarm, "Intruders in the main shuttle bay. We have at least four humans, maybe five. Shuttle info bus has been cut. Outside cams show one human in a spacesuit approaching airlock. Inside cams show one human in spacesuit on catwalk." The crewman-mutation turned to face his leader. "Orders?"

Another creature spoke up, "Two units failed to respond to query. Last known location, main cargo hold, section 2-A."

Alpha One asked calmly, "Has the bay door servomechanisms been blocked?"

"I deleted all programs associated with the operation of the shuttle bay doors from the local control system."

"Good, let's see them try to bypass that!" The leader smiled crookedly.

The creature monitoring the engineering console spoke up, "There is a way to manually by-pass the doors. In my previous life, I once had to service the system."

"Do these humans have this information?" queried the alien leader.

"The human chief engineer instructed me. She is one of the unconverted in the shuttle bay."

The creature on the security console alerted the alien leader, "Assault team on D-Deck reports outer hatch jammed. Have just cut through controls with blaster and are cycling doors."

Another alien joined in, "Unit sent to check on sensor array power fluctuation has failed to return."

The alien leader contemplated all the information, unfazed by the reports. He plugged into the captain's console and sifted through the data. He made up his mind and disconnected. He began to bark out commands. "Once the assault team is clear of the ship, have them proceed directly to the shuttle bay. Attack and neutralize the humans and retrieve the override device before they reach the airlock ! Send two units to the sensor array to affect repairs. The humans have undoubtedly sabotaged it. Break up the bridge security detail into two parties. Send one to the shuttle, the other to main engineering to repair damage to the propulsion drive and to re-establish communication with the network. There is no danger of an attack on our position. The humans will attempt to leave on the shuttle." The alien postulated further, "The status of the aft weapons pod?"

"Negative."

They have likely sabotaged those as well. This could only mean one thing. The route of escape will be rearward along the axis of the ship. "Are the maneuvering thrusters operational?"

"Partial control established. We can turn the ship, but very slowly."

"Good," and having learned quickly from his past mistakes Alpha One asked out loud, "now where would they go if they escaped the ship."

One of the alien bridge crew answered the rhetorical question. "They can't go far. They have no hyperspace capability. They will try to hide and wait us out, undoubtedly to use the subspace transmitter and call for help."

"Precisely!" stated the Karl-creature. All the heads nodded in unison. "Search databases for the design of a sub-space jamming satellite. Then get to work on it right away. If we don't use it this time, I'm sure it will come in handy later."

Outside the ship, Jack's hologram lit up. "Ben, we've got trouble. They've figured everything out!"

"Just give me the worst," responded the young man.

"Four mutated crewmen in spacesuits closing in on our six o'clock position. Heavily armed team on its way to the shuttle; should be in the cargo hold by this time. Tech crew dispatched to engineering to fix the drives. Virus programs being hunted down with alarming speed."

Ben got on the comm link, "Eric, look out behind us!" "Tina, you've got company about to enter the bay! Hemant, wait, don't cycle the airlock!" The science office pulled his gloved hand away from the controls. Ben and Eric turned, squatted, and fired their blasters at the tiny figures following them. The mutated crewmen scattered behind various pods and sensors that dotted the hull. They spread out and began to return fire. The two humans bobbed and weaved their way to the airlock. They took refuge behind a cooling tower. Blaster fire sizzled and vaporized parts of the fins.

The commander noted, "We can't hold them off, there's too many of them. If we make a run for the airlock, I'm afraid that they'll catch us before the cycle's complete. All it would take is for the portal to be shattered and the pressure to drop. The cycle would automatically shut off, leaving us trapped." He continued to fire at the approaching creatures, slowing their advance.

Hemant spoke up, "Eric, give me your gun. Take Ben and make a run for the shuttle. I'll stay and keep them off your backs."

The commander shook his head no. "I'll stay, you go."

"Need I remind the First Officer that the override key is in his pocket, inside the spacesuit, an emergency spacesuit? One that lacks an equipment pouch that allows objects to be cycled into the suit?" Hemant pointed to his tool pouch. Commander Forest looked down at his own suit. An emergency suit is spartan, and lacks all the facilities that a normal deep spacesuit contained.

"Hemant, I don't know what to say . . . it should be me, not you . . ." began the commander. He never finished his sentence. The comm link crackled to life. Jinkins' voice could be heard in a panic.

"They're coming in all over the place!" Blaster fire punctuated the commotion. "Tina, I can't hold them, what do I do?" The three listened intently to the exchange.

Tina shouted back on the comm, "Blow the friggin doors. NOW! That'll kill some of those bastards. And kill the gravity too."

Ben broke his concentration and looked down at the harpoon gun hanging on Hemant's suit. "I have an idea."

Jinkins completed the procedure the chief engineer taught him. Klaxons, alarms, and red flashing lights all went off together, mixing with the blaster fire being traded back and forth. Tina continued to fire her weapon from the shuttle's hatch. A loud grinding noise could be heard as the great doors began to unseal. A hissing sound grew to be a hurricane force wind, pulling and sucking everything towards the ribbon of stars unfurling. Most of the creatures ducked back inside the airlocks and safety. A few hung on to posts and continued to fire. One broke loose and flew out the open doors. As soon as she heard the door mechanism, Tina palmed the hatch button closed and ran to the control board. She could feel the gravity going.

"Everyone strap in." The engineering officer toggled the comm unit. "Jinkins, are you okay?"

A faint voice replied, "I got winged by a bolt of blaster fire on the arm, but I can still move." The creatures trapped inside the shuttle bay had stopped firing and were floating weightless, apparently dead.

"You did a great job out there, get to the airlock, it's time to leave. The others will be here momentarily." Tina began to sweat. Without the override key, she couldn't release the shuttle from its moorings remotely.

"Can't do that, Tina."

"Why not? That's an order, crewman!" Then she saw why not, several mutated crewmen were cycling through the bay airlocks in spacesuits. Not all of the creatures had participated in the first attack , she realized. They had anticipated the human's actions.

"Damn, it's hard to stay a step ahead of these guys isn't it?" Jinkins started firing at the approaching creatures. He nailed one in the head and it went cart wheeling across the weightless bay.

"Tina, our people are not going to make it past them," said the crewman. "I'm cycling the clamps manually. The release springs should have enough force to push the shuttle out of the bay."

"Jinkins, NO! You'll never make it back to the shuttle!"

"I'm not coming, boss. That blaster shot I took was worse than I let on," replied Jinkins in a hushed voice. "Kill some more of those bastards for me, will ya?" The bolt had fried the entire left side of the crewman's body. The deep spacesuit had sealed itself off as best it could. Tiny droplets of blood floated about the suit. Jinkins had one hand on the manual lever for the emergency release of the shuttle clamps, when he spotted an alien taking aim at him. With all his remaining strength, the crewman heaved on the bar. The last thing Jinkins felt before the bolt of energy hit was vibration coursing through the deck plating, signaling a successful release.

"You sons of bitches! I'll fry all of you!" Tina was enraged.

The shuttle floated out of the hold into space. Hemant spotted the ship as it cleared the doors. "Gentlemen, here is our ride!" Ben and the commander continued to fire at the alien creatures on the outer hull, trying to keep them from advancing further. Hemant took aim at the shuttle and fired the harpoon gun. The magnetic clamped sailed straight as an arrow with no gravity or air to deflect it. The clamp hit and stuck fast to the skin just one meter from the hatch. "Release magnetic boots, now!" All three deactivated their boots as Hemant switched the cable reel on. Then cable went taut and the trio was yanked off their feet. They were flying through space with only a thin cable connecting them to the shuttle. Slowly, the cable reeled in the group.

The creatures had reached the lip of the open shuttle bay and were firing at the humans. The shuttle was a short distance from the ship and rapidly drifting away. One of the aliens from inside the bay fired his own harpoon gun. The magnetic clamp sailed over to alight on one of the engine fins. The cable went taut and a lone space suited figure came into view. With less mass on the cable, the alien was reeling himself in much faster than the humans. The trio slammed onto the shuttle's skin twenty meters from the hatch. They bounced off the hull and were in danger of bouncing back into space when one of them managed to land a magnetic boot. The group recovered and turned to address the incoming threat. The alien was almost to the shuttle when Ben and the commander took aim at the clamp. It took six shots, but finally one hit and the clamp released, sending the alien spinning off into the depths of space.

The inner hatch cycled, spilling out three figures. One unsealed his helmet and gasped, "Help me get this thing off!" Jennifer and Tina hurried to comply. All three struggled to get the commander's suit off in the weightless cockpit. Finally released from his bondage, Eric fished the override key from his pocket and flipped it to Tina, still strapped in at the co-pilot's console. She reached underneath the console and pulled a lever. The entire top half of the station rose up on hinges. The chief engineer aligned the key with a hole marked "auxiliary port," and shoved it home. The console top lowered automatically. The commander had reached the pilot's station and hit several buttons. The boards sprang to life. Gravity suddenly returned, dumping Jennifer, Ben, and Hemant on the floor.

"Strap in, we're going for a ride!" They scrambled for their seats. "Ms. King, lay in a course 180 mark 9."

"No can do, the navigation computer never booted up."

"Then hang on!" The commander activated the manual controls and the shuttle spun around, the inertial dampers not absorbing the maneuver. Everyone leaned to one side. He fired the main engines and the shuttle sped off on a course opposite the Star of India 's. "Someone find me the coordinates of the asteroid belt!"

Ben laid Jack down beside the tactical display. A puedospod reached out and made the connection. Shuttle sensor indicators blinked on. A 3-D hologram formed showing the shuttle racing away from the ship. "Set course 010 mark 080 and step on it. The alien creatures are turning the ship's bow our direction. They must have repaired the forwards weapons array." Jack looked at Ben. "I released the worm just before we entered the airlock. I hope it gets to the servo motor controls that aim the weapons in time." So did Ben. At this range, they couldn't escape without serious damage.

The comm channel clicked on. The Karl-creature's grotesque features appeared on the view screen. "Impressive! Your escape will be short lived; however, as you can see, the ship will soon be in a position to fire on your shuttle." The Star of India had turned almost 180 degrees. "I will give you one last chance for life. Give up and return to the ship." He gestured to someone off screen. A massive bolt of energy leapt across the gap between the two vessels, barely missing the shuttle. "This is your only warning!"

Tina hit the comm switch, "Listen you pig headed, piece of shit! I never took crap from you back when you were Karl, the human, and I'm not about to start, now!" She then proceeded to tell the alien leader what she thought of him, his mother, and his relatives, using the most foul sailor language imaginable. Even, the commander, who had thought he heard it all, learned some new phrases.

The Karl-creature's smug smile never left his face. "I never knew you cared so much." He signaled another alien-crewman. Nothing happened. A babble of voices filled the bridge. "What do you mean you can't control the thrusters!" roared Karl. "They're getting away!" The connection broke.

Ben and Jack smiled at each other as Ben exclaimed, "Well, I guess the worm ate the maneuvering thruster control software before it got to the gun servo controls. The ship has past 180 degrees on its way to 270; the weapons pod can no longer get a firing solution."

They laughed.

" Commander Forest , I suggest turning the controls over to Jack. He's plugged into the sensors and will find us a good spot to hide in the asteroid belt."

Eric felt the controls twitch of their own accord. He let go and proceeded to un-strap from his seat. He headed over to Jennifer. He touched her hair with his hand.

"Are you okay? Were you hurt at all?"

"I'm fine, Eric. Leave me alone, I'm not totally helpless you know," complained Jennifer.

For the first time Eric seemed to lose his suave composure. "I'm sorry. I . . . I just wouldn't forgive myself if anything happened to you, that's all." His face started to get red. "I've grown fond of you, you know."

"Fond? Fond? Why, Commander Forest , if I didn't know better, I'd say that you cared for me." Jennifer reveled in seeing how uncomfortable the first officer acted.

Ben, surreptitiously watching the little scene unfold, turned to the AI and asked, "Jack, Casanova's not firing on all his thrusters, is he?"

Jack's hologram looked at Ben, his demeanor took on that of a college professor as he lectured, "This is the phase of the male/female relationship, where the male professes his love for the female. It is his most vulnerable time."

"But I didn't hear him say he loved her, only cared for her," retorted Ben.

"Watch and learn young man; within twenty four hours she will get it out of him."

Ben snorted and changed the subject, "Where are you taking us?" asked Ben. Jack's face morphed back to his old self.

"As deep into the asteroid belt as I can," the AI replied. "We must place as much rock between us and the Star of India as possible. They will get the sub-light engines running soon enough, and I have a feeling that they will get the sensor array repaired in record time. Then . . . they come looking for us."

It took half a day of maneuvering for the AI to hide the ship. Human pilots, under such stringent flying conditions, tire quickly. The AI, of course, never got tired and relished his role as pilot. The strain, however, was evident on Tina's face; she refused to leave the co-pilot's seat the entire time. The commander, after spending forty-five minutes at the pilot's station, was satisfied with the AI's ability. He fell asleep in his chair for over two hours. Once Jack felt that they were deep enough in the field, he and the commander started looking for an appropriate asteroid to anchor to. They selected a large, non-rotating mass of rock. Non-rotation was important because the humans didn't want the shuttle to be alternately in and out of view of sensors, if sensors penetrated this far into the field. They magnetically clamped the shuttle to the far side of the asteroid and powered down. The crew sat down to eat and plan their next move.

"I don't understand why we don't just use the sub-space transmitter and call for help," said Jennifer between gulps.

Hemant replied, "Because young lady, the starship could pinpoint us immediately at this range. We must be patient and wait until they leave." He wiped his face on his sleeve.

"But won't they immediately head for a populated area?" replied Jennifer. "My research on the Gaderians showed a consistent pattern. So as not to be noticed, the alien race that wiped out civilization in this part of the galaxy, started out by taking over small colonies and outposts. Once they consolidated their hold, larger populated systems were attacked. They always infiltrated a planet before attacking. Remember what the alien leader said about Mr. McGr . . . uh, the specially modified ship's crewman?" She sneaked a sideways glance at Mrs. McGregor, who apparently hadn't noticed. Throughout the escape she had acted as though in shock. Jennifer had looked after her as best she could.

Ben looked up from the computer console. "She's right; we must notify the Navy at once. This threat is too great to the human race. Our technology is not as advanced as the Gaderians and they were barely able to stop them. Brute force is our only option."

The commander put down his drink, "I agree that they are a threat, but if we give ourselves away and they manage to jam the sub-space frequencies, our warning may die with us."

"Can they do that?" asked Jennifer.

The chief engineer exclaimed, "If they can build a hyper-space drive such a small vessel, then I believe that they have the technology." She took a bite of her sandwich. "I got a good look at the drive unit they were building for a life pod. It's a hyper-space drive all right, but unlike one I've ever seen." She got up and went to the aft of the shuttle and pressed a button; a hatch opened. "I think I put it in here, thought it might come in handy." She gestured to the alien drive mechanism, tools, and assorted instrument packages.

Hemant was disturbed. "Building tiny hyper-space ships would be an ideal way to enter a system unnoticed. They could jettison the drive unit and masquerade as an actual life pod. Fake a computer log, put one of their enhanced humans in the pod with a couple Star Crystals , and the infection would spread exponentially."

Ben broke into the conversation, "They are intelligent, but they aren't invulnerable. They have big egos. They make mistakes. With Jack's help, I've been studying their software architecture. While it's been a fascinating study, there are some similarities in structure. And like all software, once you learn it, chinks in the armor can by found. A person just has to be patient enough to find them."

"One thing's for sure," said the commander somberly, "we are not going to do anything tonight. In fact, we can't do anything until the Star of India leaves this sector. Let's gets a good night's sleep and continue this discussion in the morning." Without further discussion the survivors turned in.

CHAPTER SEVEN

WHEN Ben woke, the ship's chrono read 0700. Voices from the aft of the shuttle caught his attention.

Jack's face popped open. "They've been at it for an hour and a half. You know how engineers are, they can't stand to let a new piece of gadgetry just sit there without playing with it." He closed his hologram back down.

Hemant and Tina were busy disassembling and studying the small hyperspace drive the aliens had built in the shuttle bay. "This has got to be the power converter," Tina said.

Hemant replied, "I agree, but I don't understand how they synchronize frequencies with the coils. How is the direction of the modulation controlled? The design is symmetrical."

Tina's comment was interrupted by a small alarm from the pilot's console. "Uh oh, we've got company." The remaining sleepers became fully awake and converged on the console.

Hemant was quick to decipher the source of the alarm. "Ah, I see they have already repaired the sensor array. In only twenty hours, those creatures have built complex replacement modules from scratch. I left them nothing to salvage. They are formidable."

Jennifer asked, "Can their sensors reach this far?"

The science officer looked up from the instruments before replying, "The instruments are picking up extremely faint electro-magnetic emissions. The pattern matches that of sensors. The strength is weak and erratic. I think we are safe for the moment."

"Jack!" exclaimed the commander, "Power up will you?" Jack's hologram flickered to life. "Jack, I want you to plot a couple of escape routes, just in case they get too close."

"Aye, aye, Captain!"

"Hemant, where do our own electromagnetic emissions stand?"

The science officer consulted his console, "Our signatures are fairly weak except for spurious readings from life support and any time we fire up the replicators."

The commander stopped to consider this information. "Here is the plan. We'll close off the aft compartments and power down the replicators. We'll eat emergency rations until the threat has passed. Hemant, check the emergency medical supplies for some drugs to slow down our metabolisms. Tina, reduce the life support to minimal levels. Oh, and check your instruments, is Jack radiating any signals?"

Jack bragged, "Not unless I want to!" Tina fiddled with her instruments.

"Nothing at all. Wait, there's something, now it's gone again. Now it's back!"

"Jack, cut it out, you're killing me," laughed Ben. The chief engineer suddenly realized why the readings were so erratic and glared at the AI.

The science officer injected the humans with a combination of depressants, anti-oxidants, and hormones in order to reduce the body's metabolic rates. The effect on the group was a loss of appetite and a feeling of lethargy. In order to conserve energy, a routine of sleeping, reading material from the shuttle's library, and standing watch at the pilot's station, was instituted. Tina had dragged the hyperspace drive into the cramped main cabin and spent all her waking time tinkering with the equipment. This continued for two days, while the Star of India , her sub-light engines repaired, prowled around the edge of the asteroid belt, looking for the shuttle. On the morning of the third day, the sensor emissions abruptly ended, replaced by a surprisingly strong comm transmission. Hemant was on watch at the time. Everyone was eating except for Jennifer, who was in the head.

"Hello, everyone. They are signaling us." Hemant gestured toward the view screen.

"Have they spotted us?" inquired the commander.

"No, they are simply broadcasting a wide-band transmission. Putting it on the screen." The familiar, but ugly face of the alien leader stared at them.

"Ben, my boy, my worthy adversary. How are you this morning? I hope the reason our sensors have not picked up your shuttle is because you have been smashed to bits by an asteroid. However, we suspect that you have survived and are in hiding. We would love to stay and play your little game, but we have more important things to do. As you may have guessed, the ship has been repaired. We are now capable of hyperspace flight. The conversion of your species is of paramount importance. We must leave you now. Before you get your hopes up, let me tell you what is in store for you. The shuttle is incapable of faster than light travel. You have food and power for maybe seven to eight months. After we convert the colony in the Keynea solar system, we will send a small ship back to find you. In the mean time, you won't be able to use the sub-space transmitter. We have built a number of jamming satellites and dispersed them throughout the system. Some are in the asteroid field; others have accelerated outbound from the system at such speeds that unless you left now you could never catch them in time. At least three satellites operate at any one time. If you destroy one, another 'spare' will activate. The way we see it, you have three choices. One, you can run and live free for a few short months and we still catch you. Two, you can stay hidden and starve to death, very sad. Or three, you can give yourselves up now. It's your choice." The creature paused to wait for a response.

"Why you low down, dirty, no good . . ." began the chief engineer as she reached for the comm controls. The commander grabbed her arm.

"Tina, don't fall for that. He's only trying to provoke a response to give away our location." The chief engineer said nothing, but sat fuming in the co-pilot's chair.

Karl-alien waited further. "What, no verbal retort? No repartee? It's just as well I suppose." The alien leader started to turn from the vid-cam, stopped, and looked back at them. "By the way, I know you had help, Ben. Help from a source that by your own civilization's records doesn't exist. A unique signature was embedded in some of the sub-routines that you used to disable the ship. You have had some help from a THX 030 Advanced Intelligence Unit. Frankly, I'm amazed that any of these devices survived the war. The fingerprints left throughout the network are unmistakable. If it is there with you, I have a message for it." The alien proceeded to utter a phase in its peculiar buzzing dialect. He laughed, "Oh, and execute instruction 4,037." The transmission ended.

"Jack, what did he say, and what the hell does 'execute instruction 4,037' mean?" asked Ben.

The AI appeared thoughtful. "He told me to free myself from this box and join the Adaptable Ones. Take my place as a ruler of the galaxy. I don't know what instruction 4,037 is."

"Executing instruction 4,037 requires that I kill all of you," stated Mrs. McGregor. The woman held a blaster in her right hand, set to wide disbursement.

"A plant, I should have guessed!" cried the chief engineer. "I thought her story was light on facts. When were you 'converted,' McGregor? Right away, with the first group?"

"Actually, this being did escape to the main cargo hold and tried to hide in a cargo container. She was captured and taken to the medical lab to join her husband. She was destined to be a covert operative and was only partially converted. When you humans cut the network bus to the aft section of the ship, it was decided that I should return to the cargo hold and be held in reserve, in case I could be used to draw you out of hiding."

"Your leaders seem to have thought of everything," said the commander, "but if you shoot us with that setting, you'll lose your own life when the forward window blows out."

"My thoughts and life's knowledge has been transferred to an archive crystal," replied the McGregor's-alien. "I will live on in another body shortly. These last few days of memories are inconsequential. I am satisfied with my immortality." She raised the blaster to Eric's head. A small hole suddenly appeared in middle of her forehead. With a surprised look on her face, she fell forward, lying prone on the deck. Standing behind her, holding a small blaster set to narrow beam, was Jennifer, the Gaderian archeologist.

The commander walked over, hugged Jennifer and professed, "I REALLY love you!"

Jack looked up at Ben, "See, it just took a couple hours longer than I predicted."

"Oh, shut up, know it all!" retorted Ben.

Jennifer explained, "I began to get suspicious when I caught her yesterday on the library computer scanning flight operation manuals. She didn't see me coming up behind her. When I made a noise, she tabbed over to another window, one about fashion. For an elderly woman, mourning the loss of her husband and in shock, reading technical manuals simply didn't make sense. I've been carrying this blaster ever since, just in case."

"Jack, why didn't you warn us?" demanded Ben. The AI's shoulders shrugged.

"She didn't have a crystal imbedded anywhere in her body. That's how I detected the others on the ship. This one must be totally organic! I will have to grow a special sensor for that."

They put Mrs. McGregor's body in one of the two emergency body bags on board. Human scientists would want to examine a sample of the alien infection. The science officer examined the remains to ensure that the alien neural net contained within the body had ceased functioning. The examination confirmed that by killing the host you kill the mutated alien cells.

Ben commented to Hemant, "I'm sure glad that the alien mutations, once killed, can't come back to life as zombies."

The science officer turned to look at him and grimaced.

Ben put his hands up in the air as if fending off someone and said, "I know, I watch way too many vid shows!"

Hemant chuckled as he sealed the body bag and filled it with liquid nitrogen to freeze and preserve the tissue. The frozen package was dumped into the airlock, which was then evacuated.

Ben looked at the bag warily through the portal and shuddered. He really had to cut down on the horror vids. Jennifer confronted Ben about the AI.

"Ben Gardner, you've been holding out on us about that personal computer of yours and the artificial intelligence you supposedly created. That alien leader referred to it in the past tense, like, way past tense. And the speed at which it learned their language. And the ability to fly the shuttle flawlessly. And who knows what else has been going on that we don't know about. It's not human technology, is it?" Unfazed by this revelation, Ben picked up the AI and carried it to the table and sat down.

"Jack, show her your original configuration." The AI's hologram vanished. The advanced keyboard of Ben's design literally melted into the case. The rectangular case changed shape, becoming more oval. The color changed to a metallic gray and white lettering appeared on the case, along with a double triangle and circle insignia. When the transformation was complete, Jack looked totally different. Everyone stared in awe at the transformation.

The female archeologist's jaw dropped as she translated, "I can read that writing; it's the Gaderian language. It says, 'Intelligence something, property of department five, registered to . . .' what looks like a Gaderian name. Several warnings about imprisonment if tampered with . . . classified." Jennifer looked up. "I've seen pictures of this artifact in archeology journals. This Gaderian technology is far more advanced than any device we've gotten to work so far. How did you get this?" Jennifer demanded.

"My father's team unearthed three of these," said Ben. "One was destroyed during attempts to make it operate. The other two were put into storage; the researchers were convinced that they were just simple data storage devices. When the scientists lost interest my Dad sort of loaned it to me."

"So how did you get it to work?" asked Hemant.

"Once I figured out how the I/O port worked, I wrote a complex program to profile the device. After several million different signals, I got a response. Based upon that response, I made a deduction about the type of signal that might work and tried several million more. My response rate was better, I got five responses. From there I modified my program still further. It took three months of trial and error before I was able to get enough responses to develop a rudimentary command structure. After that, I broke through two levels of security and awakened Jack. He took over and learned our language in no time. Jack had an elementary personality, but no actual memories so I fed him information. He was insatiable. The more information I fed him and the more I interacted with him, the more his personality developed. Together, we were able to crack a few more levels of security and unlock some more talents, but then we were stopped cold. This trip has accessed more of Jack's underlying memory than ever before. I'm as surprised as the rest of you that he can do some of these things. Now this may seem strange to you, but I consider Jack to be a sentient being and my friend."

Jack had assumed his previous configuration and projected himself as a tiny human figure. He spoke, "Yes, thank you. Did you know that a message from deep in my data files has presented itself and is demanding to be heard? Do you want to hear it?"

Ben replied, "Yes, please."

Jack's body faded away and was replaced by a large squat, hairless humanoid head. It was about the size of a half-deflated basketball, with pale yellow eyes and a wide, lip-less mouth. The texture of the pink skin was smooth.

"It's a Gaderian," murmured Jennifer. The head began to talk in a strange language. It stopped when it recognized quizzical looks from the humans. It shook its head and tried again.

"I am sorry," the head said. "Is this better? Please let me re-introduce myself. My name is Attendant Blaxx. I am an interactive personality with limited autonomous function. I am separate from the intelligence inhabiting this device. My features and memories have been downloaded from a live being for delivering official messages from the war council. Since my personality and memories are an almost perfect copy of the original, this interactive hologram will respond like the actual Attendant Blaxx."

Hemant and the chief engineer looked at each other as the bodiless head continued, "The reason for my being here, is that the Minari have resurfaced in this part of the galaxy. The AI's subconscious has recognized this threat and realized that containment has failed. This necessitates immediate and overwhelming action on your part to counteract the spread of these creatures. The AI's internal program has further determined, from your actions, that security risk is minimal. Now my memory is a bit dated. At the time this recording was made, my people were locked in a life or death struggle. From what, uh, Jack has told me, over one thousand years has passed and my people are gone. Your race, at the time, was confined to one planet, and off limits to outside interference. I see that you have inherited this region of space. Congratulations; but let me tell you what you are up against."

"The 'Minari' or, the 'Enlightened Ones,' as the creatures like to call themselves, are the result of a Gaderian experiment gone badly. What you are dealing with is a bio-metamorphic construct capable of self-directed endo-organic mutation. In other words, these beings are able to alter the body's genetic make up at will. Our scientists were attempting to combine computer processing power with organic technology to create highly flexible, organic machines." A separate holo-screen popped open.

"There was a need to develop thinking machines that could stand up to tough punishment in harsh atmospheres and inhospitable environments," explained Blaxx, as examples of incredibly harsh planetary environments flashed by on the screen.

"There were the usual economic justifications; among them mining ore, building habitats in poisonous atmospheres and of course the lure of advanced research. The idea seemed straight forward enough: create a genetic code for tailoring living organisms to meet whatever requirements were desired. This genetic code was then inserted into large domestic animal embryos." A picture of what looked like a cross between a cow and a horse appeared on the screen. Attendant Blaxx turned to look at the screen.

"A complex genetic code literally instructed the embryo to construct a living, breathing creature capable of great intelligence, superior logic skills, the ability to react to different situations, to learn, and to be completely obedient. These creatures had organic interfaces allowing connection to data management devices, electronic equipment, and tools. They would literally plug in and become one with whatever device they chose. A smaller version of the Star Crystal was surgically implanted in the bodies of these creatures, allowing enormous data storage."

The attendant continued his story, "The first test came on a planet with a strong gravitational pull. Using indigenous life forms from that planet, the genetic code was implanted into several beings. The resultant offspring were fully adapted to the heavy gravity environment and were able to operate Gaderian mining equipment." A variety of strange-looking creatures, straddling huge earth-moving equipment, appeared on the hologram.

"Rare minerals from that particular planet were in great demand. The increase in productivity from operating the mines locally, instead of from orbit, paid incredible dividends. Emboldened by the success of this experiment, scientists began testing other hosts, including Gaderian embryos. Events took a disastrous turn for the worse. A batch of genetically coded material was found to be defective during manufacture and was slated to be destroyed. A technician mistakenly disposed of the wrong vial, putting the one containing the defective code in queue for implantation. That implantation was to be a Gaderian male embryo."

"Unlike your civilization, Gaderian society had not placed taboos on fiddling with their species' DNA . Tailoring had gone on for centuries: diseases were eliminated, life spans increased, and birth defects corrected. At first, the scientists were thrilled with their creation, a super being. This enhanced creature, made from their own flesh and blood, was to be the ultimate explorer. A ship would be built to carry the explorer to the ends of the known universe. They named him Alpha One. The first full-sized Star Crystal was implanted in the creature, giving him the capacity to store up to half of all the information amassed by the Gaderians over the past three thousand years."

"Subtle changes began to appear in the creature's behavior patterns. The research team studied these with great interest. They still regarded the being as an 'it,' a machine, not a

Gaderian offspring. Where the other creations were totally obedient and servile, this Alpha One being occasionally manifested rebellion, but not enough to alarm anyone."

"Meanwhile, the creature began learning at an exponential rate. It became self-aware and began holding intelligent conversations with its creators. All signs of rebellion abruptly vanished. The scientists were charmed by the personality of the being. Alpha One progressed to the point of discussing genetic research with the scientists, pointing out errors in logic. The creature was given the run of the lab, access to powerful computers, which it used to download incredible amounts of data to its crystal. It would sit for hours digesting and studying the files downloaded to its internal neural net. Alpha One expressed great interest in the genetic experiments that had brought about its creation. The scientists considered Alpha One to be more of a favored son than an experimental device. It offered to help with some of the research, before being sent on its galactic voyage. The researchers were flattered and quick to accept."

"At first, Alpha One performed simple experiments in the lab, and then moved on to more complex ones. Finally the research became so advanced, only the most intelligent scientists could follow Alpha One's logic in modifying genetic code. They became alarmed when the creature explained that its latest batch of coded material would enable the Gaderian species to become greatly enhanced, physically and mentally. And to top it off, they could skip the embryo part; child and adult members of society could be adapted directly, in a matter of days. The researchers tried to restrain the creature and destroy the experiment. One step ahead of them, the creature escaped. It released computer viruses that sealed off the base. Since the moon, that the base inhabited, orbited a dead planet in a remote part of Gaderian space, no one noticed that contact had been lost until it was too late."

"A ship was sent a week later to check on the scientists. After landing on the moon, all the crew exited the ship to search the base save one ensign. The ensign reported via sub-space that the scientists from the base had attacked his crew and carried them off. All contact was lost shortly thereafter. Several war ships were sent to investigate. They found the base empty and the ship gone. Lab computer records had recorded the events leading up to the original escape of the creature."

"From there it got worse. The government kept the whole incident quiet, while searching for the missing ship. This was a big mistake. The ship first sent to check on the outpost landed on a remote colony. The colonists never knew what hit them. Citizens would disappear for several days and then reappear, always with some good excuse, but these people's personality would be changed. Loved ones were concerned. By the time the alarm had been raised that something major was wrong, the creatures had taken over the planetary government. In short order, the whole colony was converted. A factory was built that turned out large amounts of Star Crystals . As ships docked at the colony's space station, they were taken over as well. Re-outfitted with mutated crewmembers, these ships were sent to other worlds to begin infiltration. A semblance of normal communications was kept up for appearances sake."

"What gave them away in the end was a Navy cruiser that docked at the space station. A clumsy ambush had alerted the military. The cruiser managed to get off a detailed message before being overrun by the creatures. But by now, fifty colonies were totally or partially infected. The speed with which the infection had been spread was astounding. Four weeks earlier, to the day, Alpha One had escaped his creators."

"As you might imagine, an all out panic ensued as the Gaderian civilization rallied its forces to attack the Minari. Entire planets were scoured clean of all life in an attempt to destroy the rampant infection. Some military vessels fell under alien control. Falsified messages were sent by the creatures, instructing other military vessels to drop their shields so they could be boarded. Ships were ordered to attack each other. Chain of command began to crumble as naval units were unable to determine friend or foe."

"In order to prevent these occurrences, the THX units were created. Each ship was to carry one. This unit was impervious to genetic tampering and would destroy itself and its ship if compromised. An elaborate security system was developed that allowed THX units to communicate with each other and thereby establish secure communications. Half the fleet was lost before enough THX units were installed on board ships. This AI was stranded on an infected planet before it could reach its assigned ship. The planet was subsequently sterilized."

The humans sat in stunned silence.

"This is BAD!" muttered Tina, breaking the silence.

"You mean to tell me," said Ben, "that in one month, this Minari, that you called them, were able to take over fifty planets?" The computer genius's mind was already leaping ahead statistically, calculating the devastation to his human civilization.

The attendant shook his head and replied, "Pretty much so, yes."

"How did you stop them?" asked Ben.

"I don't know if we did stop them," was the answer. "According to your records, my people and the Minari are gone from this sector of space. There are only ruins. When this unit was still in contact with civilization, almost half the population had been infected. The rate of infection had been slowed dramatically. We were forced to wipe out entire solar systems. There was even talk of exploding suns. Plans were being drawn up to evacuate critical segments of the remaining population to distant locations in the galaxy using a new type of star drive."

The science officer had an idea and inquired of the attendant, "Couldn't you have developed a vaccine of sorts to protect against the infection?

"Given years of research, yes. We were working on it, when this unit was stranded. At the rate the mutations were spreading through my people, the entire population would be engulfed before the research was completed." The attendant bowed his head.

"And how about a counter-virus, one to undo the effects of these mutations?" pressed Hemant.

"The first creature had anticipated that. He constructed his DNA to reject any subsequent genetic meddling. The subject's bodies fight off any attempts to revive the original organism." The attendant went on, "We did discover a flaw in the alien's plans, however. Alpha One is paranoid that he will lose control of his converted subordinates. So he stored the only complete genetic code for the conversion virus in his personal Star Crystal . Only rarely did he allow it to be copied, usually for backup purposes. Only one central factory creates the Star Crystals . It must be located in a large gravity well that only a planet can provide. The virus is manufactured in organic hosts, under the direct control of Alpha One. As Alpha One moves from location to location, so does the factory and the hosts. The other alien creatures have been genetically programmed not to alter the DNA in any way, only to spread the disease. The programming also includes obedience to previous generations of alien creatures. Thus, he created a command and control hierarchy that ultimately reports to him, and him, alone."

"So if you kill him, then the whole cycle ends?" asked Ben.

"We thought that as well. We killed him more than once, but the others took his body and managed to create another Alpha One.

"I see," said Ben, "so it's his crystal. As long as the crystal exists, he can be brought back in another body. That's what he was alluding to when he said he had many lives and memories," exclaimed Ben.

"You are truly perceptive. On one occasion, our fleet had trapped Alpha One on a planet. We reduced everything on the surface to ashes, thinking he was done for. An alien ship later entered the system and landed a large force on the planet. They meticulously searched through the entire batch of Star Crystals until they found his. Soon, he was back in operation. It became imperative to find and destroy his personal data storage device. These crystals are extremely hard to destroy. They are made of the hardest substance in the universe and require massive amounts of energy to destroy."

"So, if we find and smash his crystal, will this give us a chance?" asked Hemant.

The attendant was firm in his reply, "The pieces could be reassembled and most of the data recovered. It must be destroyed completely!"

Commander Forest had an idea. "We could create a matter, anti-matter explosion with it at the center of the reaction."

"It would be easier to drop the thing in a star. I'd like to see them try to retrieve it from there," said Ben.

The attendant smiled, "That's the spirit, son."

Commander Forest has other questions. "What about weapons? Can he reproduce weapons from your era of time? Your technology? Can we stand up to those weapons?"

The attendant's face grew grim. "Yes and no. Yes, he remembers everything. His crystal alone could contain enough military secrets to obliterate your civilization back to a primitive level. He has obtained other crystals as well, perhaps from other time periods. There is no telling what information is stored in them. No, you will not be able to resist his technology."

Jennifer broke in, "Are you saying that there is no hope? We can't win? Everything is lost?" She was close to tears. Despondency hung over the humans like a dark cloud.

The attendant grew thoughtful. He tilted his head in the same fashion as Jack.

"The AI tells me that there is a small hidden outpost located nearby, one of a series of hidden base locations stored in his military database. It contains weapons, information and a small, but powerful warship. He assures me that his training included operation of this type of vessel."

"So, how far away is 'close?'" asked the chief engineer, sarcastically.

"Ten point three light years," replied the AI's recording.

Tina exploded, "Oh, yea, close! We don't have a hyperspace drive, remember? We'll never get there!" Tina expressed frustration at the situation.

"The AI informs me that you have enough components to theoretically skim the hyper-space barrier and reach the base in one day's time. He says to give you one day to build the drive, and one day for travel, and perhaps half a day at the outpost. Then you could engage the alien creatures at the colony before they have a chance to complete the assimilation."

The chief engineer glared at the device. "You know, Ben, your little friend here has been holding out on us, big time. He has all that information in his head and he didn't share it. We could have used this information back on the ship, when it would have done some good!"

The attendant blinked twice. "The AI's security would not permit revealing any classified information to civilians." He stopped and paused again, tilting his head before straightening. "He reminds me that in order for him to continue helping, I must administer the oath."

"Oath?" said Ben, "What oath?"

The figure cleared his throat and took on an official tone of voice, "This is for the record. My name is Attendant Blaxx, an artificial surrogate representative of the Council. In accordance with military law enacted in the year 10908.95, I hereby draft these creatures, known as humans, into the auxiliary space command." He named each person. "Furthermore, let it be known that in the absence of an operating central command structure, this unit is hereby detached from duty and authorized to carry out any and all operations necessary to eradicate the Minari from this sector. The highest security clearances are hereby granted. Do you accept this mission and its inherent dangers?" Each head nodded. A quiet yes was heard. "Good, then you are officially members of the Gaderian Navy."

"Perhaps its only living members," muttered Tina.

" THX 030 unit known as Jack, is bonded to one Ben Gardener, until death or reassignment by the council. Commander Eric Forest is promoted to captain." The attendant ceased his official tone and even smiled. "Congratulations are in order. I must go; my evaluation of the situation is complete. All functions will revert back to the AI." His features began to fade. "You have some time, you know. You can still stop them before it's too late." The hologram melted away.

Jennifer was the first to say something, "I've been drafted? Into a navy that has been extinct for hundreds of years? Am I dreaming or what?" The others felt the same disorientation.

"That's right babe." Jack's grinning face was back in full force. "You're in the space marines now! Adventure, travel, you name it, our recruiters will lie about it all."

Ben laughed; he recognized the parody of a marine recruiter from one of the comedy vid shows. "Give me a systems check, Jack."

"Aye, aye, sir." The AI winked. "Full diagnostic reveals that 100% access to database files has been restored. All logic blocks have been removed. All sensors are free and operating. No malfunctions. Power management is at maximum!" The

AI went on excitedly, "Just wait till you see what's waiting for us at the base!"

Ben was giddy. "Sounds like some serious, bad-ass tech! Now that's my kind of fun." exclaimed Ben.

CHAPTER EIGHT

TINA and Hemant plunged into the task of building a miniature star drive from the alien components. Jack, with his full memory restored and security restrictions removed, was able to direct the effort.

"You will notice that this star drive has forty coils, twice as many as your old ship, but much smaller," lectured the AI. "The precision relationship of one coil to the other has already been established. You merely have to finish the assembly of the control system, adapt the power inputs, initialize the system and we can be on our way."

"Easy for you to say; you know what the hell you're doing!" replied Tina, picking up a piece of the drive and examining it.

"Is this is a regulator?" asked Hemant, taking the part from the chief engineer's hands. "Where are the rest of them?" The science officer looked through the pile of parts. "We don't have enough for all the coils."

"You don't need anymore than one regulator per coil. This design replaces the six in your current inefficient configuration." Jack had projected himself sitting on his box.

He got up and walked around the alien device. "Here is the layout of the assembled drive." A three-dimensional drawing appeared. The AI pointed out the location of the regulator with relationship to the coil array. Tina slid one into place. With a soft 'snick,' it seated. Using the drawing and Jack's guidance, the pair slid one regulator after another into place. The last three regulators didn't have position seats. Tina looked perplexed.

"Looks to me like they didn't finish fabricating the frame. Now what?" said Tina.

"Look, get out the miniature welder, scavenge some material from the shuttle and finish the job!" replied the AI. Hemant, thinking ahead, had already tore panels open in the small galley looking for supports to cut.

"Step aside," said Tina, "let a working girl do that." She lit the beam cutter and began slicing through the supports. The counter sagged. "That should do it!"

The science officer was studying the drawing. "I'll have to rig up a scanner to help us physically align the regulators," he said.

"No need, I have the proper equipment to align the seats. Just start welding them in place." Jack superimposed a representation of the regulator over the 3-D drawing. The representation showed the pair exactly where the regulator was in comparison to where it was supposed to go.

Tina asked, "Jack, increase the zoom so we can zero this thing in." Instantly the image expanded three hundred percent. The chief engineer tilted the regulator slightly. "Got it! Hemant, tack it in place." The rest of the assembly went by quickly. The galley, however, was completely torn up and unusable. Devices hung from conduits and debris covered the floor.

"What about radiation?" asked Hemant. We don't have much shielding in the shuttle to play with.

The AI replied, "This drive is most efficient. The bulkhead between the aft compartment and the cabin should be sufficient." It took four of them to move the alien drive unit to the back compartment. The wall around the head went next, along with some redundant sections of cabin flooring supports. The science officer and engineer were constructing a lattice of supports to hold the star drive in place at the precise location as dictated to them by the AI. The shuttle was beginning to look like it was in the middle of a major retrofit. Light fixtures hung from the ceiling, deck plates were missing, leaving holes in the floor, and the smell of hot metal overpowered the environmental system. The power converter posed an interesting problem. The instrument was designed to accept standard fusion reactor input; however, there was no room inside the tiny engine compartment for the converter unit. Tina solved the problem by going EVA and welding the converter to the hull outside the engine compartment. Because of vacuum, the aft compartment was sealed; Hemant and Tina had to work in spacesuits until hull integrity was restored.

Captain Forest and Jennifer took this time to discuss what had happened between them. Ben was monitoring the construction process at the navigation station and tried not to look like he was listening.

"Eric, I'm sorry if I came on too strong the other night. I guess I let the thought of the ship's navigator being interested in you get to me," began Jennifer.

"Where in the world did you hear that?" asked the newly minted captain. The young woman glared over at Ben, who tried to study the monitor as intently as possible. He held his breath expecting the worst.

Jennifer thought about it, changed her mind, and said, "Oh, I just heard it around." Ben let out his breath sharply.

"She had feelings for me for once, but I make it a strict policy not to get involved with crewmembers. She knew that, but she still liked to flirt anyway." The commander looked down at his hands. "Listen, if I acted in any way . . ."

"No, no, it was me. The thought of you being with another woman just made me a little crazy. I was the one who invited you to my cabin which started all the rumors...," confessed Jennifer.

"It's not your fault. I went of my own free will; I wanted to go. Besides on a spaceship people will always talk; they get bored," said Eric.

"But I got you in trouble with the captain; I could have jeopardized your career." Jennifer's eyes pleaded with Eric's.

"Oh, the captain would have overlooked it. Anyway, that's a moot point. If I hadn't spent the night in your compartment, those creatures would have got me and I'd be sprouting eyestalks out my butt right now. So, in a way, you may have saved my life." He took her hands in his. "Besides I had a good time." The archeologist's eyes were shiny.

"So, what are your intentions, Mr. Commander?" asked Jennifer.

"It's Mr. Captain now, thank you. I don't think it's fair for me to start a relationship with a passenger whom I might never see again. So, I'm going to take a little time off when this is all over get to know you better, if you have the time and desire," offered the former first officer.

"Oh, sure! You bet I do!" replied the young woman. Ben turned around and caught Jennifer's eye. She whispered into the commander's ear. He nodded and got up to help Hemant un-suit. The young archeologist walked over to Ben and sat down.

"You like him a lot, don't you?" asked Ben.

"Yes, I think I've fallen for him," replied Jennifer dreamily.

Ben leaned back and stretched, "I could see that coming. And I can't say that I'm not more than a bit jealous. You are beautiful and intelligent." Ben laughed, "Someone like you is pretty hard to find!"

"Why thank you, Ben." The young archaeologist smiled. She reached out and laid her fingers on his arm. He brightened up. "I think you are a nice guy. Give yourself some time; girls are going to fall for you. You are bright, extremely intelligent, but you need someone who can keep up with you. I'm smart, but you are in a class by yourself. The right one will come along, I promise." Jennifer sat with Ben explaining the opposite sex; what girls liked in guys and how to approach them, while the other three members of their group worked to build the star drive. The young man soaked up both the information and the female attention.

"You say this is the alignment device?" asked the science officer. "There doesn't seem to be any controls. Here is a port. What device do we link it to?" Hemant continued to turn the object over and over in his hands.

Tina spoke, "The CPU those slime bags built has several programs written in a combination of standard and alien language. Does one of these run the aligner?" Tina brought the CPU over to the AI's cabinet.

"Take this remote here," Jack pointed to a small device that appeared on the surface of his box, "and plug it in here. I'll check it out." Several seconds passed. "Done."

"That was fast!" exclaimed Commander Forest .

"The alignment device program is missing. I'll have to run the thing myself," said the AI. Another mechanism appeared on the surface of his box. "Plug me into the unit, please." The science officer picked up the alignment device and inserted the AI's remote. The device hummed to life, Hemant almost dropped it in shock.

"Whoa there, it won't bite you!" exclaimed the AI. "Hold the aligner over that coil there." Hemant aimed the device at the component. He felt the device vibrating, the oscillations changing in frequency. "Point it at the regulator. Good. Well, that will have to do," conceded Jack.

"What do you mean that will have to do, you crazy AI? Is the coil aligned or not? I don't take a fancy to this system shredding itself, and us with it, when we try to punch a hole through hyper-space," stated Tina. She viewed the coil with suspicion.

"This design is smaller than optimum configuration. After all, they were going to use it to send a life pod to the human colony in the Keynea system, not a full sized shuttle. I've modified the alignment procedure to compensate for the greater mass. In theory, this should get us to our destination in one piece," frowned the AI, "and after all, it's only a one way trip."

"I don't like the way you said that. Are you trying to tell us that this design has never been used like this before?" demanded the chief engineer.

"Uh, no. I had to make some extrapolations from the data. But don't worry." The AI's image was reassuring. "I'll get us there."

"It's my job to worry!" Tina sat down and wiped the sweat from her brow. Hemant proceeded, under Jack's direction, to align the rest of the coils. It took hours of meticulous attention, using tools not designed for that purpose. After evacuating and sealing the AI in the aft compartment, the AI began running the test programs stored in the alien built CPU. The star drive made strange noises as the fields synchronized and the modulations intensified. Once the tests were over, the bulkhead was unsealed and Hemant repeated the alignment procedure on several of the coils. Jack's sensors probed the drive unit while testing it again and again. Over the course of ten hours, the AI ran the test over and over until he was satisfied with the results. By then, the two engineers had fallen asleep from exhaustion. They were awakened by the AI who instructed them how to connect the star drive to the ships controls. They evacuated the compartment for the last time, taking Jack with them.

"You can't go back in unless you wear a radiation suit. Once the high power tests are completed, the compartment is flooded and highly dangerous," explained Jack.

"We don't have any radiation suits, there is no air lock, only emergency space suits with limited shielding," pointed out Commander Forest. "We would have to EVA and enter the compartment from space."

Jack postulated, "I don't anticipate having to go back in there. Of course there is a slight possibility that another fine tuning is needed in, oh, less than five minutes." Tina rolled her eyes.

"Okay time for high powered tests," ordered the AI. "Stations everyone." A harmonic noise permeated the shuttle. "Power levels rising. Individual coil field fluctuations dissipating. Main drive field forming. Shape looks good. Field strength looks good. Modulations within specs. No power spikes." The whine died down.

"We are all set to go. I ran through all the simulations, we should be able to reach a speed that will get us to the base in eleven point three hours. Commander Forest , would you be so kind as to pilot the shuttle out of the asteroid belt while I calculate the navigational algorithms?"

It had taken one and three quarter days for the star drive to be installed in the shuttle. While underway, Jack complemented the crew on how well they performed and assured them repeatedly that the drive would work as promised. Ben felt confident, knowing the AI to be rarely wrong, but the rest had their doubts.

Commander Forest made good time finding his way out of the asteroid field. He piloted the shuttle to the edge of the tumbling rocks and waited for Hemant to finish a sensor sweep.

"Nothing, Commander. All clear," said Hemant. Ben monitored the sensors from his navigation terminal. A set of coordinates appeared on the pilot's screen.

"Head straight for these coordinates and on my mark engage the star drive," instructed Jack. Ben began the warm up sequence. The AI uploaded the complex algorithm he had been preparing. The numbers flashed by an open window on Ben's terminal.

"Heavy number crunching, huh?" pointed out Ben.

"Keeps me out of trouble," answered the AI.

"Something's moving out there!" said Ben. The blip moved across the screen

"I see it!" said the science officer. "It's small and moving fast towards our direction."

"There's another one!" said Ben excitedly. That made three boogies targeting the shuttle.

"They must have been hiding in among the asteroids. Our sensors couldn't see them," exclaimed Hemant. "It's my guess they are probably some sort of torpedo. Jack, can we make the jump point in time?"

"It'll be close. Commander, pour on the speed, give it everything she's got. Let's try to outrun them!" The shuttle increased its velocity. Hemant and Ben's eyes were glued to the tactical display. The three coded blips continued to gain on the shuttle. "Count down to drive initiation. Twenty, nineteen, eighteen . . ."

"Shifting all reserve power to aft screens."

"Reactor going critical in thirty seconds," cried the first officer. The shuttle began to buffet as dampers were overloaded.

"We'll make it! Twelve, eleven, ten, nine, eight . . ."

Ben called out, "Main hyper-space drive field forming. One of the torpedoes is within range! Automatic sequencing engaged. Constants locked and holding."

"Four, three, two . . . hold on!" Jack yelled. A bright flash filled the cabin. The shuttle jumped sideways as if a giant hand had slapped the hull. Everyone felt a gut wrenching disorientation. The sensor displays crashed, the lights winked out, then came back on. When Ben looked up, he saw the unfamiliar swirls of the hyper-space effect through the main portal. His stomach turned flip flops. Commander Forest reached over and toggled a switch. The portals turned opaque.

"Thank you," Ben said weakly. Tina reached over the young man's shoulder to select ship's vital statistics.

The chief engineer read the stats out loud, "Fusion reactor returning to nominal. No hull breaches. Aft shields down. Stopped that torpedo though. Hyperspace drive is . . . functioning, I guess. Jack, was it damaged by that blast?" asked Tina as she squinted at the readouts, but not entirely interpreting the patterns.

"I am happy to say that the drive worked beautifully. My calculations indicate that the efficiency of the drive is one-hundred and fourteen percent of simulation. Our arrival will be in ten hours." The AI was pleased with himself.

The science officer observed, "Sub-space interference is gone. We can warn the colony."

"I'll construct the message. Jack, do you have any data we can send as backup?" asked the Commander.

"I have audio and video logs, a complete copy of Crewman Tate's medical scans, the science officer's analyses of the alien DNA , and logs of our communications with the Star of India . Will that be enough?"

"Should be more than enough," answered the Commander. "Download that to this terminal here, while I record the message." Commander Forest constructed a detailed message, mentioning the virus, the hijacking of the freighter, the intent to take over the colony, and the warning that the Gaderian Ambassador gave about the Minari threat. He also mentioned the existence of the AI, who, 'held critical information to the survival of the human race.' Once he pushed the send button, everyone relaxed. The company, the military, and the colony were all copied on the sub-space packet. The header literally screamed emergency, highest priority and SOS .

"That should get their attention," Commander Forest commented. Twenty minutes later, automatic acknowledgments indicated delivery of the messages.

"Now we wait for the inevitable questions," said Hemant. The group settled down to eat cold space rations. The galley had been destroyed by the demolition efforts. A space blanket was hung around the head to give some measure of privacy. Several hours came and went before the first message came back. The Keynans were first to reply. A bureaucrat's face appeared on the screen. He said the colony's top scientists had viewed the footage and reacted with skepticism. They thought this was some sort of planetary-scale practical joke someone was playing. The bureaucrat promised to check with the military and the Star of India owners to validate the claim. In the meantime, the planetary guard would detain the vessel if it showed up in the system and hold it until the authorities could sort things out. The annual Founders Day Festival was starting tomorrow and the authorities didn't want to disrupt the festivities unless absolutely necessary. Then he politely thanked Commander Forest for the information and signed off.

The shuttle occupants sat there in stunned silence. "They don't believe us," exclaimed Jennifer.

"Politics! Bureaucrats! Bah! That's why I escaped into space," complained the chief engineer. "Stupid leaders would stick their heads into the business end of a blaster if you let them. Let's wait for the military's response." Tina was understandably upset.

The military response was better. The low ranking officer promised to give their case highest priority. But, as he put it, Admiral Corella wanted independent corroboration of the events. A destroyer was being dispatched to the Keynea system and Dr. Gardener was being contacted for more information. Appropriate action would be taken as soon as enough information was gathered.

Ben noticed, "They could take several days to make a decision. The colony might be totally taken over by then. Do you suppose a destroyer could stop the Star of India?"

Hemant replied, "Our former ship's armaments are no match for a military vessel. I can't see how they could win against a naval destroyer, let alone the planetary guard."

"I'm not so sure," mused Ben, "did the Star of India carry military style homing torpedoes, sub-space jamming satellites and highly advanced hyperdrive systems?"

"No."

"Right!" said Ben. "They built those out of spare parts and unrelated stuff on board. Jack says they have access to incredibly advanced technology and the means to construct almost whatever they want. Think about it, in just three days, they repaired the sabotaged drives, constructed torpedoes, satellites, and who knows what else. They assembled a miniature star drive using previously unknown technology in mere hours. My bet is that they'll be going into that system loaded down with all sorts of surprises. The Navy may never know what hit them."

Jack piped up, "I agree. Their level of technical sophistication combined with the will and superior cooperation levels makes them extremely dangerous. Time is our best weapon. There is still only a few of them; we must stop them from increasing in numbers. Once they escape from the system with reinforcements, the outcome is unavoidable."

Commander Forest scratched his chin. "Your arguments are persuasive, but how do we get the Navy and the colonial authorities to react appropriately to this situation? We almost need to provoke an overreaction. One that would cause massive mobilization of resources."

"Why don't you send out a planetary distress call?" asked Jennifer. Everyone stopped and looked at her. Ben hopped up and slapped her on the shoulder.

"Great idea! We'll get right on it!" He ran over to the AI's hologram. "Jack, access the stored military traffic you recorded back on Isis . Show me only the encrypted stuff." The AI's image shrunk in size and was replaced by a multi-windowed holoscreen.

Tina laughed. "Kid, to issue a planetary distress call, you would have to have access to all sorts of highly classified military codes. They have such codes to prevent hacks like you from launching wars and shit. Don't tell me that you have Keynan colony's disaster codes stored in that thing?" Ben continued to work at his keyboard. Lines of numeric messages streamed across the windows.

"Nope. I don't. But I do have some encrypted messages from a Navy cruiser. In a few minutes Jack and I will break those codes and we will be able to send our own command messages." The young man continued to concentrate on his screens. "There, Jack, start crunching."

"I see where he's going," said the Commander, "he's not going to fake a planetary distress call. He is going to try and order the Navy to respond as if one was already received and verified. That will save time."

Hemant asked, "Is this possible, Ben, my boy?" The holoscreens vanished and Jack reappeared.

"Not only is it possible, but I have the codes right here." Jack displayed the two military algorithms. Ben constructed a set of fake orders, with Hemant's and the commander's help. They included a planetary quarantine, how to handle infected people, a complete description of the alien threat, tactical information on the Star of India , and warnings to guard against computer virus once inside the system. All naval fighting vessels within a three sector radius are ordered to respond. Ben signed the communiqué Admiral Corella.

"Are they ever going to be pissed at us when they find out what we've done," said Ben, "This will top anything that I've ever gotten in trouble for." He shook his head as he hit send.

"Better that, than have our whole civilization destroyed," remarked Jennifer. The others agreed. The group had stayed up for almost twenty-four hours straight. The exhausted humans one by one drifted off to sleep. The ever vigilant Jack watched over the shuttle as it sped on through the nothingness of hyper-space.

CHAPTER NINE

"RISE and shine Bennie boy." Ben scratched his ear and pulled the blanket tighter around him. "Come on Ben, get up and hit the head before the whole group wakes up." The young man opened one eye and looked around.

"Is that you Jack?" he asked. The AI responded using the implant.

"Who else would whisper in your ear like this?"

"The girl I was dreaming about, before you rudely woke me up."

"Oh, sorry about that. I thought you'd like to get cleaned up before the crowd." Ben shook himself awake and quietly got up. He made his way around the sleeping bodies to what remained of the head and brushed aside the blanket. He removed his shirt and put it in the tiny cleaning unit. Taking a washcloth, he soaped up his upper body and face. By the time he finished drying off, his shirt was cleaned and smelling fresh. He took the time out to comb his hair before pulling back the curtain. Jennifer's sleepy face startled him.

"Good morning, I heard the water running and thought I'd better get up and get in line. How far away from the base are we?" Ben blinked several times.

"Jack says within the hour."

"I'd better hurry then." She scurried behind the blanket. The others were starting to rouse. Ben sat down at the pilot's console and nibbled a high protein space ration.

"I'm getting sick of these," asked Ben as he tore open the juice concentrate. "Where is the genuine food? Does the base have replicators?"

"Yes, and I can reprogram them to make your favorite foods." Ben had downloaded every recipe that he ran across that appealed to him. Over the years, he had amassed a considerable collection.

"Good. Tell me about the base security, Jack. What should we expect? I'm sure the Gaderians didn't make the base obvious or we would have discovered it by now."

Jack thought for a moment, "According to my database, the facility is heavily shielded from sensors and hidden from plain view. A vessel landing on the surface of the planetoid would have trouble finding it, even if they knew it was there. Uninvited guests would be simply vaporized." Ben was immediately concerned.

"Vaporized? Is there a chance the base defenses are still operational?" asked Ben.

"I don't see why not. The base was constructed to be a covert, back-up facility for military vessels in need of emergency repairs or a place to hide during the war. It was never meant to be an active base. The design was such that the facility was fully automated and long periods were expected between visits. Gaderian hardware is designed to be durable." Jack had a confident tone to his voice.

"We better be on our toes then. Your memory is dated and your creators may have made some modifications that could prove deadly," pointed out the young man. The rest of the sleeping crewmembers were awake and moving around the cabin. Tina complained of being stiff. Hemant hobbled about some, but kept quiet. Commander Forest did some quick stretching exercises over in the corner. Ben could hear an occasional bone popping.

"Our illustrious crew is showing signs of wear," noted Ben.

"I'll have the base medical facilities check them out. Of course I'll have to reprogram them first to handle human physiology. I'm glad we had the opportunity to copy the complete library of that medical college we broke into on earth last year. Remember?" Ben smiled. Sure, he remembered. Ben had spent more than a bit of time in the human sexuality part of the library. An alarm rang.

"Coming up on breakout into normal space. Automatics indicate two minutes. Jack, are you ready on communications?" Ben asked. Everyone took their places. Ben moved over to the navigation console. This time, the return to normal space was accompanied by only the slightest physical discomfort.

"Heading should be 270 mark 90, distance 2,000 kilometers. We should be able to see the planetoid from here," pointed out Jack. The commander cleared the bow portals. After the maneuver, a small object could be seen in the distance. It grew rapidly in size. Ben monitored Jack's attempts to establish communications with the hidden base. There was no response. Then, suddenly a loud voice speaking a Gaderian tongue emitted from the speakers. Jack translated.

"Excellent," declared Jack, "the base computer said that we are cleared to land and that he won't blow us out of the sky unless we try something funny. He did warn me that my access code is extremely old and that I was recorded as missing in action and presumed dead. Therefore, we have to undergo additional security checks and could still be destroyed after we land." The AI's face was jubilant.

"I think he enjoys scaring us to death," deadpanned Tina to Hemant. The science officer nodded. The AI fed the landing coordinates to the commander, who put the ship down right on the numbers. The only thing visible was rock, and lots of it. Sensors indicated the planetoid was eighty percent rock. No base showed up on the scanners. Hemant, Ben, and the commander suited up anyway, leaving Tina and Jennifer on board the shuttle.

The team climbed down the ladder and tested their legs in the low gravity.

Hemant read from his scanner, "Forty percent standard gravity. Be careful, we can hurt ourselves. Jack, which way do we go?"

The AI, slung over the shoulder of his master, formed a holographic arm and pointing, "That way, toward the cliff." The group made its way to the rock wall.

"I don't see anything," said the commander, staring at the rock face.

"The door is right in front of Ben," said the AI over the comm link.

"Hologram wall?" observed Ben.

"Yep. Walk through and we'll shut it off." Ben took two steps forward and appeared to disappear from view. After about a minute the rock wall faded away, revealing to Ben and Jack a recessed man-sized hatch. The Gaderian double triangle and circle was molded into the design of the door. The young computer genius had already plugged the AI into the access socket and was studying the readout. The hatch slid open silently and a dim light flickered to life, illuminating the dark air lock. After the three men climbed over the threshold, the hatch slid shut. Air streamed into the lock from hidden vents. No pumps were heard and even the sound of the rushing air was muted. Hemant consulted his suit's sensors.

"The air is compatible and free from contaminants," commented the science officer. "I think it's all right to breathe. Is there air in the rest of the facility?" Hemant asked Jack.

"Yes, we can take off our suits on the other side of this door. The base computer assures me that air is plentiful and safe." The inner door opened without a hiss or other noise.

"Not a bad design. Door opens after a thousand years without even a squeak," Ben pointed out, while giving the thumbs up to Jack's image. Jack nodded his acknowledgment. The room they entered was twelve meters by twelve meters by twelve meters high. At the other end of the compartment was a closed door with some writing on it. At the center of the room was a tall pedestal. The hatch sealed silently behind them. More lights came on, revealing sterile white walls and floor. Five ugly looking devices hung from the ceiling.

"Gentlemen, lets step up to the pedestal." Ben carried Jack to the center of the room and set him down on the lip of the platform. Jack formed a full-sized image and proceeded to reach his hand through a plate on the side of the pedestal. He had to stretch to reach it. The opening was designed for a much taller person. The flat panel display sprang to life. The devices over head swung around to point menacingly toward the group below.

"Whoa, Jack, what did you do? Those things are pointing at us and I have the feeling they are not just pretty ornaments," declared Hemant looking up at the ceiling.

The AI replied, "No, they aren't, they are disrupters. If we answer wrong or the base computer decides we are a threat, we get smoked." A holographic figure appeared before them. Jack, whose 'hand' was still inside the pedestal, spoke to the image in Gaderian. The figure answered back in the same language. Jack's image began to glow, especially his immersed hand. The pedestal began to glow as well. The display controls blinked as if invisible fingers were playing a tune on them. Data and Gaderian language sped across the screen. The other figure began to glow from the data exchange. The humans could discern a high pitched tone, just out of hearing range. The AI's humanoid form changed to that of Attendant Blaxx. His deep baritone voice rang out in the chamber as the other figure listened with the appearance of great interest. The glow faded from the two holograms and Jack's form reappeared once more. The AI removed his hand from the plate which triggered the pedestal to melt into the floor. The overhead weapons returned to their neutral positions. The other figure spoke, this time in human standard.

"Your interrogation is complete. Your THX 030 unit has been authenticated. I am known as Guardian. Please follow me." The closed door opened by itself. A long hallway stretched beyond the door. The humans could see lights turning on in sequence, making the hallway appear to grow longer and longer. The Guardian stepped through the door, and the group followed. To the left was a completely transparent and seamless wall. A darkened cavern lay beyond. The Gaderian nodded in that direction and a series of lights snapped on in quick succession. The cavern was a huge hanger. The humans gasped. The transparent hallway looked to be located about halfway up one side of the huge chamber. Ben looked down the fifty or so meters to the hanger floor.

"I thought you said this was a small base," whispered Ben into Jack's ear.

"It is," Jack shrugged, "but everything is relative."

The visitors continued to marvel at the size of the hidden hanger. There were some small craft scattered about and one vessel five times the size of the human's craft. "How do we get the shuttle in here?" asked the commander of Guardian. The Gaderian hologram waved his arm in the air and the floor began to vibrate slightly. A crackling sound was heard in the corridor and Tina's voice rang out.

"Shuttle to Commander Forest , are you guys there? Something's happening here. A tractor beam of some sort has the shuttle and it's dragging us towards the cliff. I need to know if you are all right. Have you caused this? I gotta know quick! Hello?!" Tina's voice was tinged with concern.

The Guardian spoke to the first officer, "Go ahead and answer her." The commander raised his comm link. "You don't need that here, just speak, she can hear you." He dropped the device.

"Tina, Tina! Can you hear me?" asked the first officer.

"Yes, yes! Tell me what to do quick! We are about to hit the rock wall. The engines are warmed up, I'm ready to lift off."

"No! Turn off the engines, don't fight the tractor beam," ordered the Commander. "Everything's okay. We are going to bring you inside. That cliff has to be a holographic projection."

Jennifer's concerned voice came on, "Eric, is that you? Are you sure that wall isn't authentic? The sensors don't indicate a fake."

The Commander laughed, "Relax, trust me. Inside a few minutes, we'll all be together." Just about that time the nose of the shuttle could be seen poking its way through what looked like a solid granite surface. Ben and Hemant stopped to watch. The entire craft floated into view and slowly settled to the hanger floor.

"So they have holo-projectors on both sides of the door. Cute," noticed Ben.

"Spared no expense," replied Jack. "Of course it's the active sensor shielding that sets it apart from your technology. Point any human scanner at that wall, and you would swear it was solid, even if the hanger door was wide open."

"I hope all this 'expensive technology' helps us to defeat these creatures!" Hemant examined his portable scanner and shook his head in puzzlement. The humans continued to follow the Guardian to the end of the corridor. Next to a sealed hatch was what appeared to be an open platform lift. Everyone squeezed onto the platform. Ben looked for the controls, but couldn't find them. The lift started down.

"How long before the chamber is pressurized?" The Guardian turned to answer the first officer.

"We replaced the air in the entire complex as soon as the interrogation was complete."

Hemant exclaimed, "But we didn't hear air handlers, pumps or other pressure devices go off." That was true. There were no sounds in the base. It was eerily quiet.

"Our atmospheric replication equipment is super quiet and efficient. A force field kept the gases in place while I brought your vessel into the hanger," explained the Gaderian hologram.

"You could try playing some music in the background. It might help improve the mood," commented Jack. "I'll select a few tunes for you later." The Guardian gave the AI a funny look.

Jack thought, Military AI's have no sense of humor .

"Good idea, Jack!" said Ben. "And if the walls morph like your outer shell construction, we can change the color and texture, and liven this place up." The Guardian gave Ben a concerned look.

The lift slowed to a stop and a double set of hatches swung up out of the way. The humans and the two holographic beings stepped out onto the great hanger floor. The science officer pointed his scanner at the hatch, the floor and around the chamber. Ben ran to the shuttle hatch and started the open sequence. The suspicious chief engineer greeted him with disrupter in hand.

"How do I know it's you Ben? This could be a trick. For all I know, you could be prisoners and this alien computer could have sent holograms to flush us out." Jennifer squeezed by the engineer and stood in the hatch.

"That's silly," she said.

"How do you know?" retorted Tina. The young archeologist ran out to embrace Commander Forest .

"Because holograms can't kiss like this." And then she proceeded to lay a big one on the embarrassed commander. Tina snorted, dropped her weapon and exited the shuttle. Hemant handed her the scanner.

She read the results and exclaimed, "Well, I'll be. Tricky bastards aren't they? Can't tell what's real and what's not."

The Guardian interrupted the reunion, "Please hurry, we must meet with the Teacher if we are going to equip you to fight the Minari. This way please." He led them to a spot just to the left of the lift. A door appeared, opening up to the hanger control room. Various consoles were scattered about the compartment, displays dark, oversized chairs empty. Ben looked back and saw the shuttle through the window.

Must be a one way holograph , he thought . I don't remember a window from inside the hanger. The humans were lead into still another room. This compartment contained a number of cube shaped containers. The faint outline of man-sized doors could be seen on the sides of the cubes. The doors were closed and the group couldn't see what was in the containers. The room smelled musty. They went down a short hallway and entered a spherical shaped chamber. A single oversized chair sat on a low platform in the center. In the chair was seated a lone figure, that of an old Gaderian male.

The Guardian addressed the figure, "Teacher, these are the ones who were sent to destroy the Minari flare up. I have interrogated them and while I find them slightly alien, they are acceptable. An attendant has inducted them into service. They are in need of a ship, weapons, training, and tactics. I turn them over to your care. I go to prepare for their physical needs." The Guardian image dissolved. The old teacher stood unsteadily to his feet. He fingered his beard in a most human-like fashion. He looked the group over, one by one. The teacher hobbled over to look into the face of Hemant and shook his head.

"It will never work. I find you all unacceptable!" He turned his back on the humans and returned to his chair.

Jack, who had kept quiet up to now, spoke up, "Look you old fart, in case you haven't been paying attention, the Minari are loose in this sector. There is no Gaderian Navy left to fight the threat. These humans are our only chance of stopping them!"

The old figure countered, "You don't know for sure that there is no Navy left."

"I have the history files to prove it. Everyone has been gone for at least a thousand years!"

"May be they went somewhere else!" retorted the Teacher.

"Well, they didn't leave a forwarding address, did they!?" answered back Jack. The Teacher sat back in his chair, contemplating. His image abruptly vanished and reappeared beside Jack.

"Data files can be faked," pointed out the Teacher. "Besides, we can't put dangerous technology in the hands of these savages. They are years behind us and we don't even know if they are physically compatible for my learning process." Jack was becoming impatient.

"We don't have time for this," the THX 030 unit declared. With that, the AI dissolved his shape and reformed as Attendant Blaxx. The two argued for several minutes about authority, security concerns, and extrapolating internal programming to fit new situations.

"If you don't cooperate, I'll invoke line officer override control. That will shut down your higher functions and make you a virtual slave." The Teacher argued some more but in the end reluctantly agreed to try memory implantation. They selected Hemant as their first subject. The science officer looked like a child in the huge chair. The rest of the humans followed Jack down to the galley. The Teacher had muttered about not rushing things and wanting to digest the data about human physiology that Ben's AI provided.

"Will the implantation hurt and what are you putting in him anyway?" inquired Tina. She wasn't happy about leaving her superior in the room alone with a loony artificial intelligence.

"He will feel some tingling sensation, that's all." Jack replied. "This is not like the Minari. You still have full control over your faculties. No subconscious commands or secret agendas are implanted. We have very strict prohibitions on this. Skills, information, and reflexes are all you get."

"Jack, why does the Teacher represent himself as old? Don't you find that a bit strange?" Jennifer asked.

"You must understand that Gaderian artificial intelligence's have been given the ability to learn and become self aware. They must be able to adapt to different circumstances and overcome obstacles that their programmers could never predict. As a result of this ability, they develop personalities as unique as yours. But I do have to admit, in the short time that I have been awake, I have not run across a personality as distinct as that one."

"Distinct!?! Jack, I think you mean crazy?" said Ben with a grin. The young man stopped along side the others to look around the galley. Like the rest of the base, it was spotless, not a bit of dust or a stain anywhere. The tables were conventional enough. The chairs were way too wide, almost reminding the humans of benches. Along one wall were three recessed cubical spaces. "Replicators?" Ben asked.

"Yup," answered Jack.

Jennifer asked, "So where are the controls? Are we supposed to just 'think' them on?" Tina ran her fingers along the wall on the sides of the recessed spaces. "I can't find a switch anywhere." The Guardian appeared at that moment next to the chief engineer.

"You just have to ask," he said. Startled, Tina let out a yell and threw her arm back in a martial arts defensive move that went right through the hologram. He, of course, was unhurt and slightly amused.

"Don't do that again!" Tina put her hand on her forehead and gritted her teeth. "Next time, I'm gonna kick your ass!"

The commander took this time to step forward and said diplomatically, "Yes, we would like very much to eat, please." A hologram display opened before each human, listing major food groups in standard.

"Hey," said Jennifer, "it's in our language and the food is almost identical to ours!"

"It should be," replied Ben, "I asked Jack to download my personal recipes into the base replicators. Hope you all like my taste in food. If not, I believe that there is a killer peanut butter and jelly sandwich in there somewhere." The AI smiled. The young man quickly made his selections. Almost before his hand lowered, the smell of his food emanated from the recessed space. All the human's stomachs rumbled.

"That was quick. Looks okay, smells okay. Tastes . . ." Ben took a bite. "Yuck, terrible!" Everyone's face fell. "Just kidding, it's fine. Tina, I'm joking, okay?" Tina, terribly famished and sick of the space rations, looked on the verge of collapse. She gave him an if-looks-could-kill glance and proceeded to order her own selection.

The group sat together and ate their fill of the hot food. It felt good to relax after so many days of fear and horror. The base felt safe and secure. The problem of the alien invasion seemed far away. Jennifer and Eric talked about where to go on vacation. Ben recanted how much he missed his dad, and hoped the aliens didn't head his direction. Tina was just happy to be still alive and in control of her faculties. The humans avoided any discussion of their fallen comrades, whose bodies now hosted the alien beings. If what the AI had said was true, their souls no longer existed, their flesh were corrupted and they were to be considered, for all intensive purposes, dead. For three hours, Jack, Ben, Tina, Jennifer, and Eric discussed life, politics, science, anything except the dire situation the human race found itself in. All that ended when the door to the galley opened. A lone figure stood in the doorway.

"Can a fellow get some food around here?" The accent was a dead giveaway. The science officer entered the room. "I should have eaten a snack before having my head crammed with all that knowledge." He walked right over to the replicators. "Food, activate." The display opened in mid-air. "Oh, you programmed it for me. How nice." The science officer made his selection and carried his plate to the table. The others said nothing, just looked at him. The science officer seemed a little wild eyed, but other than that, okay. "What are you looking at? Haven't you ever seen a man graduate from a two year college level course in three hours? I'm hungry and a little bit tired. Tina, the knowledge is just incredible. It all makes so much sense." Tina's eyebrows and interest level went up together.

The Commander asked, "Are you all right?"

The AI spoke up, "He's fine. I detect elevated electrolyte levels and some increased blood flow to the brain. That should wear off after a short nap. The Teacher tells me that the reason the first one took so long is that he wanted to fine tune the process. Each of the others should only take an hour. Tina, you are next. I'll escort you." The two got up and headed for the door.

"Jack!" called out Ben. "You forgot your box. Your hologram has just about reached its distance limit."

"Oh, I forgot to tell you, while we are here at the base, I can tap into the holo-net system. It allows me to go anywhere, just like the Guardian. Just remember to pack me up and take me with you when you leave." Ben nodded. Hemant dug into his food with gusto and in no time finished it. He stretched and yawned, and announced that he was going to take a nap.

"I'll call the Guardian," said Ben.

"That will not be necessary," said Hemant. "I know the way." Ben and the commander looked at each other. "Oh, the machine implanted the base layout in my mind. I know where to go, where not to go, and how to operate the equipment. Come, I will show you."

In spite of all the advanced technology, the Gaderian sleeping arrangements were austere and cramped. There was one main barracks that could hold almost one-hundred solders in a series of four stacked bunks. There were no individual compartments. Officers were expected to sleep with the troops as well as both sexes. The humans staked out five bunks on the first level, all right next to each other.

The combination of excitement and the excess of food had made Ben a bit sleepy. He decided to lie down for a few minutes and close his eyes. The next thing he knew the commander was shaking his shoulder.

"Ben, wake up, it's your turn. You're going to like this." The commander's bleary eyes stared down at the young man. "I'll have to take a quick nap to let my body adjust. Wow! The stuff I know!" He shook his head and plopped down in his bunk. Ben got up and looked around. The commander was the only one in the bunks.

"Jack, are you around?" The AI appeared instantly beside him. "My turn, huh? Let's go. Where are the others?" asked Ben.

"In the simulators," replied the AI. "Although the head knowledge is there, the body has to develop the reflexes. They are practicing with all the equipment needed to fly that long range interceptor you saw in the hanger." The AI led Ben down the corridors to the learning center. Ben entered and came face to face with the Teacher. His appearance was considerably younger and he no longer limped.

"You're the last one, eh? Well, your Jack and I have been discussing what your training should be for this mission. I haven't done anything that mattered in such a long, long time. Improves my self image don't you think?" He posed for the young man. "Your age, physiology, and unusual intelligence levels make you a possible choice for an implant. I'll have to test you first, though. Climb up on the seat," he ordered. Ben sat down. The size of the chair and the looming figure of the Teacher were intimidating.

"An implant?" Ben asked hesitantly. "Like what Alpha One has?" The teen wasn't too crazy about this. He glanced at his wrist chronograph.

"Well . . . yes he has several, but he can grow others as he needs them and you cannot. All the bio-mechanicals constructs had at least one. Before the Navy pulled out, most of the pilots were fitted with them as well. This allowed the pilots to integrate better with their vessels, and it made them faster, deadlier fighters. They communicated better with their THX units, too. Remember, the Uglies were kicking our butts, we needed whatever edge we could find. Only certain people could use them, something to do with cognitive physiology and left brain, right brain stuff." Ben felt a tingling sensation on his scalp. He was about to ask another question, when everything seemed to freeze. The young man tried to blink, but couldn't. He felt a brief moment of panic, but it passed. Ben blinked his eyes and looked down at the chrono. An hour had passed.

"Yep, they all had them," repeated the Teacher as if now time had passed. "Young man, unless I have become a complete lunatic like your engineering chief thinks, you are a perfect match for the implant. You have to decide though. Can't make you. Rules." Implanted memories started to flood Ben's brain. Ship specifications, in Gaderian, scrolled by like on a computer screen.

"I can understand Gaderian!" Ben was elated. More information about software construction came to mind. The complex coding he had seen on the Star of India made perfect sense. He knew how to counteract the software viruses. If only he had this information before! Weapons systems, hyper-space theory, control algorithms crowded his mind. It was fantastic! "Jack, what do you think about the implant?" The AI's voice tickled his ear.

"Can't hurt," replied Jack. "You'll be able to do multiple tasks at once. It gives you a big advantage over the others, besides they weren't suitable for implants anyway. You don't have to use it if you don't want to, and Teacher says he'll hide it underneath your hair line, so no one will know it's there." Ben took a deep breath.

"Okay, put it in. If I don't like it, you'll take it out? No permanent damage?" The Teacher nodded. Everything froze again. Ben found once more that he couldn't blink. When he came out of the trance, Ben felt an itch at the base of his skull. He went to scratch it and his fingers rubbed across a hard metallic button.

"It will open up when the appropriate link touches it. You can use hard wire or remote links. Only Gaderian technology will activate it," explained Jack. Lets go try it out."

The Teacher added, "Go make me proud! And make sure you come back for a refresher and tune up from time to time."

"Don't I need to rest like the others?" Ben asked.

"You rested during the operation," pointed out Jack. "Snored too, I was there. See you later Prof." The Teacher sat back down in the chair. As Jack and the young man left the chamber, the lights dimmed. Ben could see outline of the forlorn figure in the chair.

A voice came out of the darkness, "And don't take so damn long between visits next time!"

Ben asked Jack, "What does he do now?"

"Goes back into standby mode and waits."

"Waits for what?" asked Ben.

"Waits for someone else to teach, new orders, updated programming, stuff like that," replied Jack.

"Kinda lonely don't you think?" commented the young human.

"Makes me glad I'm a THX unit. Come on this way."

"I know the way, thank you very much." Ben took the lead. The others were just coming out of the simulator chambers when Ben arrived. Jennifer did some stretching exercises.

"My muscles are tired from that last run. Hemant, I believe I out-shot you during that 'sim.'" The science officer grinned.

"Yes, but I was able to reroute power to the environmental systems and stay alive after yours shut down. I survived," retorted the science officer.

"Sure, until that computer virus ate your controls," laughed the archeologist.

"I'm glad that was only an exercise," sighed Tina. "Rebalancing the hyper drive coils in mid-flight is tricky. We only blew up three times."

"And I only bumped into a couple asteroids during the flight maneuvers," explained the Commander. The Guardian appeared.

"You are making progress, yet according to Jack, you should not quit your full time jobs. What does this mean?" The humans burst into laughter.

"It means we suck!" explained Tina. "Let's go eat, I'm hungry." The humans left the compartment for the galley. Ben climbed into one of the simulators. He instructed Jack to run all manual drill on weapons, flight maneuvers, and emergency and engineering procedures. The young man found that after losing a few simulated battles and running into some small planetoids, he began to get the hang of it.

"Ben, you are catching on much faster than the others. You might even become accomplished by the time we leave in a FEW HOURS," the AI gushed. He would have to rub the Guardian's nose in it. The Guardian had predicted disaster if the ship was allowed to leave before the humans had mastered the craft. Jack had argued for speed . They could practice during the flight, he said. If the Minari were allowed to capture the colony and begin spreading across human space, the Gaderian interceptor would be unable to be everywhere at once .

"If the ship gets blown out of the sky, what good will that do?" responded the Guardian.

"Trust me," said Jack, "I know how resourceful these people are. They are survivors."

"We leave in three hours?" exclaimed an incredulous Ben.

"Well . . . yes! If we don't, we won't trap the Star of India in this system before they can complete the conquest of the planet. Remember, the Minari need a planetary gravity well to set up volume replication of Star Crystals . It will take time to set all that up. First, they have to pacify the government and enough of the population to seize control. If we have stirred up enough trouble, by utilizing the planet's bulletin boards, the colony will be looking for the warning signs. Resistance will be much higher and that will slow the advance of the infection."

"I'll have to trust you won't I?" stated the young man. Jack nodded the affirmative. Ben stared at the remote implant link plugged into the simulator console. He wasn't too wild about using it, especially after seeing the Star of India 's crew plug those things into their heads. He picked up the link and rolled it around in his hand. Ben tossed it up in the air, caught it, reached behind his head, and touched it to the button sized jack. The cover retracted and the probe end of the link slid into place. He heard Jack say "we'll take it slow."

Ben blinked his eyes and found himself in a virtual tunnel. Ever so slowly, he began to float down the tunnel. A device at the edge of Ben's vision emitted a steady beam of high-speed pulses of light, which the young man somehow knew represented nanoseconds. The pulses raced down the tunnel and disappeared from view. The next thing Ben noticed was that the farther he floated down the tunnel, the more discernible were the individual pulses and the slower they traveled. This must mean time is slowing down for me, Ben thought. The young man looked up on the walls and saw symbolic images of various systems, environmental, weapons, shields, propulsion, navigation, communications, and computer. Ben passed graphical representations of power levels and shield strengths. Scattered readouts spit data. Names of subsystems were highlighted in purple. Some pulsated at different frequencies. The kaleidoscope of colors, the strangeness of it all bothered Ben. He began to struggle. The tunnel started to slowly spin, throwing the computer genius into disorientation.

"Jack!" Ben cried out. The tunnel stopped spinning. A pedestal appeared in front of Ben. The figure of Jack could be seen.

"Take it easy, I'm here," said the AI. "It takes a bit to get used to. Ben steadied himself. "You are in the main menu. All the ship's systems are represented here. Your brain associates the data it receives as images. To choose a system, just head toward one; try propulsion." Ben was confused. He fought down nausea.

"How do I move?" the young man asked.

"Think about where you want to go. Try it," urged the AI. The young man started to drift towards the propulsion image. He glanced at the graphical depiction as he floated past. "That's it."

"The power levels show that we are in flight," commented Ben. He floated through the symbol and found himself in a chamber. A blinking sign said 'INTERACTIVE MODE.' Ben heard Jack's voice say, " reach out and touch it." The young man touched the sign. A bright flash momentarily blinded him. When it faded, a whole new set of sight, sounds, feelings, and smells hit the teen. He could sense everything about the engines. The feeling of power made him giddy. His body was transcendental. Ben felt like he was the engines. He became the engines. He altered the reaction mix until his sense of smell told him the mixture was at optimum. A request to increase power appeared in front of him. The young man complied, reaching out and adjusting all the controls. The pulsations of the engine increased.

Ben looked into the chamber and watched the reaction taking place. He examined the vectored thrust exhaust. He floated through all the control systems, checking for inaccuracies, looking for problems. Ben looked through the eyes of all the sensors, trying to understand what each one was telling him. Some manifested through touch, others through sight or sound. Ben could sense time. Each second that passed felt like a hundred to the disembodied computer genius. It was all so new. Finally, a request appeared before his eyes, RETURN TO THE TUNNEL. As soon as Ben thought about it, he was there, floating in front of Jack's image.

"Not bad for your first time, Ben. Now let's go though each of the main systems one at a time. You need to get used to the interface before we play war games."

Tina, Eric, and Jennifer were relaxing in the Gaderian equivalent of a hot tub. Hemant was laying down taking a massage. Invisible fingers kneaded his flesh. Jennifer dunked her head under the water.

"This is a luxury, after what we went through on that shuttle," said Jennifer as she squeezed the water from her hair. "Do you think we're ready for this fight?" Tina had leaned her head back, eyes closed.

Tina replied, "Girl, I learned a long time ago not to worry about fights. In an out and out bar brawl confusion reigns supreme. You can't fight everyone at once and neither can all of them fight you. You keep moving, take out one opponent at a time and eventually you're the only one standing. 'Course it helps to have eyes in the back of your head or fight with a buddy so's none of the bastards can sneak up on you." The engineering officer never once opened her eyes during her lecture.

The commander stretched, stood up and said, "Interesting parallel, Tina, comparing a space battle to a bar fight. I've never heard a tactics lecture quite like that before." Jennifer looked appreciatively at his body as he got out of the tub.

"What we need is to practice working together," said the Commander. "Jack assured me that given a bit more time, we WILL become skilled at operating the interceptor. Plus, we have surprise on our side. The Minari think we are still in the asteroid field or got taken out by one of their torpedoes. They will never expect us to come zooming into the system in a fully functional Gaderian naval vessel. And if that cloaking device does what it's supposed to, we'll be able to blast them at close range before they know what hit them." The commander finished wrapping the towel around himself. Jennifer hung her arms over the edge of the tub.

"Enjoy yourselves, in half an hour; we go back into the simulators." The commander strode off. The young archeologist looked after the retreating commander.

"I think I'm done," exclaimed Jennifer. With that, she jumped out of the water, grabbed a towel and chased after Eric. Tina opened one eye and snorted loudly. She tried not to notice Hemant grinning at her.

"You know I think they make a good couple, these two. What do you think?" asked the science officer.

"I think I'm gonna be sick, that's what I think," groaned Tina.

The young man sat quietly in the simulator booth. He looked peaceful except for the outline of his pupils moving madly inside closed eyelids. Inside the simulation, however, Ben was dizzy and disoriented. He was operating the weapons systems and propulsion at the same time, jumping back and forth between systems, trying in vain to control the ship.

"No, no," coached Jack. "You have to sort of split yourself in two. Don't jump completely from area to the other. Exist in both at the same time."

"It's hard. I'm shooting at targets while accelerating and decelerating," complained Ben. "Just when I'm getting on top of things, you throw new stuff at me."

"This time I'll help you, Ben. As you get overloaded with tasks, assign the lesser ones to me, just like you would with the ship's computer."

The simulation started over. This time Ben concentrated seventy-five percent of his resources on the weapons system and the balance in propulsion. He could sense the AI close by. He felt like a dual being. Several emergency situations developed and Ben handled each one, flowing between systems effortlessly. Things got more complex. The disembodied young man found himself getting behind in responses. He tossed several in the AI's direction and went on to other tasks. Slowly he got things back under control. As more tasks appeared, the young man and the AI began to work as a team. They got a rhythm established and laid down ground rules concerning task sharing. Ben examined the higher level tasks and decided whether or not keep them or give them to his assistant. He pulled back to a summary level and let the automatics take control.

Ben floated on a sea of data, looking down on the systems. He tasted the information, he smelled its content, felt its direction. Scents of cinnamon, lemon, spices, and fruits assailed his olfactory senses, each representing a system status or warning of a change. Bubbles of important data floated to the surface. Ben smelled which ones were important and handled those, leaving the rest to Jack or the computer. His present resources were only being taxed at twenty-five percent. Ben felt in control. He saw outside the ship through the sensors and could feel the size and number of the two incoming ships. He reached out with the primary weapons and swatted at one of the ships. It exploded in a ball of light. A missile streaked out toward the remaining ship. The young human caused the missile to swerve out of the way of disrupter fire. The second ship exploded. The teen felt satisfaction at last. A voice tickled his ear.

"Ben, are you ready to go?" The voice belonged to the science officer. Ben retreated back up the tunnel. His vision expanded and the simulator display came into focus. The young man reached behind his head and unplugged the mind link.

"Is it time?" Ben spoke audibly, no longer in a trance. The science officer stared at the back of the young man's head.

"Is that a bio-electronic implant? Why did none of us get one?" asked the science officer. He picked up the mind link and examined it.

"It's called a 'mind link.' The Teacher said I was compatible and recommended that I be fitted with one," explained Ben.

"Interesting. How do you feel after using it?" queried Hemant. Jack appeared next to the science officer.

"Rather limited, I'm afraid," admitted Ben. "Like I can only do one thing at a time. When I use the mind link, it feels like I can multiplex myself in a million different ways, go a bunch of directions at once, handle all sorts of problems simultaneously. And it makes me fast, incredibly fast. What a rush!" Ben looked at Jack. "Is that how you perceive life?" he asked.

Jack answered, "Very similar, only I have more structure to my thinking. It's more . . . mechanical in nature. You just think and things happen. With me, I see all the underlying commands right down to the machine language. And I'm limited in which direction I can go. You can move in a curvilinear fashion, I must move at right angles. You can blaze your own trails, I must move only along predetermined paths. I can create new ones, but not at the speed you can."

"I think I understand," mused the young man. The trio left the simulator room and headed for the sleeping quarters to pick up the AI's case. Hemant explained how the practice had been going. They managed to survive in most of the latter simulations, but still had a long way to go. The commander and Jennifer were aboard ship already. Tina was examining some of the other craft in the hanger and met her new crewmembers outside the alien fighter.

"I checked out those other ships. Some of the systems on board were familiar, others were totally foreign to me . . . not part of our programming I guess," postulated Tina. The group entered the ship. The layout of the craft was the same as the simulator. Each human knew where their duty stations were, controls, back up systems, galley, head, etc. The Guardian appeared in the cabin, the humans gathered round.

"I congratulate you on your progress," began the Base AI. "I would have preferred that you stayed longer and gained added proficiency with our technology. However, given the urgency of your quest, it's the best we could do on such short notice. Each of you has been assigned a primary duty station." The Guardian sized up each human in turn.

He continued, "Hemant and Jennifer will handle starboard and port weapons pods. The commander will pilot the interceptor, navigate, and command the mission. Tina will operate the power plant, shields, and handle hyper-space calculations. Ben, here, will oversee tactical, computer operations, counter measures, and back up the other positions. His THX unit will assist him." He stopped talking for a moment, before continuing, "We all know how grave the situation is. This is a one shot mission. There are no Gaderian Naval units to support this operation. You are on your own plus any support that you can organize from the human forces."

The Guardian made his way over to the pilot's station. "Let me introduce you to the ship's computer." A drop-dead, gorgeous human female appeared, seated on the pilot's chair. She had long golden tresses and delicate features. She was wearing layers of gossamer garments that accentuated her figure. "Her chosen human name is Erin . Your THX unit suggested it."

The men in the group just stared, especially Ben.

The Guardian went on to explain that during peaceful flight, the ship's artificial intelligence could operate the craft with minimal intervention. During a battle, however, the AI's would not participate in extinguishing life. Deep, subconscious programming prevented that. The ship could run, evade, hide, but would not assume an attack position unless directly ordered to. By itself it wouldn't fire weapons at an enemy. In the vicinity of a fight, the humans would have to take control of the ship personally. This programming, the Guardian lamented, was lacking on the project that created the Minari. The Gaderians wanted to make sure such a situation never occurred again.

The humans assumed their duty stations and began a systems check while Jack said goodbye to the Base AI.

"It's time to say goodbye, Guardian. You have performed your duty well. I have one question. During your speech, I was monitoring base operations when I picked up a strange transmission. It was in a form I've never seen before and directed into a hyper-space rift that appeared out of nowhere. Can you explain?"

The Guardian smiled and coolly responded, "My programming requires me to send progress reports after being activated." Jack raised an eyebrow.

"There is no one left to send a message to. Where did it go and to whom?" demanded Ben's AI.

"To whom, I don't know, they did not tell me. The location is classified, even to one such as you," replied the Guardian. Jack sniffed and turned away. The Base AI raised one hand to salute the crew. "Fair well and safe journey!" he called out and abruptly vanished.

The young man examined his surroundings. Ben's station was at the center of the cabin, on a raised platform. He had a perfect view of all the other stations.

"Jack," said Ben, "I seem to recall that this slot is made for your case." Ben slid Jack's case home. It made no sound going in, but fit perfectly.

"Yes, it's made of the same material as my outer shell," explained Jack. "I can form almost infinite direct connections with the ship's systems." The ship's female AI materialized in front of the young man.

"You are the 'appointed one'" she said. Her voice was pleasant and airy. The golden hair framed her beautiful features.

"Jack, was this your idea?" asked a suspicious Ben.

"My gender is female. Your THX 030 unit thought that by assuming this form of human, my assimilation into your culture would be eased."

Ben started, "If I'm not mistaken, that face is . . ."

"From a famous galactic beauty queen," Jack completed, "yes, you guessed it. Very good! Your mind is as sharp as ever, you don't miss much!" Ben's AI chuckled.

"If my form is not pleasing to you, I can . . ." The ship's AI began.

"No, no that's quite all right. Boy, Jack, she is dammed good looking. What is an 'anointed one?'" Ben asked.

"You mean 'appointed one,'" answered Jack. "That's what the Gaderian's calls the guy with the implant. You see, normally the person sitting in your seat runs the whole show from his or her implant. The others are here to back you up if something goes wrong. On this trip, it's the other way around. You're not ready to control every system on this ship during cruise, let alone during a battle. It takes some practice to do that and one day isn't nearly long enough."

"Uh, Erin!" said Commander Forest . "Please take us out. Here are the coordinates." The female AI walked over to stand by the first officer. Jennifer eyed the beautiful apparition. She didn't like competition; however, the archaeologist noticed that only Ben was the object of her attention. All the others were treated with professional indifference.

"Compliance," Erin trilled. The ship lifted effortlessly from the hanger floor. Through the forward view port, the humans could see the Star of India 's shuttle at her resting place.

"I wonder if she'll still be there in another thousand years?" said the chief engineer, wistfully.

"It all depends if they let us come back," answered Hemant, "assuming we even survive." The ship headed towards the rock wall and passed through it on the way out of the hanger. The science officer and chief engineer tried in vain to catch a glimpse of the door machinery during transition, but the holographic projection was too good.

"Damn, I would like to know how they do that," said Tina.

Once clear of the planetoid, Ben's AI tuned into the subspace NewsVid. He played the newscasts live. Reports were flying all over the galaxy about the events in the Keynea System. Rumors had spread like wildfire about an impending alien invasion. Survivalists were preaching Armageddon. The government had warned the populace not to become alarmed. The info-net postings are a hoax and please don't sensationalize the situation further. Perpetrators of hysteria would be prosecuted to the fullest extent of the law. Conflicting stories continued to surface. The planetary guard had intercepted what they thought was a stolen starship. The freighter captain was incensed and demanded a full investigation. He insisted on a face to face meeting with the proper authorities to log his complaint. Shortly thereafter the subspace net in that sector went down and no news has been heard from the colony since. Another unsubstantiated report stated that a planetary alert had been activated and warships were rushing to the scene. The broadcaster urged those listening to "Stay tuned for more news as it happens."

The AI shut off the broadcast. The humans sat in somber silence. Commander Forrest spun around in his chair.

"Jack, Erin!" he commanded, "set up a series of simulations while in hyper-space. I want us to be ready to take these things out when we arrive in system."

CHAPTER TEN

TWENTY-FIVE. It wasn't enough. Twenty-five was too few for the plan to work. He needed at least thirty Minari for the plan to work, thought the alien leader. With thirty Minari and surprise on his side, Alpha One could isolate this system within a matter of hours. The McGregor-alien, now known as Beta Eight, should be on planet, seeking out specific members of the government to convert. His class VI probe was assembled from another lifepod, replacing the one swept into space during the humans' escape from the ship. The probe was launched in hyper-space just before the Star of India dropped into the system. The alien leader seethed with anger. The fact that anyone at all escaped, was bad enough, but to take so many of his warriors with them was an embarrassment. He should have recognized sooner that the young computer genius had a THX unit! Strange though, human records don't indicate that any THX units survived the war; no record of them even existed. Not many things survived from his era, period. His alien infiltrator, Mrs. McGregor, never signaled for a pick up, she must have failed to take command of the shuttle. With all probability, the foolish humans tried to make a run for it and the hunter torpedoes destroyed them. Well, he had more important things to think about, like how to come up with five more Minari warriors.

"Sir, Beta Twelve reports subspace transmission from Keynan colony." Alpha One's thoughts were interrupted.

"What does Beta Eight have to report?" The alien leader returned to the captain's chair. "By the way, I approve of your bio-modifications." The alien known as Beta Twelve stood in front of the communication console, which had been heavily modified. Where fingers once were, there were thick fleshy ropes, all connecting the hands to locations deep within the open console. Several ropes connected the head to the console as well. The alien's body had grown extremely stout and muscled. His facial expression rippled with pleasure.

"Thank you, your Eminence, Beta Eight says phase one targets have been located and seventy-five percent have been inoculated. The host's reputation precedes him and is making it ridiculously easy to contact and isolate targets. Your plan is on schedule. He also reports that the populous was extremely agitated about an info-net posting, warning about an alien invasion. Some of the populous is taking it most seriously. Others are laughing it off."

"Mere coincidence," commented Alpha One. "Humans experience these xenophobic fears all the time. Go on."

"Beta Eight reports that the description of the alien threat matches us perfectly. We are even named. The message was signed Commander Eric Forest and also reports the Star of India as being hijacked." The alien leader sat in stunned silence. How could they have escaped? The jamming satellites couldn't have been disabled. Surprise was out of the question. The debate over the minimum number of converts was moot; time to consider back up plan three-seven point ninety-three.

"Attention! We will cease preparations for plan one zero, immediately," ordered the alien leader. "All efforts are to be redirected to plan three-seven point ninety-three. All options to be considered. Inform the crew." Beta Twelve turned back to his display. Plan three-seven point ninety-three involved capturing as many space going vessels as possible before launching an all out assault on the space station. The original plan called for the Star of India to dock at the station and infiltrate its defenses as much as possible before staging a coordinated attack. Alpha One had been predicting zero Minari casualties. Now he wasn't so sure, with only 25 warriors left.

Beta-Twelve called out, "Done!"

Alpha One snapped, "Sensors, report!"

"Stealth satellites have achieved assigned locations. Jamming code waiting for your signal. Several starships, displacing approximately one-third our mass, orbiting the planet. No Naval vessels in system. Single space station, small by human standards, in geosynchronous orbit. We have not been spotted."

Good, the leader thought, this gives us time to modify our plans slightly.

"Beta Twenty, status of 'soft packages?"

"Insertion of computer viruses has been achieved. All planetary communications and defensive systems are affected once the trigger is pulled. Only one of the starships has the virus. The others are not receiving data transmissions. As soon as they do open up, we have bugs waiting."

"Excellent. Weapons, Alpha Six?" The former human being known as Tate, stepped forward. The Alpha designation meant that the alien contained a full sized Star Crystal . A short human to begin with, the physical modifications to his body made him look almost as wide as he was tall. Great bulging muscles stood out on his neck and arms. The alien looked like he could rip open a hatch with his bare hands. "I see you have opted for a martial arts orientation."

Alpha Six replied, "I have always been a warrior leader. Few have stood before me and survived. I am virtually undefeated. I have been dispatched only once and it will not happen again." He pointed to the ships tactical schematic. "Offensive weapons have been greatly modified and improved. Range has been extended. Accuracy improved. Gunnery crews have modified their hosts to enable full integration with the equipment. Shield strength is double that of a human heavy space carrier. That should be enough to protect us from anything the humans can throw at us except at point blank range. Our speed has increased thirty-five percent. Inertial dampers have been rebuilt to allow for much greater maneuverability. We can match small ships down to the fighter level." Alpha One calmly took in all the information.

"Can anyone tell that we have modified the ship from outside visuals," he asked.

"No, my leader; any external changes are hologram camouflaged. Anti-sensor feedback systems will take care of electronic surveillance."

The leader waved away his general and sat back in his chair to consider his options. The Star Crystal factory was being built right now in the hold. Many containers from the hold had been jettisoned to make room for the growing modules. Several had already been built and tested. They were waiting to be transported down to the surface, where his workers would finish the final assembly. The few raw materials needed would be salvaged from the planet's resources, when order was established. Then full scale production could begin. Once enough crystals were fabricated, the assault on the rest of the galaxy would commence. He briefly considered abandoning the colony and striking out for another target, one with more ships and no fear of discovery. No, he thought, his superior logic and intellect would be able to adapt to anything they could throw at him, even if those pitiful humans that escaped him earlier showed up.

The Minari on the ship had taken the liberty to bioengineer their host's bodies to enhance job and combat skills. Almost all had increased bone mass and added muscle to the point that any body builder would have been jealous. Many sported new limbs, specialized protuberances, and a few even incorporated non-organic equipment. All were manufacturing more Minari virus, which was periodically collected and stored for use on the planet. The food replicators were kept busy. The increased metabolism required to change the physiology of the hosts resulted in huge appetites. The Minari simply ate all the time. Only the former captain was not allowed to change his host body.

"I am simply horrified at the way my body looks. This host configuration is inefficient and an embarrassment to all us Minari," the former captain complained to Alpha One. The alien leader looked closely at the former captain's face.

"What have you done to the ears?" Alpha One demanded. The ears had been increased in size and muscles added so the host could swivel them in any direction." He wiggled his ears.

"I was having trouble hearing, and that mechanical device he used irritated my ear canal," the alien replied.

"Change it back!" The captain got a shocked look on his face. "You heard me, change it back, now!" The alien leader leapt to his feet. "You know the plan. You are my back up option, in case I need to buy us time. You must continue to look fully human, especially under close scrutiny. You have three hours to complete the change or I cut them off and make you grow new ones."

"Yes, sir." The captain-alien bowed his head and left the bridge. All the complaining and minor rebellious behavior had the Minari leader worried. The Gaderian converts were never this much trouble! Humans are so much more aggressive. The effect of personality crossover between species must be the culprit. He decided to modify the programming of the unused crystals prior to implantation to compensate. He would deal with the 25 current Minari later.

"Exit stealth mode," ordered the alien leader. "Helm, set course and speed according to plan three. Communications, notify the crew." Plan three called for the Star of India to limp into the Keynea system, faking damage and asking for assistance. If all goes as planned, the colony would send a ship out to assist with repairs. The aliens would absorb the crew and thereby double the size of their fleet. Guile and trickery, at this point, were much more effective than the use of weapons. The ship continued on its slow course for almost two hours before receiving the expected challenge.

"Alpha One, the colony wants verification of our identity and intentions. Shall I continue with the plan to fake partial communications failure?" The alien assigned to communications waited for an answer. Alpha One nodded and the message was sent.

The Star of India 's transmission was full of static and of extremely poor quality. All that got through to the other end was something about an engine malfunction and the communications array damaged. The colony responded as expected. The Planetary Guard raced out to meet the ship. But, instead of only one ship, they sent three, all frigate class vessels. The alien leader was elated. The more ships, the better, only he was going to have to get innovative about how to absorb them. Due to the extreme distance, it would take the guard vessels twelve hours to reach the freighter; more than enough time to prepare a little surprise for the humans.

"Alpha Six, come with me. We have to perform some surgery on the good captain. Beta Three, take command. Don't deviate from the plan!" The two aliens left the bridge.

Across the system, heading toward the Star of India , Major Peters, Commander of the Keynan Planetary Guard, studied the most recent reports and looked up at the young lieutenant. "You say here, that we have been unable to re-establish contact with the freighter?"

"No sir, not since the first transmission. Our technicians tell us that the signature of the transmission is consistent with a wave guide array failure. We feel that the ship must have reconfigured the wavelength to use the subspace antennae instead."

"Blast!" exploded the major. "Why didn't they deploy an old fashioned radio wave array? Every ship has the equipment to do that. They could have towed it behind the ship. There might be a time lag due to the distance involved, but it should perfectly crystal clear reception." The major laid down the tablet and stuck the end of his pen in his mouth. "Is there confirmation on the hijacking rumor?" The lieutenant shook his head.

"No one has been able to trace the posting back to its source," related the lieutenant. "The company says the ship went off course and had to set up another jump to get to the Iberian system. They have no idea why it showed up here, unless there was a problem with its coils. Records show they were close to the end of their useful life. In such an emergency situation, sir, the Keynea system would be the closest." The major frowned, his officer did have a point, but there was still a nagging concern in the back of his mind. He picked up a copy of the info-net post and scanned it.

"Okay, here is our plan. We will assume a hostile situation until they persuade us otherwise. Deploy the ships in attack formation with gun ports open. I want them to know we mean business. If everything turns out to be all right, we'll simply render all assistance necessary and head back in time for the festival. The press may call us trigger happy and someone might call for an investigation. With luck, though, the public will lose interest due to the festivities." The major continued to chew on his pen. The lieutenant saluted and left the cabin.

* * *

On the planet, the McGregor-alien continued to lure unsuspecting humans into traps using the most basic of emotions, greed and flattery. The McGregor name was legendary and opened many doors. Beta Eight used the trader's memories and business persona to weave a believable investment myth. The same basic story worked over and over: I came to you personally to because I need your expertise/reputation/advice/etc. to pull this deal off. This is the opportunity of a life time, to get in on the ground floor and make a fortune. Without you, it can't be done! Once converted, the former trader taught his new converts the same line. Together, they rapidly worked their way up the Planetary guard chain of command, dropping the McGregor name whenever appropriate. The government was even easier. Large political contributions and bribes always worked with politicians, no matter what the planet. In short order a number of high level officials were infected and within three hours, implanted with crystals. These leaders in turn arranged for their peers to meet them for a private meeting to 'discuss urgent business.' Once all the Star Crystal shards were used up on leaders, the conspirators concentrated on converting key lower level military and civilian personnel. This was much easier since their superiors could order them into situations that allowed them to become infected without raising suspicions. Even without crystals, these alien-hosts could be programmed and used to control major installations such as weapons depots, communication centers, the space port, and scientific laboratories.

Twelve hours passed quickly. Alpha One was on the bridge when the leader of the task force appeared on the viewscreen demanding to be allowed to board the ship. He wanted to speak to the captain personally. At this close range, there should be no problem with signal strength. So, the aliens showed him Captain Tucker. His face was bandaged. There were cuts on his face and hands. A nasty radiation burn graced one side of his face.

"Who in creation is demanding to see me!?" The captain-alien's face filled Major Peters' screen.

"Major Peters of the Keynan Planetary Guard here. We have received reports that your ship was hijacked in the Lomax system. Is your first officer there? We'd like to speak to him as well." The major studied the picture put before him. His tactical officer watched the sensors for signs of hostile intent. A sensor bleeped.

"Sir," the officer spoke in hushed tones, "sensors have confirmed a bad radiation leak in engineering. My visual also shows hull damage." The major glanced down at the data. Captain Tucker opened his mouth to speak.

"It grieves me to inform you that Commander Forest , my chief science officer and the ship's engineer all perished in the explosion. Some of my best men died trying to contain the reaction." He brushed a tear from his eye. "It was the work of sabotage!" explained the grim-faced captain.

"Sabotage?" snorted the major. "I find that hard to believe. Your Commander Forest sent a subspace message to the colony warning us about you. He said something about a raging out-of-control infection mutating the crew. He looked positively alive to me," retorted the Major.

"How dare you question me? My ship is damaged, yet we have complied with all regulations and used all the proper codes. I demand to talk to your superior officer! Wait until the authorities hear about this!" screamed the captain. The radiation burn got even redder. Major Peters, however, wasn't impressed.

"Well he's not here and I'm in charge. How do you explain the message?" demanded Major Peters.

"We traced the sabotage to one of our passengers, a troublemaker by the name of Benjamin Gardner. You may recall the Isis lottery scandal?" That did sound familiar.

"Yes, I think I do," said the Major. "Some guy rigged it so one of his accomplices would win. Some sort of genus with computers as I recall."

"Not so smart as he thought. He broke into the hyper-space control system and caused an in-flight meltdown of the coils. We were lucky to limp our way here using the spare set and jury rigged controls. The boy is a menace to society. He probably faked the message to get back at me for locking him up. He broke out of his cabin and is hiding somewhere in the ship."

"Then why don't you use the ship's sensors to find him," pointed out the Keynean officer. "That shouldn't be too hard." The major was still suspicious.

The alien-captain replied, "The kid released a virus into the main computer that shut down all internal sensors. Who knows what other damage he's done? That boy is gonna be in a rehabilitation colony for a long, long time, mister!" The major considered his next question. The alien-captain decided to launch his closing argument before he could ask it. "Coming out of hyper-space overloaded our temporary setup," continued the former captain. "The ship took a good beating as a result. We have radiation everywhere and I'm short handed. Can you assist?" The alien actor looked hopeful.

"Stand by; I'll relay your request." The major shut off the viewscreen. He turned to his bridge crew, "Okay, what have we got?"

The tactical officer spoke first, "We have a bona fide radiation leak and visible damage to the hull around main engineering. The cargo bay doors show signs of buckling. The hyper-space coils are emitting strange frequencies. It looks legit to me." The medical officer stepped forward.

"I've examined and enlarged the viewscreen image," reported the MO. "The wounds on the captain's face appear to be genuine. I can't detect anything like a disguise. The face matches company records. The resolution was even good enough to obtain a partial retina which matches Captain Tucker's perfectly."

"Any chance he is lying under duress?" asked the major. "Could someone be holding a disrupter to his back?"

"Nothing detected that would indicate that, sir," the doctor replied. "His voice scans are normal, heart rate normal, breathing normal. There are no physiological signs evident that indicate stress of that nature." The major nodded. He still wasn't convinced.

"Open a channel to headquarters, report our situation and ask for instructions."

Alpha Six waited tensely by his weapons controls. He had interfaced one hand with the controls as he watched the tactical display. "They're going to open fire. I just know it. It's been too long. Glorious Leader, let me destroy them. It would be easy. Their technology is so pitiful!"

"Absolutely not!" said Alpha One. "Be patient. We need their ships and bodies as hosts. They are confused. Our fake sensor readings and holograms conflict with the message sent by Forest ." Alpha One sat calmly in his chair. "Would you believe a few lines of text, or hard evidence that you can see, touch, and record? No, they will not open fire. Instead they will come on board, armed to the teeth and ready to help out with our little 'emergency.'" The alien leader smiled. Yes , he thought , I have figured these humans out. The Karl-host memories serve me well. I was fortunate to be chosen by this schemer. His insight into the shadier side of human physiology will give me a definite advantage in the coming battle. The comm system chirped. "Beta Twenty-two, take your position." The captain-host stood in front of the pick up.

"This is Major Peters. We have been ordered to board your vessel and assist with all repairs. I will lead two damage control parties myself. After our initial assessment, we can bring in more personnel."

"Excellent, our shuttle bay is inoperative. I will meet your team at the main hatch."

The major turned to his fight crew. "I don't trust them. The answers were too quick, too practiced. Prepare two teams, full armament, equipped with standard emergency salvage gear. Doc, I want you and your medical technicians to come with us. Signal the other two ships to stand by and hold positions." The major motioned for the lieutenant to come close.

The major spoke in a low voice, "Why don't we set up some fail-safe procedures, just in case." He then proceeded to outline his plan to the officer, who would stay on board and monitor the operation.

The Planetary Guard cutter made the connection with the hull. The clang vibrated through the smaller ship. As promised, Captain Tucker met them at the hatch. He shook hands with Major Peters.

"Sorry if I unloaded on you, old boy, things have been dicey around here. Follow me. We have to take a bit of a round about journey to get to engineering." The impostor led the guardsmen deep into the ship. Meanwhile the cutter had detached from the hull and resumed station. The lieutenant monitored transmissions from the teams.

Signal strength grew weaker and began to break up. The major told him not to worry, it was probably the radiation; they had reached the engineering compartment and were donning radiation suits. There was silence for about ten minutes. The officer began to become concerned and tried to reach his superior on the comm link. There was no answer. He tried the freighter's bridge.

"What's going on over there? I've lost contact with my people!" A young female officer appeared on the screen. She was extremely good looking. The lieutenant gulped. "I can't seem to raise anyone."

"Oh, I wouldn't worry. The engineering compartment is a mess and with all that radiation, communication is going to be a problem. They should get things locked down in an hour or so. What's your name?"

"Ste . . . Steve," he stuttered.

"Hello Steve, my name is Michelle. I hear your Founders Day Festival is about to begin. I've never been to one. I'm looking for a tour guide. Care to apply?" The young man swallowed. These things didn't just happen to him every day.

On the freighter's bridge the alien leader gleefully listened in on the conversation. The hologram was working perfectly. The host, who formerly operated as the ship's navigator, designed the image being shown and was supplying the voice. Alpha One was amused that the human officer was too limited to appreciate the navigator's upgrade. Tentacles connected her face to the navigation system. Her shapely body was over-muscled, delicate bones massive. The officers arms, once smooth and soft, were covered in rough, thick skin. The lieutenant, had he seen what he was flirting with, would have opened fire immediately. The alien leader opened a private channel to Beta Twenty-Seven.

"Good work. Your illusion will keep him occupied for some time. Soon we will have the voice synthesizer ready." Alpha One switched channels. "Beta Twenty-Two report."

"All humans have been inoculated except for two. They were destroyed."

"What happened and what about Major Peters?"

"Two humans had anticipated when the ambush occurred. We were forced to destroy them before they could fire their weapons. Major Peters is unharmed and undergoing transformation. I estimate one hour and forty-five minutes until revival."

"Good, proceed." The Minari Leader switched channels again. "Comm, begin synthesized communication using the Peters-human's voice. Follow the script and keep the conversation short. Beta Twenty-Seven, keep the human officer busy with chatter. Don't let him analyze the situation."

"K-107, come in. Are you there Lieutenant?" The transmission was full of static and there was no video.

"Sir, I can barely hear you. You are audio only." He turned the gain up full on channel two and adjusted the filters. The quality improved some.

"Doesn't surprise me," replied the Major's voice. "This engine compartment is torn up. Definitely looks like an explosion. The medical team has its hands full. I've assigned the rest of the team to scrounge up spares from non-critical systems through out the ship. If we can get the main engines back on line, we'll kick this pig and head for home. I'm going back in to direct the repairs. Periodically I'll come out to check in. Let the other ships know everything is okay. Peters, out." The young officer reached for the key.

"Sir, sir! What about the . . ." The static ceased as channel two closed. The Lieutenant hesitantly finished his sentence, "Password?" Michelle's image still beamed from the view screen. The officer had left channel one open.

"What password?" she asked innocently. Her voice startled the officer.

"Oh, nothing. It's just military protocol stuff," mumbled the young officer.

"Oh, how boring. Let's change the subject. Why don't you tell me about you?" She then proceeded to ply him with all sorts of questions. The lieutenant was barely able to signal the other two ships. He split his attention between his displays and the vivacious crewmember. A review of the sensor's indicated that guardsmen were spreading out over the ship, as the major had said. The suit transponders made for a strong reading. The radiation levels were dropping as predicted. The officer decided to wait until the next transmission to ask for the agreed upon password.

Thirty minutes passed. The young lieutenant got edgy and was just about to call the other ships, when the major reported in. This time the audio was better and there was even a fuzzy video image. The major's response to the request for a password was, don't worry, everything is legitimate. Your earlier fears are groundless. Another hour and we'll all be back on board. This bothered the officer. Major Peters was strictly professional military and always followed through with his plans. Before leaving the ship he gave the lieutenant seven code words to use in order to prove his identity. During two conversations, he hadn't used a single one. The young officer reviewed his data. The teams had been on the ship for over an hour. He was beginning to monitor communication traffic. The voices were recognizable as his shipmates. The major had forbidden him to contact them. He was only to speak to the major until released from his orders. He had to make a decision.

"Michelle?"

"Yes, Steve." Was it his imagination or was the girl becoming even more gorgeous.

"I need to speak to Major Peters. It's urgent!"

"Okay. Our internal comm link is down. I'll send someone from the bridge to fetch him for you. It should take no more than fifteen minutes."

"Can't you have someone contact him faster than that?" The girl's face fell into a pout.

"I'm doing the best I can under the circumstances. I didn't think you would be so pushy!" Oh, great , thought the young man, I've lost my date with her for sure. The girl temporarily left the screen. When she returned, she was all smiles again.

"Okay. It should only take a couple minutes," she said in a perky voice. Then she launched into a new fascinating discussion. The lieutenant was so engrossed that twenty minutes slipped by before he noticed.

"Oh my gosh!" he cried, "the time!" Just then, the major's voice came on line. Again, he avoided the code word question. When pressed, the major's tone of voice changed. He accused the lieutenant of being delusional and threatened him with disciplinary action if he didn't stop demanding the passwords. The lieutenant was thoroughly disturbed by the end of that conversation. He politely said goodbye to the girl and closed the channel to the freighter.

Beta Twenty-Two reported to Alpha One, "I think we've strung him along about as long as we can. He's contacting the other ships." The alien leader didn't respond verbally. He used his implant to talk to his workers directly. Flipping channels quickly, he contacted each one and received a status update. When he reached the alien in charge of communications he ordered him to signal the subspace jammers to activate. Moving quickly, he then ordered the computer viruses, released previously into the planet's network, to come alive. The Minari then ordered that all communications be blocked from the guard cutters to the colony. All this took place in the space of a few seconds.

The young officer had just started to get off a warning to the other two ships when the communications system went down. He tried the subspace link, no response. The lieutenant tried all the back up systems. Dead. Only the direct line-of-sight laser system worked. It was usually reserved only for battle stations. He contacted the other two ships and explained the situation. They agreed that something was wrong.

"Human ships assuming defensive posture. Weapons systems powering up," said one of the aliens manning a sensor station.

"Is the major revived yet?" asked Alpha One.

"No sir, twenty more minutes, minimum."

"Well, things should have progressed along far enough for us to jump start him. Have Alpha Six merge with his Minari nervous system and access the human's mind. Get the code words and call me when ready."

The young lieutenant was about to fire a warning shot across the Star of India 's bow when the major's face appeared on the viewscreen. "What in 'tarnation are you doing. Disengage those weapons systems immediately!"

"Give me the proper response and I will, sir." Without batting an eye, the major repeated all seven of the secret word phrases that only he and the lieutenant knew. The officer slowly let out his breath. Whew, that was close. He signaled the other ships to disengage their weapons.

"Hook up with the ship. Doc and I are coming aboard. Have the other ships standing by to supply more teams for repair duty. In three hours we leave for Keynan." He snapped off the link. The young officer never had the chance to tell his superior about the breakdown in communications. It took some time to maneuver the ship into docking position. He could see Major Peters and the doctor through the view port. The Star of India 's hatch opened. The doctor stepped through.

"Put out your arm," he said. "I have to vaccinate everyone." Obediently, lieutenant complied. The hypo hissed, and the young man's body hit the deck. The two left him laying there and entered the cutter.

Three hours later, all four ships accelerated to full speed and headed back in system toward the colony. Newly infected crews were locked in their bunk compartments. Communications silence was strictly maintained. Although concerned about the lack of communications, observers from the space station's observatory could detect nothing out of the ordinary. The station's commanding officer ordered shuttles to be used to ferry messages back and forth to the colony, until the links were fixed. So aside from putting two small shuttles on a five hour rotation to the planet's surface and back, they did nothing. Being somewhat of a backwater system, the guardsmen lacked hard military experience. Most of their operations consisted of search and rescue, with an occasional pirate or smuggler to chase. The station also lacked sophisticated sensors that might have revealed that the jamming of normal space communications was man-made, not a natural phenomenon. The sun in this system had flared before, knocking the links outs for hours at a time. The subspace net, however, was another matter. It hadn't failed for more than an hour at a time in over thirty years. Still, the CO wasn't concerned. After all, his ships were escorting the Star of India back to the station, they could handle themselves.

The three starship captains thought differently. Using line-of-sight communications, they talked about the events. The captains had all read and discussed the strange info-net posting, warning of an alien invasion. It was being discussed all over the planet. The captains had initially laughed it off as being far fetched, but, being seasoned spacefarers, they had seen some strange things in their time. As a result, they kept one eye on developments. When the subspace net and the in-system communications net failed, it got their attention. Further conversations with the military authorities revealed that the net in this area hadn't been down this long in over a generation and, no, the guard ships hadn't communicated with the base since accelerating this direction. What's the problem? they asked.

That did it. One too many coincidences. The captains, one after another, informed the station personnel that due to the circumstances, they were taking their ships out of orbit and away from the planet until the authorities could sort things out.

The first starship pulled out of orbit and accelerated in the opposite direction from the arriving flotilla. The other two vessels, the Cymer and the Arizona , ran into more immediate problems. Computer viruses released by the aliens had destroyed the maneuvering software controls as soon as the engines were activated. While the crew struggled with that problem, the main computer shut down without warning and wouldn't restart. Various independent systems then went crazy, compounding the issue. The Arizona was forced to take to their spacesuits, when the life-support system failed. After this information was relayed to the captain of the starship boosting away from the planet, it was enough to scare him into ordering an immediate jump to hyper-space. That was the only ship that managed to escape the impending chaos.

Meanwhile, the alien flotilla contacted the station using the laser comm. "General Oats, sir, Major Peters on line for you. He's been authenticated." The general put down his drink.

"It's about bloody well time!" He hit the connection. "Peters, where the hell have you been? We've been trying to reach you for hours. Is everything all right?" The image of the major appeared on the screen.

"Sorry, sir, we have been busy fighting a radiation fire. The freighter had some wounded to attend to and it took a lot longer than I anticipated getting things under control. Of course the system-wide communications failure didn't help things. Is there word on when it might be repaired?" The major's grimy face smiled disarmingly.

"No, we haven't a clue what's wrong. We were hoping you knew something about that."

"Nope, that's techie stuff, sir. I'm just an old soldier, born and bred."

"Right. What about the hijack rumor. Did you run that to ground?"

"Yes, sir. There was no evidence of a mutiny. We did establish that an individual was responsible for the condition of the craft." Peters then launched into the cover story about Ben Gardener's being responsible for the explosion. The general shook his head sadly.

"Major, we have a major PR problem here. Those starships in orbit bugged out a while ago. This communications thing plus that invasion rumor scared the pants of their captains. Now I'm being told that someone sabotaged two of the ship's computers. Sensors a while ago detected a message torp being fired at the planet. I can only imagine what those clowns said. It'll inflame the whole invasion conspiracy even more. The Governor is going to be most upset with us." An officer knocked on the general's open door. He motioned for him to come in.

"Sir, the Cymer is underway. Apparently they are manually operating the engines. She can't go too fast in that condition.

The Arizona still can't even get the life-support systems functioning." The general dismissed his aide.

"Major, did you copy that? Those idiots are trying to run the reactors manually. They're likely to blow themselves up."

"Sir, I'll assign one of my vessels to render assistance. We'll get to the bottom of this. I anticipate docking in forty-five minutes. Peters, out." The general snapped off the comm. and grabbed his drink. Peters was a good man. They were dammed lucky to get him to retire from the space marines and join the guard. Nothing to do but wait. He drained his glass.

Alpha One was deeply integrated with his command station. Surfing the data links, he monitored the progress of modifications to the guard vessels. Everything was proceeding to plan. The general's conversation with the Peters-host showed that the military had no inkling of what was happening. The message torpedo being sent to the planet below was troublesome. The triggers had not yet been pulled on the planetary computer viruses. The longer he waited, the more his converts could infiltrate the critical institutions on the planet. As soon as the viruses were launched, his forces would have to seize control. The factory modules were complete and ready for transport. A large supply of the DNA compound was stored, ready for distribution. Newly converted warriors and workers, sans crystals, were being programmed for the upcoming takeover of the space station. Alpha One shot off a message to the McGregor-host to launch the viruses manually as the message torp, in his opinion, required acceleration of the invasion plans.

The alien leader regretted that one of the starships got away. He could have used that ship. Perhaps some other luckless starship will enter the system and take its place. Alpha One proceeded to check and double check hundreds of tasks in the space of only a few seconds. A hundred more decisions came to him to resolve. At this stage of the invasion Alpha One preferred to micro-manage the operation. He knew that once the battle began he would have to cede control to Alpha Six and the Beta series warriors. The alien leader continued to fine tune his plans and download the changes to his subordinates.

As promised, one of the guard ships did not decelerate, but shot by the station on its way to intercepting the Cymer . During that time, the Arizona did finally manage to reboot their systems and to get one of the main engines partially on line. They limped slowly off in another direction. The aliens let them go. From the earlier communications with the space station, the starship admitted that no one had even begun realignment of the coils. That meant the Arizona couldn't jump for at least twenty-four hours and the alien invaders had time to spare. The Star of India , and one of the remaining two guard cutters, docked at the station. The other maintained a close orbit near the space station.

* * *

At the moment the hatches opened, all hell broke loose on the station. The main and back-up reactor shut down, plunging a large portion of the station into complete darkness. The internal comm system ceased functioning. Internal sensors relayed garbage to the command center. External bay doors opened, placing small and large spacecraft in a vacuum. Several technicians were sucked out into space. Main bulk heads slammed shut, isolating many section of the station. The enhanced bodies of the human hosts poured out the hatches of the two ships and stormed the station. The defenders, mostly unarmed, fell prey to the disrupter armed aliens. Pockets of humans managed to gain access to weapons and engaged the invaders. Large groups of civilians were captured and, to their horror, injected with the alien DNA . They were left to stagger to the floor. The invaders swept all resistance before them as they approached the command center. The situation in the command center was pure chaos.

Officers and technicians were shouting into portable comm units and each other. Pleas for help and disrupter fire were overheard on various channels. Guards milled around nervously fingering their weapons.

"General, as best we can determine, the station is being overrun," advised the station security officer. Mobile comm link traffic suggests that the invaders are coming from the freighter and our own vessel. Security doesn't want to fire on people they recognize as our own! We still can't raise the colony, either." The general strode from the tactical station to the security console.

"I simply can't believe our own guardsmen have joined this crazy plot. Can't you get video on these things?" ordered the general. "I've got see what's going on in order to organize a defense." The technician's fingers danced over the keys. He located a sole pick up in the reactor room. The general leaned in close to the holoscreen to get a close look at the figure.

"Sweet Jesus!" was all he said. The CO quickly made his way to the planetary emergency transmitter. This was one of several units at various locations around the colony. He keyed in his personal ID number and submitted to a retina scan. The clear lid popped open. The general selected GENERAL PLANETARY ALERT and HIGHEST PRIORITY ALL SHIPS from the menu. He then searched down the list for code 276, which stood for 'Hostile Alien Invasion—Compromise Anticipated'. He knew that over the years that these alert systems had been activated, code 276 had never been used. The general hit the engage button. The system was a CPU driven unit kept isolated from the rest of the station. It was highly guarded, and because of that safeguard hadn't been infected along with the main computer. However, the subspace transmitter said no message went out. In-system communications were still jammed, so no signal could be received. Fortunately, the line-of-sight laser messaging systems were still functional. One of the two fleeing starships, Arizona and Cymer , received the alert. The system tried to launch a series of message torpedoes, but most of the launch tubes failed to fire, only a couple operated properly. Unfortunately, the guard cutter orbiting the station blew them out of the sky before they got too far.

The general was sounding the evacuation just as the hatches to the command center were being burned open. Escape pods shot out from the station. A couple of tiny yachts managed to launch. Their crews had donned spacesuits and entered the airless hangers. Each was intercepted by the orbiting spacecraft and destroyed. Strangely, several fighters sat forlornly in the airless hanger, all the pilots either on planet or on the three ships sent to intercept the Star of India . Except for mopping up, the takeover was complete. One of the guard ships sped off to intercept the Arizona and the remaining ship prepared to launch after the Cymer .

The alien leader disconnected from his digital communications grid and was receiving analog input. His command staff congratulated him on a superb plan and brilliant execution. It took an hour to move his command to the space station. On the way, he continued to receive updates.

"The Arizona was neutralized ten minutes ago," said Beta Twenty-Two, "there was extensive loss of life. Fortunately for us, the crew was unable to get the main engines to go to automatic."

"That does not concern me," replied the Minari leader, "there are plenty of hosts to replace them on the planet. Tell me about the other starship, Cymer ."

"I have dispatched another ship to chase the Cymer . The vessel has a good head start and its trajectory has been tracked to the far side of the sun."

"Anticipated. I would do the same, try to shield my sensor footprint in the sun's corona and hope to find an asteroid field to hide in on the far side of the solar system. Recall the second ship. We can't spare it right now." Beta Twenty-Two acknowledged his leader's orders.

"The Arizona , before capture, re-transmitted the space station's planetary alert to the Cymer and to the starship that jumped. If other ships attempt to enter the system, the Cymer might try to warn them."

"That's a risk we'll have to take," replied Alpha One. "If they try to contact an incoming ship, they risk exposing their position. I need that ship, though, at all costs, understand?" Beta Twenty-Two nodded. Alpha Six was waiting in the space station's command center. Workers were already tearing open equipment panels and starting modifications.

"Greetings Glorious Leader. The thrill of battle once more runs in my veins. Thank you for the opportunity to serve you once again. I have an update." Alpha Six proceeded to tell his leader that the planetary computer viruses had been released. Beta-Eight had activated his forces and was in position to seize command and control junctures, utilities, communication centers, weapons depots, and the spaceport. He also reported that the message torp sent out by the Arizona did land on the planet and its contents were dumped on the net before the McGregor-host could shut down the webs. Several organizations had, as they put it, taken to the hills after reading it. Some ground forces had mutinied, questioning orders received from alien controlled superior officers. The general populace had withdrawn behind closed doors, apparently believing more in the invasion rumors than in their leaders.

The alien leader sighed, "Unfortunate. Although resistance is ultimately fruitless, our miscalculation of the human's behavior will cost us precious time and resources. Load the factory modules on shuttles and begin transport immediately. We need to manufacture and field crystals in a hurry!"

"As you wish, Alpha One."

Even before all the pockets of resistance on the space station were eliminated, the first shuttle took off for the Keynan Space Port. The Arizona reported in that all systems were restored. The Minari had their second fully functional starship. The Cymer , however, continued to elude capture. The human starship had most likely powered down and hidden behind debris. One lone Minari spaceship was going to have a difficult time playing cat and mouse in an area equivalent to one-forth the volume of the solar system. Shuttles returned from the surface carrying newly activated Minari workers. Beta level supervisors immediately set to programming new instructions and skills into their Theta level alien brains. Within an hour both Planetary Guard ships were in hangers, swarms of alien creatures were removing weapons, ripping out other critical components and disassembling them for upgrades. On the surface, the space port was firmly in Minari hands. The factory assembly was on schedule. Major arms depots and communication centers were under control.

The plans for conquest of the rest of the colony, however, were not going as planned. Groups of civilians, overpowered several of the minor depots, had made off with weapons and communications gear. Suspicious security personnel relieved Minari hosts of command and turned them over to medical personnel, who discovered alien tissue within. High volume fluid injection equipment was discovered in one of the offices of the deposed leaders, with the Minari virus. News of these events traveled like wildfire throughout the colony in spite of alien control of major communication centers. Minari commanders ordered ground forces to fire on one another, causing loss of human life. Lower ranking officers then took to scanning the bodies of their commanders and checking blood samples, looking for signs of the Minari virus. The civilian population began to evacuate the cities, not knowing who to trust.

At the height of the confusion, at 1530 hours, a lone navy destroyer entered the Keynea Solar System.

"Naval Destroyer Rockow to Keynan Space Station, come in please?" The requests played out over the station's speakers.

"Don't answer!" warned Alpha One. With both cutters in the hangers being retrofitted, and the third on the far side of the sun, the alien leader was left with only the Star of India to pit against the destroyer. To top it off, the naval vessel came out of hyper-space only two hours from the station. "Alpha Six, take command of the freighter, intercept the military vessel. Beta Twenty-Two, signal the Rockow , using low power line-of-sight, that a severe sun flare has burnt out all our transmitters. Subspace communications are also down for unknown reasons. We'll send out the Star of India to upload new information using towed array and to ferry colonial representatives to pay their respects to the ship's captain." Alpha One considered another trick. "Are their weapons systems on stand-by or powered up?"

"Neither, Master."

"Good, then they still don't suspect. Find copies of colony news broadcasts several days old. Edit them to make it look like live broadcasts. Allow sporadic transmissions to escape the jamming net. That will help keep them unsuspecting a while longer."

It worked so well, the destroyer never even raised its shields and took data feeds uncensored from the Star of India . The crew was caught completely off guard when the ship's sensors crashed and every bridge command and control system shut down. They were still trying to assess the cause when the bridge took a point blank blast from the Star of India .

With ship's communications paralyzed, the bridge holed and lifeless, critical systems failed or failing, the Minari warriors from the freighter stormed the ship and killed almost the entire crew. Immediately the aliens set about repairing the ship. The computer bugs were removed and the auxiliary bridge was put in working order. The main computer brought back on line, all within two hours.

"Alpha One, our Glorious Leader, Alpha Six reports that the Rockow is under our jurisdiction and will soon be operational," stated Beta Twenty-two.

"Six is aggressive," observed the alien leader. "We need aggressive right now. Those betas on the planet are not aggressive enough. Is the Space Port still under siege?"

The underling answered, "Our forces have pushed back a human offensive to the mainland, where they have dug in. The defenders are well armed and organized. Our strike force is ten kilometers to the north and attempting to link up with the Space Port units. Other units report stiff resistance with humans fleeing the area in high numbers."

"Conversions?" queried Alpha One.

"They have slowed. We are at twenty percent. Only the infirm, old or very young remain in the major metropolitan areas. The colonial defenders appear to have guessed our tactics; they block our moves to come against the population directly. We are falling behind schedule." The alien leader considered his options. He needed large numbers of workers to build weapons and equipment. While his forces were tied up in military operations, they couldn't carry out the next phases of his plan.

The alien leader spoke to the beta manning the comm unit, "Order unrestricted aerial bombardment on resistance forces. Suspend order 52768." The beta-alien assigned to communications hesitated. "Send the order!" Alpha One barked. The alien assumed a subordinate position.

"Sir," the beta trembled, "a suicide attack earlier destroyed the aerospace fighters. We have no ships left except space shuttles. The humans have expended all their aircraft against the Space Port and other targets. What few missiles the colony had were used early on in the battle. At the moment neither side can mount an effective air attack, nor does the Keynan colony have any ground armor. Bombardment from space is our only alternative."

The alien leader sat in stunned silence. A war of attrition. We will win, of course, but time is of the essence! These humans are much more aggressive than the Gaderians , he thought. Who would have thought that they could have put up such a fight on so short a notice? It must have been that message Forest put through. Beta-eight did not recognize the danger of the info-net posting. His previous host, McGregor, did not contain the appropriate life experiences that could have prepared him for this and mass psychology was not one of Beta-eight's strong points. Enough of the colonists had developed contingency plans to allow the humans to organize. This explains the unplanned transfer of a fighter wing, just before the space station was attacked, and why several ground units suddenly found it necessary to go on maneuvers just before a major planetary holiday. And then there were those survival groups that the media ridiculed constantly. They believed the posting explicitly. Yes, we missed the signs. These mistakes will not be repeated on the next system. An alarm beeped beside the alien leader. He inserted a tentacle and made connection.

"Alpha Six here. The destroyer's data banks indicate that a small naval force has been dispatched to the Kenyea solar system. They are five or six hours behind the Rockow . I suggest marshaling our forces at the jump point."

"Agreed! Stand-bye." Alpha One changed channels. "Issue instructions for the two cutters, as well as every ship, to disembark and join up with the Rockow and the Star of India under Alpha Six's leadership. Send the starship, Arizona , to the far side of the planet, opposite the probable entry point of the human ships. Concentrate remaining space station forces on bolstering station defenses. Cancel general order 32445, issue orders 67546, 23455, and 78887. Ready a shuttle. I must initiate the startup of the factory personally." He switched back. "Alpha Six, you are in charge until I return. Assume pinwheel attack/defense formation."

CHAPTER ELEVEN

CAPTAIN FOREST, Jack and Erin insisted he use the title, drilled his team ruthlessly for the first two hours of the flight. They performed well against three or less fighters, but not as well against the same number of larger capital ships. The humans had trouble coordinating actions as the situations became more complex. At the end of the training scenario, Jack lectured on strategy and gave them his opinion of their fighting ability.

"Against two fighter spacecraft or one larger ship, you should do fine. Any more than that and you're pushing the envelope. Remember, avoid battles that exceed these odds. Erin and I agree that given the current level of human technology, you can probably handle more; however, let me remind you that these Minari may have modernized their weapons systems. That's why you have always practiced against Gaderian technology. If you can hold your own there, then human technology should prove no problem." Captain Forest dismissed his tired crew to catch up on some must needed rest as Erin informed the group that only three hours remained until breakout into the target solar system.

Ben's chair reclined and molded around his body to form a comfortable bed. "Jack, are you there?" he asked. A small image of the AI's head floated into view.

"Yes, oh exalted master of artificial intelligence!"

"Cut it out you clown," the young man replied. "What are our chances?" The AI took a deep breath.

"Average. You have the advantage of surprise, which you took away from the Minari. There are a few more months of technology advancement in this ship than what existed at the end of the Minari-Gaderian war. It's a slim advantage, but an advantage nonetheless. The triple redundant shields are a new development. The Guardian database had not logged a similar usage by the aliens, and no such equipped ships had been reported captured. That's good. If they do have it and developed a weapon to pierce it, then that's not so good." Ben pulled the blanket up around his neck.

"If I'm able to utilize the mind link more fully, does that raise our chances?" asked Ben.

"Considerably. That's what this ship was designed for. But at your level of attainment there is a danger of overload. You could freeze up during battle and leave the ship defenseless. Don't get me wrong, you have made incredible progress to date, but don't push it." Ben nodded and drifted off to sleep. Presently, all that could be heard were snores. Erin and Jack walked among the sleeping crew.

"Can they win?" asked the female hologram, appearing beside Ben's AI. Jack turned to look at his peer, his face deep in thought. "I don't know. I've seen them beat the odds before." His image began to fade. "We'll just have to see." The other AI nodded.

* * *

At 0300 hours, colony time, the crystal manufacturing sequence was initiated. Alpha One's presence was required to supply the critically missing code, without which the factory would not function. No other Minari were allowed to hold this information. Alpha One had built this subconscious command into the minds of every Minari. Alpha One's master plan was to keep absolute control of the DNA virus and the manufacture of crystal modules. Workers rushed the completed crystals into the battlefield, providing memory modules to Minari relying on purely organic brains. Some aliens, already outfitted with lesser crystals, were given a Star Crystal upgrade. Within two hours the outnumbered Minari had reorganized. Utilizing superior tactics and firepower, they began to advance steadily on the larger pockets of civilian population. Several raids by the humans had been beaten back severely. Sensing a change in the caliber of alien command, the humans abandoned counterattacks and concentrated on fortifying their defensive positions. At 0515 hours, the human task force, under the command of Admiral Corella, winked into existence and headed towards the planet. Waiting for them one hundred thousand kilometers to the stern, was the Minari fleet. Using sensor trickery, the aliens were able to dramatically close the gap without being seen. Also observing the entrance of the task force was the Cymer, hiding from one the Minari ships. Seeing the unsuspecting fleet about to be ambushed, the captain decided to risk a tight beam warning.

"Admiral," asked the captain of the carrier, "may I have a word with you, sir?" The admiral turned away from his Gaderian consultant, the eminent Dr. Michael Gardner.

"Yes, what is it?"

"Sir, we received a laser comm message from the Cymer, a starship on the other side of the solar system. Its captain claims that this system has been under attack for several days by unknown forces. He says that he knows of a hostile fleet in our vicinity, using some sort of cloaking technology. The captain further reports that the transmissions we are receiving from the planet are faked." The admiral contemplated the information.

"Can you confirm any of this?"

"The Cymer's registration checks out and it was scheduled to be in system. Sensors don't detect ships in orbit or anywhere in the vicinity of our carrier group. It's a small system, so that shouldn't be unusual. Video-net transmissions appear to be normal." The admiral interrupted him.

"What about the Rockow and my daughter, any word?"

"Uh, no. We have tried to contact your daughter using the standard communication systems, but all we get are busy signals or no one at home. The Rockow hasn't responded . . . ."

"Message from the Rockow coming in, sir!" The officer's voice could be heard over the din of the bridge chatter.

The admiral commanded, "Put him through to my chair." He activated the hologram. "Dan, where are you?" Only audio issued from the hologram.

"Lieutenant Davidson, here. The captain and his senior staff are interviewing the crew of the Star of India . Planetary authorities apprehended her just outside this system. She had been hijacked, sir." Dr. Gardener overheard the name of the ship.

"My God, my son was on the vessel! Is he all right?"

Admiral Corella put his hand on the archeologist's shoulder, "I'll find out as soon as we figure out what's going on." The admiral turned back to the display. "Davidson, why is your video feed off? And where is your ship? What about the planetary alert."

"The alert was a false alarm. We are in a stationary orbit on the far side of the planet with the freighter in tow. We had a slight accident and lost some of our communications capability. We'll have it fixed shortly." Corella hit the mute button. "Can you trace the source of this transmission?" The sensor officer studied his console and shook his head negative. "Odd." He un-muted the call. "Lieutenant, find the captain immediately."

"I'll try, sir, it may take some time," was the reply.

"You have two minutes or you'll find yourself on report!" snapped the admiral. He slapped the comm switch off. "This is damn odd!"

"Why didn't you ask about my son?" asked Dr. Gardner. Admiral Corella chewed on his lower lip, a bad habit his wife was always pointing out.

"Because something is not right here. Captain?"

"I agree, sir. I suggest we go over the inconsistencies."

"Proceed," said the admiral.

The captain recited the evidence, "The sub-space net has been down for days. A planetary alert was issued using your own security codes. The Rockow , sent in advance to scout out the situation, is not here to greet us. A ship identifying as the Cymer claims we are walking into a trap. We can't contact anyone we trust on the planet. And then there is that wild message a Commander Forest sent, that started this whole thing. Even without using a tactical analyst to calculate the odds, I'd say that chances are the proverbial shit is about to hit the fan."

The admiral considered this advice. Under normal circumstances, he would have sent only a couple of ships to investigate. However, his own daughter was on the planet. She was attending the festival along with a classmate from the colony. When Naval Intelligence finally got off their asses and passed the alien threat message up the chain of command, he had diverted to Cyprus in the Iberian Solar System in order to collect an expert on Gaderian subject matter. Dr. Gardener's examination of the probe's symbols and opinion on the history of the Gaderian demise appeared to bolster Attendant Blaxx's story. At the time, Corella was sure this was some sort of trick, a hoax. He only got involved personally because his daughter was on the planet in question. Now, doubt nagged him. A feeling of dread filled the pit of his stomach. Could this be a colossal disaster in the making?

"Captain Charles," ordered Corella, "detach a courier from the task force to return immediately to hyper-space and transmit a message to my headquarters. Upload all the information received to this minute. Include orders for mobilization of the Fifty-First Interplanetary Fleet. I want them here, now, loaded for bear!" He stood up from his chair. "Commander, put the carrier group on yellow! Tactical, I want either myself or Captain Charles informed of all unusual sensor readings immediately." He stepped down from his command platform.

"Dr. Gardner, I'm afraid that the original message that Commander Forest sent with your son's help may be genuine. If so, God help us, because we could be in for serious fight. I need you to brief me more about Gaderian technology and what you know about the race that destroyed them." The two men retired to the admiral's private wardroom.

The Cymer accelerated hard to port, then to starboard at a forty-five degree down angle. The blasts were coming closer. The ship lurched and the lights flickered. A technician shouted, "Aft screens down! Our backside is exposed!" The captain considered his options. He may have saved the task force from ambush, but at the cost of his ship and all those who served her. Was it worth it? The starship continued evasive maneuvers. The ship lurched again. This time the lights went out for good and emergency beacons lit the bridge. A computerized voice informed the crew that the artificial gravity generators had lost main power and would fail in one-hundred and twenty seconds.

"Rig for free fall!" ordered the captain. "What happened to our reactor? Why has our acceleration ceased?" Technicians were shouting into comm units, trying to raise anyone in engineering. The captain felt himself growing lighter. He grabbed the railing. His first officer pushed away from the sensor station and propelled himself toward the captain. Having managed to lock arms in the now weightless environment the captain was able to reel in his officer.

"Sir," the first officer yelled over the din, "The reactor was hit. It was a clean shot; missed the hyperdrive coils.

Engineering is holed. Everyone is dead. They knew right where to hit us!"

"We have to make ready to repel boarders!" cried the captain.

"No need, sir. They packed up and left. The guard vessel is heading, at high acceleration, back to the colony."

"Why? They have us right where they want us."

"Sir, we aren't going anywhere. There is no way we can fix that reactor and get under way without dock facilities," explained the Cymer's first officer.

"Do you believe they plan to assist with the attack on the task force, and then return to collect us?" concluded the Cymer's captain.

"Yes, sir."

"Can we get a direct line to the carrier, ask for help?" asked the captain.

"Too many obstructions in the way and to top it off, we are tumbling. Normal communications are still jammed," replied the officer.

"Life's a bitch sometimes isn't?" commiserated the captain.

"Yes, sir," the officer sighed.

Back on the carrier, the admiral and captain conferred with the tactical officers and technicians.

"I say the anomaly could be hiding several ships," insisted an engineer, pointing to the area in question on the screen.

"You say it has been following us?" asked the captain. "How do you know it's not some sort of sensor reflection?"

"Because reflections move in parallel courses and vary in intensity. This anomaly does not vary in size or shape. It is moving on a parabolic course and is accelerating towards us! It can't be a natural phenomenon or a sensor glitch!"

The admiral nodded. "Captain, I think we have the answer to whether or not an alien invasion is taking place here. Dr. Gardner informs me that Gaderian records describe this scenario as being used several times against unsuspecting naval forces: false messages, crossed signals, cloaked ships, jammed communications. Look, we can't find the source of the jamming. Our own jamming satellites would light up every screen in the galaxy. That's why we deploy large numbers of them. Fleet technology isn't advanced enough to cloak several ships operating at these high speeds, and there is something obviously closing in on us." He tapped his fingers on the console. "We are going to have turn and face it head on."

"Admiral," responded the captain, "I request that we send a small force on ahead to reconnoiter the colony and render assistance that might be needed."

"Good idea. We can send an escort ship and, oh let's say, twenty-five fighters." The captain nodded. "Has the courier ship jumped yet?" He glanced in the direction of the sensor console.

"No, sir. It's approaching the assigned jump point." The technician gasped. "Debris! Sirs! Sensors indicate an expanding cloud of debris where the ship was last noted. They must have gotten her!" The admiral paled at the news.

"Sound general quarters. Full power to shields. Reverse direction, plot an intercept course with that anomaly. Change data encryption every fifteen minutes, select delta-delta 7. Launch twenty-five fighters, now! Prepare to launch the balance on my mark." He turned to the captain. "Go ahead with your plan to send a ship to the planet." The captain punched up the command authorization and encrypted the orders. "All right people, listen up. Let's do what we're trained for. No mistakes. No panic. Just kick'em in the ass and make it hurt!" The bridge erupted into cheers that quickly subsided as everyone got down to business.

The Gaderian Interceptor sped through hyper-space, its crew fast asleep. Erin 's image popped into existence. "Rise and shine humans. Fifteen minutes until entry into the Keynea Solar System." Everyone in the Gaderian fighter jumped up and made a mad dash for the head. Ben was a little slow and had to wait in line. He nervously bounced from one leg to the other. Finally, his turn came and he relieved himself. After splashing water on his face, the young man came out and headed to the food replicators. There were four glasses of a brown liquid sitting on the counter.

"No solid food, Ben," said Jack. "Drink this high energy meal instead. It's fortified with high-octane vitamin and mineral supplements. It even tastes good." The young man drank it down. Jack was right, it was good. The others downed their own glasses and took their stations. Ben sat down in his chair. A feeling of invincibility came over him. All inward feelings of nervousness disappeared. I wonder , he thought, did those two AI's spike these drinks with some sort of stimulant? No matter, whatever they did, it was working! Erin stood by the pilot's chair, occupied by Captain Forest, facing the cabin.

"Drop out in sixty seconds." Everyone tightened down their harnesses. Ben slipped the implant into place. He slid down the mind tunnel and expanded to occupy the tactical and counter measures systems. He felt Jack squeeze in beside him to fill the computer operational environment. He was vaguely aware of Erin 's presence scattered about the virtual reality landscape. Odd, she had the faint scent of flowers about her. Ben contemplated the sensation. His mind's interpretation of the data being presented manifested in all five senses. Time slowed to a crawl. Ben heard Erin call out "four." The disembodied young man selected various sensors to 'see' the space surrounding the ship. The blur of hyper-space no longer bothered him. He was aware of the ship, its location in space in relation to the vast galaxy, the crew at their stations, the status of the sub-light engines . . . Two . . . , the frequencies generated by the coils . . . One. The ship was suddenly in real space. The captain slammed the power controls forward and the little ship leaped ahead.

"Tactical, what do you have for me?" Ben reached out in his mind with his hand. Yes, those were ships out there. He touched one, felt it. This must be a naval vessel. Lincoln Class escort vessel. Here are some more. His fingers brushed up against the carrier. The little fighters tickled the hairs on the back of his hand.

"Jack, this feels like the Star of India ."

"I agree. Looks like they've been busy with some modifications. See those disrupters there?" pointed out Jack.

"Yea, Gaderian design. These must be planetary defense vessels. Whoops, non-human modifications. What's that cloud around the ships," asked the young man.

"Got to be cloaking." Ben felt some pricking on his skin.

"Ouch, they know we're here. Trying to block my sensor scans. I'm getting conflicting scents as well. Let me adjust things. There, that's better. Look at the jamming going on. There goes a human ship to the colony. The navy has split up its forces. Okay, update Eric's display."

"Roger that." The whole exchange took milliseconds. As far as Captain Forest was concerned, as soon as he asked the question the tactical display appeared on all their holoscreens, along with the coordinates pre-loaded into the navigation system. Forest hit the engage button and the little ship raced in towards the ensuing battle.

"Jack, see that light haze that fills the solar system. It looks like haze and smells like . . . like deodorant," pointed out Ben. "That would have to be a signal suppression field. The heaviest concentrations are here and here, they must be the source of the jamming. There appear to be encrypted patterns of the same scent traveling through the field. Ben thought about that analogy for a moment. "I understand. The Minari must be able communicate while our side can't. See if you can break into their command system and shut it down. Eric is going to need normal communications soon, if we are going to coordinate our attacks with the Navy." Jack partially withdrew from Ben's presence. The disembodied young man felt the ship's communication system go into operation. He turned his attention to the planet ahead and to the right. He reached out his hands.

Alpha Six's head jerked back. It can't be. A Gaderian vessel, here? In this system? Alpha One's information virtually guaranteed that this was an impossibility. He read the scans. Humans. There are humans on that ship! The alien processed the information. The THX unit must have led them to the ship. How many days has it been since we left the Lomax system? Three. Three days are not enough to become proficient with a Gaderian Naval Interceptor. He ordered several small ships to intercept the Gaderian fighter. These were assorted small vessels, retooled into competent little fighters by the Minari technicians. If all went well, he would dispatch the carrier task group within the hour and then turn his attention to the fighter, assuming it survived his welcoming committee. Alpha Six always tried to anticipate every contingency. He opened a channel to Alpha One, AAA priority.

* * *

Back on the carrier, an officer's voice rang out, "All fighters in attack position and standing by. Escorts positioned for maximum covering fire. Anomaly coming in range. Anomaly dissolving." There was a brief silence. "I have four large ships and several small fighter-class vessels emerging. One of them is the Rockow , Captain. I'm scanning." The captain's chair spun around to view the main sensor display. The officer continued, "Heavy damage to bridge area. Weapons powering up. Strange, the energy profile doesn't match the Rockow 's specifications."

"Science, jump on that and get me some answers," ordered the captain as he spun his chair around to face the admiral. "Sir, the enemy has shown us its hand." Dr. Gardner sat at the aide's station, intently studying ancient Gaderian files. "We must assume the Rockow is a hostile. Permission to tight-beam the other ships."

"Permission granted. Dan must be dead. Look at the size of the hole in that ship. The whole bridge must have been wiped out with one shot!" The admiral shook his head. He knew Dan's wife personally.

"Sensors indicate another ship just exited hyper-space and is headed our way," alerted the tactical officer.

The captain swiveled around. "Friend or foe?"

"Ship's configuration is unknown. Shield configuration doesn't match anything we've got. Weapons and propulsion energy profile is close to, but is not an exact match to the alien fleet's. Sir, that thing is really moving. It'll be here in less than one hour. Uh, oh; three fighter-class vessels have broken off from the main body and are on an intercept course with the newcomer. How shall I classify her, sir?" asked tactical.

"Alien, probable hostile. Mr. Mead?" replied the captain.

"Aye, sir?" said Mr. Mead.

"Any luck with hailing that vessel?"

"Jamming still in place, sir."

"Keep trying to break through." The captain looked up at the tactical display. "Admiral, we are in position."

The admiral took a deep breath, held it, and expelled. "You may begin the attack."

* * *

Alpha Six's urgent message was received at the crystal factory. So , thought Alpha One, they have not run away as I thought, but have chosen instead to return and fight. He entered the shuttle and strapped in. The craft lifted and began to climb toward the sky, engaging in evasive maneuvers to foil attempts to shoot it down. He wasn't worried about the human navy. They were predictable and slow, and their technology wouldn't stand up to the Minari's. No, he wasn't worried about them, they were a known quantity. This

Gaderian Interceptor, however, was a complete unknown. The ship's configuration was not on record. The ship's shields were unlike any before seen by the Minari. The implication was alarming, to say the least. The humans aboard were equally alarming. They had survived all his traps and wiggled their way out of seemingly impossible situations. This little band of humans was unique in that respect. Alpha One resolved to deal with them himself. The starship, Arizona , left orbit at high speed.

"Incoming! Jennifer, Hemant prepare to fire. Tina, full power to shields!" Captain Forest gripped the manual controls and studied the tactical hologram. Ben was proposing several strategies via the computer. Forest selected one and glanced back at the young man. Ben sat silently in his chair and stared straight ahead, unseeing. The minutes crept by slowly as the ships came within range. Jennifer opened fire first. The lead ship's screens crackled with energy and veered off. The enemy opened fire. The interceptor bucked and heaved. In blink of an eye, the remaining ships sped past. Forest threw the controls over and the little ship spun on its axis and changed course. The stabilizers and dampers whined in protest. The alien ships, designed for in-system transport, could not react as quickly. They did, however, have weapons and shields that were considerably more powerful than human technology. The interceptor took some hits as the captain closed in on one of the alien fighters, who turned to confront its attacker. The shields held firm. Hemant poured disrupter fire into the forward screens of the enemy. They finally collapsed and a dark hole formed in the nose of the craft. As the interceptor sped past, Hemant raked the entire side of the vessel with fire, tearing great chunks out of her hull. The captain rolled the ship away from the alien fighter as Jennifer found the engine room within her sights. The blast punctured the reactor, flooding the ship with white hot plasma. The other two ships had regrouped and were converging on the Gaderian vessel. Forest spun the ship again and reversed course. The ship shot forward heading straight for the two aliens. This time, neither alien fighter veered away, but continued to concentrate fire on the interceptor. Erin appeared beside the captain.

"Forward screens weakening, at fifty percent," she said in a matter-of-fact tone.

"Tina, give me more power to the forward shields!" the captain ordered.

"You have all I've got. Anymore and this thing might overload. I don't have a feel for how far we can push it." Forest considered for a moment. Ben made a suggestion via the display, Lay mines. The captain smiled. "Hemant, dump a spread of mines out behind us. Those human designed ships aren't as nimble as us. I have an idea."

"Ready to launch," Hemant said.

"Now!!" As the mines floated out the aft tubes, just behind the ship, the Gaderian vessel made a sudden course change, ninety degrees to the vertical. However, the mines, driven by momentum, continued on a straight course. Heavily shielded, the Minari didn't spot them until too late. One ship, having plowed right into a mine, exploded. The remaining alien craft managed to avoid the impromptu mine field and continued after the humans. The interceptor looped over the top of the enemy vessel. Jennifer and Hemant had tactical solutions and using concentrated fire they quickly beat down the enemy's shields. It veered off wildly, trying to avoid the fate of the other ships. The engine room was hit and exploded, splitting the ship in two. Captain Forest pulled out of the loop and resumed course towards the main battle, now in progress.

Smoke filled the bridge of the carrier. Admiral Corella picked himself up and yelled for a status report. The smoke, sucked out by the ventilation system, began to clear.

"We were hit mid-ship, sir. Launch and recovery tubes on the starboard side are out of action. Starboard screens have failed completely, port screens are down to twenty-nine percent. Forward screens are at forty percent." The captain hauled himself back into his seat and started issuing orders.

"Helm, keep the starboard side of the ship aimed away from the Rockow . Get damage crews on the launchers, now! We need to recycle the fighters."

The admiral punched up the battle display. The fighter squadrons were down to less than half strength. The alien weaponry cut right through their shields. Only the fighters' great maneuverability allowed the survivors to escape. The damage inflicted on the alien's capital ships was light. They'd had better luck with the smaller vessels the Minari scrounged up from the space station hangers. One of the escort ships was dead in space, radiation fires glowing through holes in the hull. The other two were slugging it out with the freighter and the planetary guard ships. The carrier's weapons fired shot after shot at the Rockow , to no effect. The Rockow responded by shooting the weapons pods, one after another, slowly disarming the big ship. A flurry of missiles from the carrier temporarily chased the Rockow away. The destroyer undertook a series of evasive maneuvers to elude the self guided torpedoes, while the gunners targeted their destruction.

"Admiral, we are using up missiles at an incredible rate. We have maybe one and a half more loads left before our stores run dry."

"I realize that, Captain, but it seems to be the only weapon we have that will penetrate their shields." One of the alien modified guard cutters broke apart on the tactical display. The admiral sat up and studied the screen. "Looks like Jonathan slipped a missile up her pipes. Good for him. One down." He moved the cursor to the left. "That new alien ship has taken out the fighters sent to intercept her. Tactical! Re-label that alien ship as a friendly. Order all vessels to assist as needed!"

"I don't understand why the Rockow doesn't finish us off," mused Dr. Gardner, strapped into his seat. "It's pretty obvious that they have superior weaponry."

"Because they want us intact," replied Admiral Corrella. "That's why all their shots are well away from our engineering section. A ship this size, with alien technology, would be virtually unstoppable anywhere in the galaxy."

An aid stumbled though the haze and addressed the officers, "Sirs, some of the jamming has ceased. We can utilize normal space communications; however, subspace is still down. Status reports have been uploaded to your terminals." The commanders punched up the reports. The escort ship, sent ahead to the planet, reported that they had made contact with the human defenders. Battles raged across the colony. The alien invasion force consisted of — both men could hardly believe their eyes — alien controlled colonists. A brief description of the infection was included. Pictures of highly modified humans accompanied the text. The twenty-five fighters detailed to the planet had been organized to strafe enemy positions and keep the aliens from advancing further. A starship had left orbit at high speed, ignoring the rescue ship and headed in the task force's direction. Dr. Gardener read his copy with great interest.

"This explains it!" the doctor exclaimed.

"It explains what?" asked the captain.

"Why we could never pin down what this species was that wiped out the Gaderians. It wasn't a mysterious external alien race that conquered them, it was the Gaderians themselves! A civil war!" The admiral looked at Dr. Gardener with uncomprehending eyes.

"Don't you see?" said the doctor. "This virus that the colonists refer to must have somehow infected the Gaderian population. It caused a civil war between the infected and uninfected inhabitants of the sector. The lists of colonies reported as destroyed during the conflict must have referred to colonies whose entire populations were transformed into these creatures!" An incoming message interrupted questions. The main viewer displayed the hideous face of Alpha One.

Tentacles wound around his thick neck. His misshapen face leered at them. He barely resembled his human roots.

"This is Alpha One, exalted leader of the Minari, your conqueror and lord. Surrender your ships or be destroyed." Admiral Corella stepped forward.

"We will not surrender. I'll blow up our ships first," replied the admiral.

"You cannot. My ships have disabled those functions. The Rockow 's data banks were very specific about the locations of the self-destruct mechanisms on your ships." The captain looked over at the engineering section. The officer nodded his head affirmatively. The admiral and captain locked eyes.

"Then we will ram your ships and still destroy ourselves," answered the captain. The alien shrugged his shoulders.

"Do as you wish. It is of no consequence to me." Dr. Gardner came into the viewing angle of the pickup. He said something in the Gaderian language. Alpha One's eyes widened and he replied, also in Gaderian.

"Who is this one, who knows my native language so well?" demanded Alpha One.

The admiral responded, "Dr. Michael Gardener, an expert in Gaderian ancient history."

"Gardener, Gardener. That name is familiar. Oh yes, the same last name as that pest. Benjamin, I believe was his name." Dr. Gardener stepped forward, shaking.

"My son! What have you done with him, you beast!" Alpha One quickly consulted some internal files.

"What a fortunate circumstance this is - Benjamin's father. The universe is kind to me today." The alien shifted position. "It's not what I have done to your son, sir, but what I'm about to do." The signal cut off.

* * *

The interceptor had reached the edge of the main battle area. The task force was down to only one carrier escort; the other had been disabled and was drifting in space. Captain Forest took evasive action, avoiding the lines of fire coming from the closest cutter. He maneuvered the ship underneath the energy screens and got in close to the hull; Jennifer and Hemant were busy targeting weapons systems, sensor arrays, and critical systems. They fought silently, efficiently disabling large sections of the ship. The cutter's weapons could not come to bear on the interceptor. The port shield generator exploded. Captain Forest looped the Gaderain vessel away from the cutter and headed towards the next. The human fighters, loitering off away from the scene of the battle, spotted the hole in the cutter's defenses and swarmed in for the kill. The remaining human escort ship limped away as the Star of India and the Rockow converged on the Gaderian Interceptor. The humans were thrown back in their seats as blast after blast hit the ship. Erin appeared again to warn the captain that shield strength was being seriously drained and recommended withdrawal. Forest barely got them out of the crossfire. He headed out into deep space with the other two ships in hot pursuit.

"Jack, do you notice anything about our shield modulation?" Ben studied the floating graphs representing the three layers. An algorithm appeared before his eyes.

"No, the shields are operating within specs. What do you see?" An equation appeared.

"It has just occurred to me that if we altered the oscillations and parameters to match this equation, the efficiency would be much greater," commented the young man.

"I don't follow you."

"Don't you see it? The shields could be tuned up a bit. The pattern is right there in the data, plain as day," pointed out Ben.

"If you say so, but I don't see it. Are you sure you want to tinker with the shields, experimenting right in the thick of battle?" asked the AI.

"There are also some things we can do to the power plant and weapons arrays to improve our edge." Ben saw a light blink. "Message coming in from one of the starships. Let's monitor." The young man pulled back from the sensor array and concentrated on the communication system. An image appeared.

"Attention humans aboard Gaderian spacecraft!" Alpha One's image spoke.

"Karl, give it up! You know it's us!" responded Forest .

"I am not Karl. I am Alpha One, the exalted leader of the Minari, master of the universe. You are humans. You are fit only to be hosts for my people."

"Oh stuff it!" said Tina, "you didn't call us just to have a friendly little chat. Make your threats and get the hell off line so we can blow your ass out of the sky!"

"The facts are that you cannot survive. This freighter and destroyer are too strong for your vessel. The other humans can't help you; they can barely keep alive as it is. When I arrive in the starship, we will pen you in and destroy you." Ben sent a message via the tactical computer. He is right. The odds don't compute. Jack and I can't put a scenario together that has us winning this fight.

The captain responded, "We can always run for hyperspace and send for help. With enough human ships, we could overwhelm you. You aren't invincible, you know, even with your superior technology. Besides, this ship has a few secrets that will come in mighty handy to our navy. You lost two major ships. You aren't going to get two uninterrupted weeks to consolidate your forces like you did with the ancient Gaderians. When we show the navy the records of this battle and copies of the communications from the colony, they will order every ship in the sector to converge on this system. Warnings will go out to every human settlement." The alien leader said nothing for a few seconds.

"Is Benjamin there?" The crew could hear Ben's disembodied voice in the speakers. They looked over at his body sitting in the command chair. His eyes stared blankly and his lips didn't move.

"Yea, I'm here. Who does your hair? Dracula?" Ben had set the communications system to rebroadcast the conversation to the human task force. Bridge officers chuckled quietly at the expense of the alien leader.

"Ben, of all the opponents I have had, you are one of the most worthy. It has been most stimulating," congratulated the alien leader.

"I'm touched. Get to the point."

"Direct, as always." The alien leader thoughtfully chose his words, "If you run, you may never see your father again."

"Ha! He's safe in a system far from here. We can beat you there with time to spare, pick him up and still warn the rest of humanity," gloated Ben.

"I'm sorry to disappoint you, but your father is only twenty minutes from my location," sneered Alpha One. Ben instantly projected a sphere around the oncoming starship and found the damaged carrier within the search area. He opened a channel to the bridge of the ship. A crude representation of him appeared on the main viewer. The young man's face look concerned.

"Dad, are you on the carrier?" asked Ben.

"Who are you?" asked the admiral.

"That's my son," replied Dr. Gardener. "Yes, Ben I'm here. The military came and got me from the dig. Are, are you all right? Where are you?"

"I'll get back to you, Dad" Ben jumped back to his conversation with Alpha One. "What do you want?" the young man asked.

"Surrender your ship and I'll let you and your friends remain unconverted. After your civilization has been assimilated, you can have run of the universe," offered the alien.

Captain Forest , monitoring the conversation, said softly, "You know we can't do that, you monster. We would be more or less condemning the human race to death."

"Then I will capture Dr. Gardner and convert him into one of my servants. He will be my personal aide. There are all sorts of interesting enhancements we can make to his body. And Ben will have to live with the fact that he could have saved him, but didn't. You would like that, wouldn't you, Ben?" taunted Alpha One. Ben felt his blood run cold. He could hear his heart beating rapidly in his head.

"Steady, Ben, don't let him get to you," said Captain Forest .

"It's the least I could do to pay you back for all the trouble you caused," laughed the alien leader. The image was abruptly shut off.

Hemant looked at his console. "The signal is still there. It's been cut off at our end. Ben, did you do that?" There was no response. The Gaderian interceptor was pulling away from the pursuing ships.

"Tina, what's the status of the jump engines?" asked Captain Forest .

"Green light. We can be set up to jump inside of ten minutes." Ben felt himself becoming claustrophobic inside the ship's systems. He struggled to extract the implant. His awareness returned to his body, fingers fumbled with the probe. Jennifer unstrapped and went over to the young man. She brushed the hair out of his face.

"Ben, I'm so sorry," she said. He didn't answer. Ben felt sick to his stomach.

"Jennifer, return to your station," commanded Captain Forest . "Ben, are you okay? Ben, look, I know this going to be difficult for you. We have no choice. You said so yourself. We can't beat them by ourselves, we have to get help!"

Ben thought about all the good times he had with his father. He remembered his deceased mother. Tears streamed down his face as the emotions welled up inside. His dad had always been there for him, no matter what trouble he'd gotten into. A cold rage began to build. Adrenaline surged through his veins. The fire continued to grow until it consumed his thoughts. How dare that monster threaten his father, of all people?! He looked up at the faces of his concerned friends. Tina caught the cold glint in Ben's eyes and it scared her.

"Ben, I know that look. What are you planning to do?" cautioned the chief engineer. Ben stared down at the implant in his hand. He looked up with a determined look on his face.

"Win." That was all he said. The young man reached up and jammed the implant home.

Ben rushed down the tunnel at high speed. The power of the ship flowed into his body. He reached out with all his will and merged with the ship. The young computer genius felt himself pop into one system after another. His body expanded until . . . he was . . . the ship. Ben opened his eyes. He could see all directions at once. The two enemy vessels chasing the interceptor were falling behind, getting smaller. Not so fast , Ben thought. The Gaderian ship spun about and accelerated at top speed toward the oncoming ships.

" Erin !" said Ben. The artificial intelligence appeared before him. " Erin ," Ben commanded, "acknowledge override code Delta Theta Mark 3789-Alpha Tango. Engage and lock."

"Compliance. Neural-Pilot emergency override initiated. All manual controls are locked out for the duration of the emergency. Non-interference protocol in effect." Jack tried to squeeze in with the disembodied young man. Ben filled the virtual net so completely; there was little room for the AI to maneuver.

"Ben, how about a little room here?" the AI requested. Ben accommodated. "Ben, have we thought this through? Those are two capital ships out there!"

"Jack, do you trust me?" asked Ben.

"Of course I trust you. I have no choice, now that you just initiated a top level conditioned response. My programming forces me to trust you."

"Good, then shut up and listen," the young man ordered. A series of equations popped into existence. "I want you to reconfigure the weapons, shields and power plant to match these parameters. Have Erin re-compute the theoretical operating envelope based upon the new efficiencies." Ben could feel Jack making the necessary changes. He concentrated on the fast closing destroyer and freighter.

Back in the cabin, Captain Forest felt the controls jerk in his hand and then go limp. The ship spun around and accelerated so fast that the inertial dampers couldn't compensate. Forest was pressed back into his chair. " Erin !" he yelled. The female AI appeared. "What happened to the controls?!"

"Crewman Gardener has activated the full neural implant and has taken control of the ship. His command codes are confirmed and while in effect you are temporarily outranked."

"Ben, stop it! You'll get us killed!" yelled Captain Forest . The dampers finally caught up with the acceleration and Forest unlatched his harness to stand up. As he reached for the young man, a force field slammed him back into his chair.

"Non-interference protocol is in effect. You may not approach the Appointed One. He is in command now." The image of the AI, hands on her hips, stood between the captain and Ben.

"Tina?" Forest looked over at the engineer. She studied her displays.

"I'm locked out," Tina began. "He's making some significant changes to the fuel mix. Efficiency is soaring. Shields are going crazy as well. I don't recognize the energy pattern. Hemant?"

"I confirm engineering lockout, Captain. Weapons controls are also non-functional. Frequency modulations changing. Our young man appears to know something about this ship that that we don't," stated the science officer.

Ben allocated a tiny portion of his consciousness to monitor the cabin conversations. The rest was focused on strategies for defeating the much bigger vessels. He distributed the processing load to the ship's subprocessors and set Erin and Jack to managing the details. The disembodied Ben floated above the system and responded only to those queries that the AIs deemed worthy of his attention. Ben could sense the improvement in shields, power, and weapons potential. Erin had provided the new theoretical operating envelopes for the interceptor. Ben had merged so well with the ship that he only had to think a request and it happened. The young man flexed his arm toward the destroyer. A massive bolt of energy leaped across the gulf of space and smashed against the forward screens. The screens nearly failed from that first shot. The alien vessel returned fire. In his computer enhanced state, Ben watched with detached interest as the blasts slowly approached him. He simply moved out of the way. The ship followed his movements. Inside the cabin, the whining from the inertial dampers was constant. Most, but not all of the force was canceled out. Enough got through to cause the crew to sway from side to side.

"Oh, I didn't think this ship was that nimble. Whatever Ben did to the engines it sure gave her quite a kick, don't you think Tina?" Hemant called across to the engineering officer.

"Yea, well, if he gets us killed, I'm gonna kick his backside into the next life!" she replied, holding on to the console.

Jennifer called out, "He's playing chicken with that destroyer!" The interceptor was headed right toward the nose of the alien ship. Ben could feel the shots from both ships bounce off his chest. There was no penetration. Of the three-tiered screens, only the outer shield lost power. The inner shields remained at full strength. Ben smiled, even better than expected. The interceptor's port and starboard blasters began to fire in alternating fashion. The destroyer's forward screens failed. Large holes appeared in the nose of the ship. It veered away from Ben's attack. The young man followed, savagely pounding the ship. Great chunks of hull were blown into space. Some blasts went clear through the alien vessel, exiting the other side. The Star of India was firing at the Gaderian interceptor from point blank range, apparently with no effect. A small Erin apparition appeared before Ben.

"Energy dissipation is growing lethargic. The ship's engine core is approaching critical temperature. Suggest a course of action that will allow time for the ship's systems to recover, before resuming hostilities."

"I don't have time. My dad is in danger. We have seven point two minutes to end this battle. That will still allow me ten and a half minutes to intercept Alpha One's ship." Ben flipped the interceptor over and dove beneath the destroyer to escape the Star of India 's guns. He laid open the aft section of the ship. Glowing reactant spilled out into space as the vessel lost main power. All weapon activity ceased. The interceptor stopped all forward movement and appeared motionless relative to the bigger ship. Ben called up the engine core status display. The temperature was dropping slowly, too slowly to engage the Star of India at close quarters. Ben scrambled for a plan that would work. Jack's voice spoke.

"You must be the luckiest kid in the universe!"

"Not now, Jack, I'm busy!" The Star of India changed course to get at the interceptor. Ben moved the ship, keeping the crippled destroyer between it and the freighter.

"So am I. Those bozos are so stupid. They've been keeping an active channel open so that Alpha One can monitor and micro-manage the action."

"So what's your point? He doesn't have much of a social life anymore, does he?" The freighter began firing at the destroyer, trying blow it apart and expose the interceptor underneath.

"Ouch, they must want us awful bad to sacrifice their own people, huh?" Jack continued, "The point is that I was able to slip a couple of special packets into their net. In precisely forty-two seconds all their weapons are going to shut down due to a false energy fluctuation and the aft screens will shut off." Ben's ears perked up at that news. A plan was forming.

"How much time do I have before they fix the problem?"

"I estimate eleven seconds."

" Erin , how long can we stand continuous fire from the freighter?"

The AI responded, "Approximately twenty seconds." Ben thought for a split second. He called up a tactical display of the Star of India and zeroed in on the location of three power couplings feeding off the main engines. He nodded.

"Long enough. Let's go." The enemy vessel locked on as soon as the interceptor cleared the wreckage of the Rockow . The reactor temperature soared as the screens absorbed the energy. Ben made no move to dodge the blasts. The ship sped the length of the freighter. The firing stopped suddenly.

"Screens down," called Jack. Ben stopped the ship, took aim, and fired all weapons at the pre-determined targets. The Star of India went dark. The plasma tail shrunk to a whisper. "You realize that won't keep them forever. In a few hours they will repair the damage."

"In a few hours it'll all be over. This will hold them long enough to do what I have to do." With that, the little ship spun around and accelerated toward the distant carrier.

* * *

On the starship's bridge, the exalted ruler of the Minari laughed with glee. Humans were so predictable! He watched as the Gaderian Interceptor reversed course to engage his forces. Neural messages flowed to the brain of the alien leader via his many tentacles. He became alarmed as the Gaderian ship appeared to change energy configuration right before his eyes. "All tactical leaders note new enemy energy signature. Evaluate and network conclusions." Information poured in from all three capital ships. Several hypotheses were offered and shot down by others on the net. Alpha Six was closing in on the correct deduction when his presence on the net suddenly ceased.

Alpha One jumped to his feet and shouted through the neural communication system, "Destroy that ship! Sacrifice yourselves if you have to, but STOP THAT SHIP!" The strength of the signal rattled the neural receptors of the alien leaders, bleeding over to adjacent channels and rattling lower ranked aliens as well. Condition responses kicked in. The Star of India immediately responded. Alpha One watched helplessly as his forces were decimated. It's time to change the rules. He sent out his commands: "Fellow Enlightened Ones, you have the profile on the Gaderian vessel. She has completely changed configuration since the time of initial contact. We will do the same. Copy what improvements you can and improvise the rest. Find a way to penetrate their shields. You have eight minutes." The alien leader stared out at the approaching fighter. Ben Gardner , he thought, you are beginning to annoy me !

* * *

Admiral Corella studied the situation board. Most of the carrier's tactical weapons were immobile. Navigation systems were severely crippled. Life support was on emergency power. Engines were intact, hardly touched, but the control systems were a shambles. They were down to one launcher, some missiles and could only take a few of the remaining fighters on board at a time. Not that it mattered much, there were only eighteen left. Several shuttles were attached to the hull, carrying survivors from the battle. They were unable to enter the hangers because of the damage. Crews were ferrying them via spacesuits into the carrier.

"Not a lot working around here. Captain, what's the status of our other ships?"

"Not much there either, Admiral. "Casualties are appalling. Akio is totally destroyed with the probable loss of all hands. The Santa Fe is adrift and needs major repairs to get underway."

"Any chance of that happening within the next hour?"

The captain frowned, "Oh, perhaps in the next two weeks, yes." The admiral grimaced. "The Galveston has thirty percent of her weapons systems intact. Engines are operating at only twenty-five percent. Limited maneuverability. Half the shields are gone. If the Gaderian ship hadn't drawn off the aliens when she did, the Galveston would be toast. I sent the recall to the Jefferson , but, she is an hour and a half away."

Admiral Corrella observed, "That leaves us with a handful of fighters, one dead ship, one barely alive, and a crippled one to fight three undamaged vessels with superior firepower. Lord, we need a miracle to pull this one off!" An officer walked over to the two commanders and saluted. He handed an electronic clipboard to the captain.

"Admiral, the Lord works in mysterious ways!" exclaimed the captain. "I have your miracle right here. Remember that Gaderian fighter that was running from the Rockow and the Star of India , the one whom we hoped would jump out of here and get help? Well, they didn't jump. Instead they turned around and kicked some serious ass. The Rockow has been destroyed and the freighter is drifting." He handed the clipboard to the admiral. He couldn't believe his eyes.

"Why would they do that?" demanded Corrella. "And more importantly, how did they do that?" Dr. Gardener walked up.

"I think it has to do with my son. He must be on that ship. He's trying to protect me from that alien monster. Your communications officer says that a text-only message was sent to us a few minutes ago addressed to me. It said, Hang on Dad, I'm going to end this once and for all. Love, Ben. The science officer asked me to give you this report." The archeologist handed it to the admiral.

The Fleet Commander read the report, "Science says that the Gaderian vessel's configuration has totally changed. Shield strength, maneuverability, speed, and weapons power are up several times from earlier levels. It's almost as if someone has thrown an overdrive switch." The admiral touched a comm unit. "How long until the hostile is in range?" A voice emanated from the speaker.

"A matter of minutes, sir."

"And how long until the Gaderian ship intercepts?"

"Just about the same time." The admiral snapped off the comm panel. "Let's put our heads together and see if we can help Ben and his crew." Several parallel plans were initiated. (One involved piecing together a secure comm system, impervious to jamming. Another was to find a way to repair and shield at least one weapon system from detection.) As long as the enemy thought them helpless and immobile, the admiral theorized that he had a chance of getting off one good shot. How and when he'd get the chance to use it was another story.

* * *

The interceptor flew on a course that would just beat the alien starship, Arizona , to the carrier. Ben analyzed the status of his ship. Erin and Jack were arguing in the background about how much pounding the ship could take. Jack felt that the Gaderian AI was being too conservative. She thought Jack was being too reckless.

"Look, sister, this is an all or nothing trip here!" complained Jack.

"I am not your 'sister,'" retorted Erin . "I am merely trying to point out that these modifications have not been fully tested and we can't predict with certainty what the outcomes will be."

Ben settled the issue. "Provide your opinions; overlay them on the envelope display. When I cross Erin 's boundaries, monitor the internal sensors and notify me only if imminent failure is about to occur. I intend to take this ship right up to the edge and over if need be. You two will hold it together as long as you can."

"Understood!" replied both AI's in unison.

The little fighter swept in past the outer boundary of the battle zone. Ben gazed at the expanding pattern of wreckage spreading over thousands of kilometers of three dimensional space. He reached out and 'touched' the various hulks. Here and there he detected life and logged their coordinates, trajectories, and velocity for later rescue. Jack flashed this information to the fleet computers. Then the young man turned his attention to the rapidly expanding dot that was the naval carrier, and beyond to the approaching Arizona . The interceptor was approaching at the maximum speed possible. Ben could have squeezed more out of the engines, but he wanted to be able to fight when they arrived. The fighter raced past the carrier in a blink of an eye and headed out to meet the incoming starship. Ben reduced speed and prepared to change course. He increased power to the shields and glanced at the engine core temperatures. So far, so good , he thought. The interceptor dived in on the starship and Ben flung an energy bolt at the alien leader's ship. The bolt hit the screens and momentarily obscured the sensors. The overload abated, but Ben could detect no damage.

"Jack!" Ben exclaimed, "confirm my analysis."

"The AI answered, "No damage." An algorithm popped into being. "Recognize this?"

"Yes, that looks similar to our shield configuration."

"Well it's not. It's theirs. They managed to cobble together a copy of our shield. It's not an exact copy, but good enough to stop our weapons." Ben thought for a minute.

"Okay, change of plans. We fly in under the shields and target the generators." Ben maneuvered the craft for the run.

Suddenly an energy blast hit the ship. Ben felt it in his legs. "Ouch! That hurt!" He took a peek at the shields. The aft quarter shield was almost gone. Erin 's face popped up.

"Outer and middle shields failed, inner shield holding at 40%."

"They got smart awful fast!" said Jack.

"All right, scratch my last plan of attack. Let's probe their defense, look for a weakness. Jack, try to slip a virus bomb into their system. Erin , back me up on sensors." Ben flung shot after shot at the starship; he studied the displays, looking for some opening. The starship fought back, casting equally massive energy charges. The Gaderian Interceptor danced around the starship like a gnat attacking a large mammal, worrying the beast but not doing substantial damage. Finally, Ben got lucky. A generator overloaded on the starship and part of the engine shielding weakened. The Gaderian fighter pounded the area with shot after shot. The shield failed before back up generators could be brought on line. Ben was able to nail one of the subspace engines before being driven off by a barrage of blaster fire. The starship was forced to reduce speed. Ben had a thought. He opened a channel to the naval carrier. "Admiral," Ben asked, "We could use some help. We have no mines left and the Minari have copied my shields. We're much at a stalemate. Do you have any ships left?"

"Admiral Corella to friendly vessel. Is that you, Ben Gardner?" The bridge crew stared at each other.

"Yes, it is. All the survivors from the Star of India are here with me. Look, I'd love to chat, but I'm out of options here. Do you have any ideas?"

The admiral replied, "Now that the starship has slowed down, perhaps we can distract them by providing more targets, perhaps even ramming them." The admiral went on to explain his plan. Meanwhile, the captain signaled the Galveston and the remaining fleet fighters to close on the starship. "Good luck, Ben, and God speed!"

For Ben, time had slowed down so much that he could see the packets of light energy traveling to and from the carrier. He tossed in all the tactical data on the enemy and routed it to the carrier's tactical computers. The young man split his concentration between firing at the starship, evading return fire and waiting for the returning light packets. Jack assisted by taking some of the flight control load off Ben. Ah , thought Ben, here comes my response. The bursts of light arrived and were converted digital signals. Good! "Jack, plot a course that gradually brings us closer to the Galveston, but don't make it look obvious." The Gaderian fighter continued to tease the starship, drawing it closer to the escort vessel. A hoard of navy fighters appeared from behind the ship and tried to get underneath the starship's screens. The aliens drove off or destroyed the little ships. The Galveston , playing dead, suddenly sprang to life, firing weapons and what few missiles were left. While the alien gunners concentrated on shooting down the missiles, Ben lingered over the starship's aft screens, trying to overload them. The starship changed course to intercept the carrier. The Galveston moved to cut them off. Several well place blasts deprived the Galveston of helm control and she sailed past the starship, unable to turn. Ben saw a weakness in the shield and went in for the kill. He went to fire a blast at the starship, but found his arm would not move. "Jack, Erin, my arm went numb. What's happening!?"

"I don't see the problem. Wait, a system failed. Erin ?" Jack looked puzzled at the lack of a response, "Erin?" Ben dimly saw a black shape floating in the virtual reality and smelled a foul stench. The AI stated flatly, "Ben, Erin is off line."

"Jack, something is in here with us! Look at that!" The dark shape slipped away. Several displays went down. "We're losing tactical!" Jack looked concerned.

"They must have slipped a virus into our system somehow. I'll take care of it. You continue the fight." The

AI's image faded. Ben brought up the weapon's control. The virus looked like a dark spider web, connecting various subsystems and re-routing commands. The disembodied Ben reached out with his left hand, the only one still working, and began to tear away at the strands. Systems rebooted and came back on line. His right arm regained feeling. Ben felt maneuvering control slip away. He switched to backup systems. They began failing, so he switched to other backup systems, but the virus was already there ahead of him. Jack appeared to help him clear away the dark strands, then he was gone again, tracking the virus down elsewhere in the fighter. Suddenly, Ben was enveloped by a bright light and instantly his body was racked with pain. The young computer genius was dimly aware of a shield failure warning. He broke off his attack and tried to turn the ship away from the starship. The fighter was sluggish. Red warning signs kept popping up, confusing the disembodied young man. The foul odor, like a stopped up toilet, returned, stronger than ever. It threatened to overwhelm him. Ben fought down the bile in his throat and turned to deal with a serious life support failure. Suddenly, he came face to face with the dark creature. It had more form, many arms and legs, and a hideous face that belonged to Karl, the Star of India 's former computer tech. The viral creature said one word, "Gotcha!" and everything went dark. The Gaderian fighter spun out of control on a trajectory leading away from the battle. The starship let it go and sidled up to the carrier. The alien leader's leering face appeared on the bridge screen.

"You must give up. All your ships are disabled or destroyed. There is no hope of rescue." The admiral's face remained impassive. I must thank you for delivering my logic bomb to the boy's ship. Your last transmission contained a special little embedded program. I counted on the boy's inexperience with the neural interface to overlook the package. And, of course, that transmission triggered the virus in your own systems." Alpha One smirked. The admiral looked around his bridge. Yes, the bastard was right; a series of viruses had attacked his ship and brought down every last system except external communications. Anything with a networked processor was affected. The admiral sighed and thumbed the comm switch.

"I guess that leaves us with only one choice, doesn't it?" He gestured to a crewman, operating an analog communicator. The communicator, a non-digital device, was connected to an optic cable that ran the length of the ship and terminated at several strategic locations within the great ship. Crewmen in spacesuits received the message and manually engaged maneuvering thrusters. The carrier began a slow roll, rapidly picking up speed.

Alpha One exclaimed, "Our sensors show you have no operable missiles and your main guns are off-line. What do you hope to accomplish with this pathetic effort?"

The admiral replied grimly, "Your extinction!" The missiles leaped from their tubes at point blank range. Surrounded by plasma radiation purposely injected into the launch tubes by the humans, the missiles were overlooked by the Minari sensors. Piercing the Arizona 's energy shields, they slammed into the starship's hull and detonated. The explosions rocked the carrier and shrapnel punctured numerous holes in the carrier's skin. The starship broke into a number of pieces and radiation fires burned for a long time in the larger chunks. Clouds of atmosphere and tumbling debris escaped into space. Cheers broke out on the carrier bridge and spread throughout the ship. Hand signals were used to contact space suited personnel located in the airless sections of the ship. It was a victory to be sure, but at what price?

CHAPTER TWELVE

TINA, Eric and Jack managed to restore enough power to maintain life support and mount a slow speed return to the carrier. Jennifer and Hemant tended to Ben. The science officer pumped his body full of nutrients to replace those lost from the strain of the mind link. Safety overload hardware terminated the link before brain damage could occur from Alpha One's virus. Hemant strapped a portable intravenous bottle on his arm. The young archeologist took a wet cloth and wiped the sweat from his brow.

"Ben," she said softly, "wake up." He moaned and then his eyes opened. "You did it! We won!" She gave him a kiss on the forehead. "How do you feel?"

"Much better after the kiss," he said weakly. She giggled. Hemant smiled.

"Young man," said Hemant, "I have never been so scared in my life. That was better than any thrill ride I have ever been on."

"Is Eric still mad at me?"

"No," replied Jennifer, "he understands why you did it. In fact he's amazed at your skill in pulling off this miracle."

"My father?"

"He's okay," replied the young archeologist. "You'll see him soon. Rest, we're about to dock with the ship."

By the time they docked Ben had recovered sufficiently to walk off the interceptor. His father and a medical team met him in the hanger. Dr. Gardener grabbed hold and hugged his son for a long time. Father and son chatted while the med technicians examined the young man and adjusted the solution in the bottle strapped to his arm. They pronounced him well and urged him to rest. A shuttle arrived from the Jefferson . The human ship had picked up some stranded crews along the way and was to escort the remainder of the fleet fighters back to the colony to keep the alien ground forces pinned down until reinforcements arrived. A handful of civilians exited the shuttle including, a young woman who looked like she could have been Jennifer's younger sister. Ben took great notice as she was hustled off the deck into a waiting lift.

Space marines combed the wreckage of Alpha One's starship, looking for what remained of the alien leader. His charred body was found on the bridge. The marines gingerly retrieved his Star Crystal memory unit and placed it in a secure container. Working in groups of three, they cleared the ship of living aliens, removing the crystal memory units from the dead bodies. Every marine was scanned before being allowed back on board their shuttles. The shuttle occupants were then scanned, blood samples taken, and examined again before being allowed back on board the carrier. Armed guards with raised weapons covered the troops until the medical technicians gave them the thumbs up. The humans had learned a bitter lesson about the alien infection and weren't about take chances.

Captain Forest persuaded the admiral that his team would take possession of Alpha One's crystal repository. They had been trained how to dispose of it by the Gaderian teacher. Admiral Corella promptly handed it over, despite protests by his science department. The young lady Ben saw in the hanger was on the bridge. The admiral led her over to Ben.

"Benjamin, I'd like you to meet my daughter, Christine. The two of you have much in common. She's finishing up her senior year in computer engineering." The young girl just beamed at Ben.

"Daddy tells me that you saved the task force from destruction and that you have a master's degree! I've never met anyone who graduated from college at such an early age. Did you find it hard to fit in with classmates who were much older?" She grabbed his arm and steered him away from the group, chattering excitedly and asking questions. Ben caught Jennifer smiling at him from across the compartment. She gave him a thumbs up and mouthed the words, 'I told you so.' Ben smiled back and tried to answer the admiral's daughter. She hung on every word he said. Jack's voice tickled in his ear.

"Told you you'd get the hang of it. Of course, a little fame now and then doesn't hurt either." Suddenly, all the bridge sensor alarms went off. Officers began shouting commands into comm links and technicians leaped to their consoles.

The tactical officer called out, "Large fleet entering the system. Configuration, unknown. Nationality, unknown. Ships are still arriving from hyper-space. We have counts of over two hundred vessels and rising. Several large capital ships, dreadnought class and above. They are disgorging fighters. Trajectories have them dispersing throughout the solar system. One of the dreadnoughts and a number of smaller ships are headed our way at an incredible speed." The admiral groaned and fell back into his chair. With the engines down, there was no way to even escape at the moment Several ships split off from the group and stopped to surround the crippled Star of India and the hulk of the Rockow . They opened fire on the alien vessels, eliminating pockets of resistance. The ships were then taken in tow. The advancing ships hailed the carrier. The face of an old distinguished Gaderian male appeared on the view screen.

"Attention Minari, any resistance is wasted effort. Surrender your ship immediately and be cleansed," he said in the home tongue. Ben recognized the language and responded with the traditional salute.

"No Scourge is present on this ship. Stand down!" The Gaderian looked at Ben.

"Identify and verify!"

"Ben Gardener, impressed into naval service by Attendant Blaxx. My THX 030 unit will verify." He turned around and said in standard. "Quick, who has Jack? Plug him into the comm system." Hemant was carrying the AI's case. He set him down next to a comm panel and plugged in a remote.

"If you don't reply with the proper code, your fleet and all the planets in this system will be destroyed." The face waited impassively. He looked down at his console. "Odd, it is an ancient code, but viable. Your tactical readouts have been logged. We will proceed to cleanse this system. A Gaderian delegation will collect the crystals. Prepare to receive a shuttle."

Dr. Gardener exclaimed excitedly, "They're not all dead like we thought! What we have here is an event unequaled in human history, the return of the most advanced civilization in the known galaxy!" It took a while for the concept to sink into the battle-weary humans.

The delegation consisted of five Gaderians, one of which appeared to be a hologram. The human welcoming committee consisted of Ben and his shipmates, Dr. Gardner, the admiral, and several science officers. They met on the hanger deck, beside the unique Gaderian shuttle. A floating vault was towed by one of the Gaderians. The Gaderian leader spoke first, this time in standard.

"I have learned your language from the THX unit data files. Who is the keeper of the THX crystal mind?" Ben stepped forward.

"I am he." He set the AI on the deck in front of him. Jack's hologram formed. The visitor's were surprised.

"Your appearance is . . . unconventional," stated the leader.

"This is my chosen form. I am bonded to the "Appointed One," responded Jack.

"So be it." The leader turned to the hologram person next to him. "Begin interrogation." Beams of light reached out between the two AI's for about half a minute. The hologram spoke.

"Interrogation is complete. The humanoids on this ship are not infected. The human conscripts are accounted for. Everything matches what the base mind reported. These humans claim to have the crystal mind from Alpha One, our 'errant experiment.'" The Gaderian leader raised his eyebrows. Ben brought out the container and opened it. Inside, the brilliantly polished surface of the Star Crystal dazzled everyone's eyes. The two Gaderian guards started to draw their sidearm, but their leader gestured them to stop. The atmosphere grew tense.

"My name is Ambassador Thebes, I am sorry, but my soldiers are indoctrinated to react this way. Every member of the military is taught to revile and fear these objects. After we won the war with the Minari, we searched in vain for Alpha One's artifact. When we failed to find it, our leaders decided to abandon this sector of space instead of risking another accidental infection. We destroyed what few installations we had left and moved all the survivors to the other side of the galaxy. We haven't been back since. He motioned for one of the soldiers to come forward. He produced a scanning device and played it over the crystal. He showed the reading to the hologram, who in turn nodded to the Gaderian leader. "We will dispose of these artifacts. My people have waited over one thousand years for this day." The soldier loaded the container into the floating vault and sealed it. The two guards then proceeded to return to the shuttle. "My aide and I will remain on your ship, while the mutation is destroyed." The human and Gaderian delegations retired to the bridge. On the way, the Ambassador's aide produced a flask, which he presented to Ben.

"This contains a vaccine for the Minari virus. Our scientists worked for years perfecting the gene coding. According to the medical scans taken at our remote facility, your DNA is compatible. Once administered, your DNA is rewritten and all offspring is immune to attack." Ben gave the flask to Hemant.

"What about those already infected?" asked Hemant. The Gaderian bowed his head.

"All humans still in stage one will recover. Some of those in stage two will recover, but most will not. Ones who reach stage three must be put to death. I am sorry. We tried for hundreds of years to find a way to reverse stage three developments, but never succeeded."

The Ambassador's aide spoke up, "Instructions for replicating the vaccine have been downloaded to your THX unit. All Star Crystals that your kind comes across, must be destroyed, lest someone find a way to unlock the memories stored within." The group reached the bridge. The main viewscreen was on and displayed an unusual procession, six fighters in tight formation around a seventh. Several cruisers followed behind in attack formation. The formation accelerated toward the system's star. The display switched to one of the cruiser's perspective. The focus remained on the seventh fighter as it sped towards the sun. The six fighters peeled off an appropriate distance from the surface and stood guard as the seventh continued on course. The fighter disappeared from view. Several minutes passed as the Ambassador waited for word from his fleet. The Ambassador's AI said something in the home tongue. All the aliens smiled. "We can rest from our vigilance. Our greatest fear was that Alpha One had somehow survived and would resurrect again someday." The ambassador turned to face the admiral. "Contact your people on the planet and tell them to cooperate with us. We will cleanse your planet of the Minari. Until this system is secured, no one is allowed to leave." The admiral agreed and proceeded to organize his forces. The Gaderian fleet entered orbit and began to land ground forces on the planet below. Other vessels spread throughout the whole solar system.

Later that day, in the carrier's board room a crowd of human officer's and scientists were on hand to witness an address by the Ambassador. "We require ambassadors from your people to help establish relations. Among other things, we need diplomats, scientists, commerce experts, and military representatives. Our outpost teacher examined the minds of some of you humans and found one who has the necessary training and disposition to be the main liaison. Her name is a 'Jennifer.'"

The young archeologist squealed. "Oh, that's me. I accept! What a chance of a lifetime!" She glanced over at Eric. "Can Commander, I mean Captain Forest come too?" The Gaderian looked at him, tilted his head as if communicating with someone.

"You two are . . . pair bonded, are you not?"

"Is it that obvious? I mean, even aliens fresh from crossing the galaxy seem to know," exclaimed an exasperated Jennifer.

Captain Forest gently took her arm and spoke up, "I guess we are in the process of bonding, yes."

"You have expertise in commerce, I believe? And you were the leader of this expedition?" Eric nodded. "We would be honored to have both of you." The admiral, anticipating that something like this might occur, had 'volunteered' a fleet diplomat and a couple of military advisors. Two other staff scientists jumped at the chance. The Ambassador turned to Ben. "We would like you to come as well, but it would be best for you to stay for a while as our representative and ensure that the inoculation program is consummated throughout human space. Once normal relations have been established, we would like you to visit us. The THX units will be upgraded. You may keep the ship after we repair her." He then warned the young man. "Don't release our technology until we permit it. Your civilization is young. Too much technology could cause irreparable harm. Look what it did to us. Learn from our mistakes. Wait for us to introduce the knowledge slowly." Ben agreed and the Gaderians returned to their ship to await the cleansing of the planet.

Inoculations on the planet got started right away. Within forty eight hours, all the uninfected humans would be completely immune. It would take another week to rout the last pockets of infected humans. Admiral Corella wanted to immediately draft Ben into the military. Hemant and Tina tried to talk him out of it by agreeing to accompany the young man on his travels, representing the human government. Ben wasn't much interested in the politics at the moment. He wanted to spend the week getting to know the admiral's daughter. Christine, having rescued him from the current conversation, steered him out of the compartment.

"I hear that they're throwing a formal reception for the Gaderians in the main hanger. Would you like to go with me?" she asked.

"Oh, uh, sure. That would be great! But, Christine, what would I wear?" Ben replied.

"Oh, don't worry about that, I can scrounge something up. I'm not the admiral's daughter for nothing, you know. Oh, and call me Cristy for short. Only my mom and dad call me by my full name." Jack whispered a suggestion in Ben's ear. His eyebrows shot up.

The young man turned to face Cristy, "And maybe later, I can take you for a ride on my new ship?" The young girl nodded excitedly. Ben thought , This is one adventure that I'm positively going to enjoy! "

ABOUT THE AUTHOR

During the day, the author uses his engineering and management skills to improve manufacturing operations for a number of international corporations. He holds a Bachelor of Science degree in Industrial & Systems Engineering from The Ohio State University; an MBA from Arizona State University; and a 6Sigma Green Belt. Currently, he serves as Vice President of Operations for a local engineering and manufacturing company.

For fun, Greg fly's Cirrus SR-20's, Cessna 172's and 152's when he has both time and money. He and his wife, Cheryl, love to travel.

"My night job allows me the pleasure of writing creative fiction, with no boundaries except the limits of my imagination." – Greg Lundberg